Footprints from the Bible, by Cynthia Davis:

BELOVED LEAH

IT IS I, JOSEPH

MIRIAM'S HEALING

MIRIAM'S HEALING

Cynthia Davis

FOOTPRINTS FROM THE BIBLE

Americana Publishing, Inc.
303 San Mateo Boulevard NE, Suite 104A
Albuquerque, New Mexico 87108-1382 USA
(888) 883-8203
www.americanabooks.com

The books of the Footprints from the Bible series are also available on audio cassette from Americana Publishing, Inc.

ISBN: 1-58943-065-4

Library of Congress Control Number: 2003113819

Thanks to my husband of 27 years, Ken,
whose love and support are a constant source
of inspiration.

Also, thanks to Ann for her encouragement.

Prologue

"My mother, see what bounty the land has provided." The eager words awakened the old woman dozing on a mound of pillows and blankets in the warm desert sun.

"Look, dear mother," a woman's gentle voice added a plea. "Caleb has brought grapes and olives."

The young woman reached out to smooth a strand of hair off the wrinkled brow. Once a deep rich brown, the thin strands were now almost white. The woman's frame was still slender despite the many years that bowed the erect body. She was a tall woman, although it was not so obvious as she lay on the pallet. The gnarled hands had once been smooth and many in the encampment knew the gentle touch of healing they had brought. Years of travail had not dimmed her interest in life and the brown eyes were bright when they opened to study the handsome couple crouching beside her. A smile appeared on the creased face.

"My boy, it is good to see you." The words were raspy with age, but full of love.

The young man presented a platter full of grapes and olives with a flourish. His dusty tunic and robe were evidence that he came straight to this tent from the road.

"Truly the land is as rich as the first time we entered it," Caleb proclaimed enthusiastically.

A thin hand reached out to take a bunch of plump purple grapes from the plate. She popped one into her nearly toothless mouth and savored the juice, then proceeded to stuff her mouth with the delicious fruit. Munching happily, the old woman listened to the report.

"Yes, my mother." The honorary title was given with affection as the scout continued, "The fields are green and broad. They are filled with grain and cattle from horizon to horizon."

A sweep of a tanned hand indicated the extent of the wonders he had seen.

"Rich vineyards and olive trees dot the hillsides. The cities are fortified with earthen battlements and thick walls of brick. This time we do not fear them."

"The children of Israel have learned to trust the One Living God," the old woman sighed happily. "The years in the wilderness have formed a community. Those who sought the false security of the old ways have died out."

Her eyes strayed to the large encampment. So many tents were pitched in the valley that the people seemed to stretch beyond view. Miriam turned to the beloved couple beside her.

"When I am gone, you must continue to keep the story alive. Recite it often to your children and children's children. Only then will the people remember the mighty deeds of our God."

Taking her daughter's hand, the Prophetess stated, "My generation will not enter the land. We lacked the faith necessary to accept all the blessings of the One God. Every one of us murmured against Moses even though the Living One chose him to be the prophet. I saw for myself the destruction such dissatisfaction can cause in the community. My own lips spoke spiteful words against my brother and caused dissension and death. God disciplined me for my evil." Seeing the sad look on the devoted faces, she continued, "Do not grieve for me. I have seen and know that God will complete what He has sworn."

She selected another bunch of grapes and a smile came to the old face as she savored the sweet juice.

Caleb looked with concern first at the woman he called mother and then at his wife. Miriam saw the look and patted the blankets at her side. The girl knelt and the man squatted nearby.

Shaking her head, the young woman insisted, "I have never seen your faith falter. Surely you, of all people, deserve to see the land of Canaan with your own eyes."

"My children, I have doubted the very existence of God many times." The confession was no longer difficult to make. "When I was a girl, I listened to my mother sing of Abraham, Isaac, and Jacob. Once I watched Egyptian soldiers rip a baby from his mother's arms and cast the infant into the Nile. A huge crocodile came up. The baby was gone in an instant. All that was left was the pink, foaming water and the mother's wails. That's when I screamed and fled to my mother's arms."

Even now, eight decades later, Miriam shuddered at the memory.

"I was terrified for her and for the baby that would be born in just a few months. I prayed that it would not be a boy to be cast into the river to appease the gods and the King."

The silence stretched out. The man and his wife had no words to ease the sorrow of these memories. After a minute, the woman raised her head.

She continued, "Then Mother sang to me of the promise of God. Joseph the Honored knew that the One God would bring the Children of Israel out of Egypt. 'God will visit you and bring you up out of this land to the land he swore to Abraham, Isaac, and Jacob.' It was the faith that sustained her. When she held me and sang I was comforted," Miriam remembered. "When my brother, Moses, was born I learned how different my life was from the lives of the Egyptians. Even the poorest of the people along the Nile were freer than the children of Israel. The tales of a free people seemed mockery as I saw my neighbors beaten under the lash. We had dreams, my mother and I. She dreamed that Prince Moses would be the Deliverer of his people." The old woman bent her head in chagrin. "I dreamed *I* would be the one to rescue my family from bondage. I sacrificed myself willingly for the safety and preservation of my family. Yet, God chose my brother to lead the Children of Israel from Egypt. It did not seem fair."

The young man bent forward to say something. An old hand held up to stop him.

"Our ways are not God's ways and our plans do not always fit in the pattern the Living One weaves." The wisdom was spoken with a smile. "The hopes of my parents vanished like a river mist. My brother seemed lost to us. All my grand plans were buried under the unremitting work and blood and sweat." A sigh slipped out. "At my mother's side I learned the herbs to cure and comfort. I devoted

11

myself to healing the hurt and soothing the dying. My mother's faith was something I could not grasp as easily. God seemed as distant as the mirage of water in a desert."

Seeing the appalled expressions on the young faces, Miriam brought her hand up to touch first the well-loved bearded cheek and then the smooth womanly face.

"It is true," she admitted. "I gave up believing but my mother never did. Almost with her final breath, Jochebed instructed me, 'wait for God's Deliverer.' Still we served the King of Egypt. The cities of Raamses and Pithom were raised on the scarred backs of the sons of Jacob."

A restless movement of the wrinkled hand brought Sarai to smooth the blankets and lift the pillows.

"Thank you child," she spoke humbly. After a moment the old voice admitted, "I never gave up beseeching my mother's God for help, but there was never a response. The work, whips, and heat never slackened. The God of Abraham, Isaac, and Jacob was far away and unreachable. Pharaoh was the one who had the power of life and death over us. Him I feared and hated. Sometimes I even wondered if perhaps he *was* the god that all in Egypt claimed."

There was a pause. Still the young woman stroked the blankets. Her eyes were full of unshed tears.

"That is all in the past." Huskily the man tried to offer comfort. "Surely God will not keep you from the land because of that."

"Do not grieve for me. I am not sad that I will not see Canaan with my eyes. My heart has already been filled by knowledge of the fulfillment of the promise. Truly, the One God blesses the people in his own time and his own way. Hear then and remember so you can tell to all the story of the Living God's deliverance of the children of Israel."

Seeing his beloved friend so intent on speaking, the young man lifted her to a more comfortable position. Sarai gave Miriam another drink from the fresh water drawn only a few hours earlier. Then they settled down to listen.

Looking into the past, the old woman began.

"I never understood my brother. From the beginning he was different."

Chapter 1

I remember holding my brother after our mother brought him into the world. That day I left behind my childhood and assumed the mantle of guardian of my brothers and my parents. We were alone in the house. The midwives had not been summoned.

"No," Jochebed told me when her labor began and I offered to run for Puah. "They have their orders and I will not put my friends in danger. You will help me."

I was only a ten-year-old girl and terrified. My father had gone to the monuments to work as he did every day. Aaron, my seven-year-old brother, was out in the fields with the other children. Every day they gathered straw for the endless supply of bricks needed to build the temples and treasure houses.

Throughout that long, hot day, I gathered the blankets and water as Mother directed. Sweat ran down my back as much from fear as from the heat. She smothered her cries in the pillows.

Finally she panted an order. "It is time. Help me up."

Using all my strength, I helped the woman lever herself into the squatting position for delivery. She clung to the table and bench I had positioned earlier for this moment. Usually midwives supported a woman at childbirth on a special stool. In that strange afternoon, I was the one to catch the baby as he emerged. Rapidly, I wrapped him in a blanket I had ready. His first cry was cuddled to silence against Mother's breast after she lowered herself back onto the mat of twisted blankets.

"Take him quickly," she urged after easing his first hunger.

My mother was still panting from the exertion of the birth, and I was afraid to leave her. Loving hands stroked the tiny red cheek briefly.

"Go." The word was a command. "Pharaoh's midwives must not know that a live child was born."

Grabbing a wool blanket to wrap my brother and the sugar tit for his grasping mouth, I slipped between the houses. With the now quiet baby in my arms, I huddled near the river. Tall stands of bulrushes hid me from all except the exploring, buzzing insects. I sat so still that a curious river rat scurried across my leg, but I dared not move.

In the tiny house, I knew my mother prepared to lie and declare that the child was stillborn. She would say that I had been sent to cast the body into the Nile. No one would question the story. It was what the midwives themselves were instructed to do with any male child, living or dead.

I knew that Puah and Shiphrah did not always follow the edict. Once I overheard them tell Pharaoh's captain, 'These Hebiru women are too strong. They deliver before we can attend them to the birthing stool. A newly borne babe is easy to kill. One that has had suck is more difficult.' Not that such deceit saved the boy babies. Bonal, captain of the guard, was thorough in his duties. I feared his scarred face more than the crocodiles in the Nile. More than once I saw him leave a home with blood on his sword. The wailing from a bereaved mother always brought Jochebed to offer comfort. My mother provided the herbs that stopped the milk and brought dreamless sleep to quiet the first grief.

The day ended and the night breezes from the river cooled my skin. Dampness, unnoticed in the heat of the day, now chilled my legs. Gently I rocked the sleeping child and softly hummed a lullaby. A rustling in the rushes made me freeze in fear.

"Miriam." The sharp whisper came from my brother Aaron. "Come, it is safe to go home now."

Swiftly I rose and followed the boy. He was a sturdy child and large for his age. Both my father and mother worried about the day he would join Pharaoh's workforce on the scaffolds. So many of the young workers died in their first season of labor in the heat and from falls or from the lash.

Jochebed and Amram insisted, "It is not right for the sons of Israel to be in bondage to the King of Egypt."

I heard their endless prayers on behalf of all the slaves.

"God of Abraham, Isaac, and Jacob, why have you forgotten us? By the hand of Joseph you saved your people from famine. Why do you now leave us in harsh bondage?"

The agony of the clay pits, quarries, and monuments was forgotten in the little house that night as the newest son of the promise suckled happily. Amram and Jochebed sat cheek-to-cheek watching their son.

"He is safe for now." My mother smiled triumphantly. "The silly Egyptian cows believed that I would rush to throw my dead son into the river!"

"It is how they would propitiate the god Hari," my father replied, stroking the cap of black curls on the baby's head.

"Alive or dead, every newborn son of the children of Israel is to be thrown to the crocodiles." I spoke partly in fear and mostly in anger. There were tears in my voice. "Has the God of our Fathers forgotten us because so many of the Hebrews no longer worship the One God but instead seek the Egyptian gods?"

"Do not condemn others, my daughter," Amram answered gravely. His hand reached over to stroke my brown hair in comfort. "We can never understand God's purpose or another's heart."

"Who knows when God will rescue his people?" Jochebed rocked her son, never dreaming that she held God's Deliverer.

The words of my parents silenced me, but an idea began to grow in my mind. I would find a way to save my brothers and my parents. Then Aaron and this new baby would not have to serve the King of Egypt. How I would do such a thing was unclear. Prayers for inspiration were raised nightly to God.

"Help me to make a plan so that Aaron and the baby will be free. Use me to liberate my family. Tell me what to do," I demanded.

Although I listened intently, no response came from the stars and evening breezes.

The baby was strong and healthy. Too soon it became unsafe for him to live with us. I heard my parents whispering late into the night when he was three months old.

"My love, we must act before Pharaoh's spies hear of the child and we all die."

Mother's tears made me burrow into my blankets to shut out the sound of her sobs. In the morning, however, she was calm.

"Miriam, bring me the pitch." Her voice was steady and only a slight redness in her eyes indicated that she had spent a sleepless night.

I watched in amazement as she took a new basket and covered it with the tar. I couldn't understand why we needed a new watertight basket, especially one that was so large.

"How will we carry such a big basket when it is full of water?" I asked.

My mother gave no reply, grimly continuing with her task. When she wrapped my brother securely in a new blanket with a sugar tit in his mouth, I stared in confusion. The baby dozed off contented. Then she placed the infant inside the basket. A brief kiss on his forehead was all she allowed herself before turning to me.

"Come, Miriam, bring the other water baskets," she ordered. Lifting the precious basket to her shoulder she walked out the door. From the street, she called to me. "We will go to the river and bring water for our garden. I have neglected my duties in my mourning."

The words were spoken loudly for the benefit of any listening ears. I balanced the smaller baskets on my shoulder and followed her down the hard-packed dirt street. Every little house was just like ours. Each one was built of packed mud bricks squatting brown and humble in the dirt from which they were formed. Unlike the homes of the Egyptians with the colorful painted scenes of gods and victories decorating the sides, ours were hardly even whitewashed. No one had the time or energy to spend on such decoration. When cracks appeared, more mud was plastered over the sagging walls.

Gracefully and in no hurry, Mother proceeded toward the river. Smiling and calling greetings to friends, she acted as though the day was no different from any other.

"Jochebed, so good to see you again."

"Sympathy for your loss."

"Better stillborn than killed."

"Blessings on your head, Jochebed."

I could barely breathe as she nodded and answered each woman. We didn't stop until we were out of sight of the town. Finally, she paused and looked around. We were alone on the riverbank. Across the delta, the King's monuments gleamed gold and white. The wind carried the rough shouts of the workmen laboring in the blazing sun. Far up the river, I could see the sails on some boats.

My mother slipped into the bulrushes beside the road. I followed, still wondering what we were doing. The height of the plants hid us from any passerby nearly as soon as we stepped into them. Down to the very edge of the river Jochebed walked. A cloud of birds rose up and she froze in place.

"Mother," I whispered but she put a finger to her lips.

Another nervous look around showed me how frightened the woman was.

"Put down your baskets and help me," she hissed finally, lowering her precious load carefully to the ground.

Tenderly she tucked the blankets more securely around the baby and moistened the sugar tit. Then she rapidly laced a shallow basket in place as a lid.

"God of our fathers, into your hands I give this child. You gave me the courage to save his life." A tear trickled down her cheek. "Now, I give him to you. Rescue him from the river and slavery to be yours."

I caught my breath as I realized what the plan was. My parents planned to set the baby adrift and trust the One God to keep him safe. Jochebed took a deep breath and closed her eyes for a moment. Releasing a shuddering sigh, the woman gave a gentle shove to the basket. In a moment, it was caught in the eddying current.

With a catch in her voice my mother whispered, "Follow and bring me word."

A quick glance confirmed that she was crying. Then I ran along the riverside watching the basket bounce and twirl in the lapping waves.

The little vessel continued its journey, here caught in a pool, there almost capsized in the wake of some grand barge. Buoyantly it continued until a wave drove my brother's ark into the enclosed pool of a rich Egyptian house. Low walls kept the river creatures at bay and offered a secluded place for the noble owner to bathe or swim.

I wanted to dart out and put the basket back into the river. The appearance of several scantily dressed young ladies stopped me.

"God of Abraham, Isaac, and Jacob." I breathed the prayer again and again. "Don't let them see him."

The girls were laughing and chatting as they splashed about in the pool. I barely listened I was so intent on my petition. Then a sharp question caught my ear.

"What is that at the end of the pool?"

One of the ladies languidly waved her hand toward the basket bobbing in the little waves created by their games. I noticed the questioner was young and lovely.

"Great Princess," a tall black woman responded. "I believe it is a basket."

My head jerked up when I heard the title. Fearfully, I looked from my brother's basket floating just out of my reach to the lady and beyond her to the tall columns of the house. The paintings on the walls and gold emblems on the doorways confirmed that this was the royal palace, just a few miles north of On. It had been built in the days of Joseph the Honored so Pharaoh could visit his governor even in Goshen.

"How odd." Tilting her head prettily to one side, the Princess smiled suddenly. "Perhaps it is a gift from the river god."

"What would the god Hari send?" another of the companions asked with a laugh.

The Princess shrugged, "Who knows?" She waved her hand toward the object. "We are curious. Bring it here."

I cowered back into the reeds as one of the serving women waded to the basket and towed it back to her mistress. Everyone gathered around with high-pitched questions and exclamations.

"Do be careful!"

"How odd, it's a lidded basket."

"Even the top is covered with tar."

"Is it safe?"

"Look at the workmanship, so tightly woven"

"Do you think it's an asp?"

"In a basket on the river? Don't be silly, Eranth."

The Princess herself drew the basket with its precious cargo onto the lowest step. Kneeling beside it, she undid the lacing and lifted the lid. I wondered if my brother was asleep when no cries issued from the blankets.

The collective question, "What is it?" was followed by sighs of womanly adoration for the baby that was lifted out.

"A baby!"

"Isn't he cute!"

"Look at the tiny hands and feet."

At last, a young woman, whose beaded hairstyle and fine linen tunic proclaimed her nobility, asked the question I desperately wanted an answer to.

"Princess, what will you do?"

The royal response was reassuring. "Bring me that blanket."

A wide-eyed maid handed the linen wrap to her mistress.

Enfolding my brother in the royal cloth, the Princess stood up and announced, "We will keep him for our own."

The calm statement was greeted with a gasped question, "Your father...?"

"Surely you know this is a Hebiru boy child," another girl remonstrated boldly.

The women were silenced as the Princess drew herself up proudly. "Of course he *was* the son of a slave. Now he is *our* son. He will learn the ways of Egypt and not know the ways of the Hebiru. The baby is a gift from the gods to us. It is a blessing to keep and care for him." Silence greeted her announcement.

"Who will nurse him?" One of the women asked, seeing the baby start to squirm and seek to nurse.

Without conscious thought, I stepped out of the bulrushes into the royal pool. "I know a woman," I began. Belatedly remembering to bow, I bent forward until my forehead touched the water.

"Come here girl." The royal voice was not angry.

Cautiously I waded forward, ignoring the hissing whispers on every side. A raised hand quieted the women. Sitting on the top step with my brother in her arms, the royal lady actually smiled at me.

"You know a woman who would nurse our son?"

Although the tone was kind, I found myself unable to speak and could only nod.

"Would this woman bring back the child when he is weaned?" A smile accompanied the question.

"Y-y-yes, my lady." I finally found my voice to stammer a reply.

Gradually hope was overcoming fear. Maybe this was the way to save my family.

Triumphantly the princess looked at the gathered women.

"You see," she stated, "the river god not only brings a son but also provides a nursemaid." With a smile for me, she promised, "The woman will be paid well for her duties and have our protection."

I bowed again, shy before her glowing smile, and stunned by the speed of events.

"Come." She held out one hand.

My brother was nestled safely in her other arm. The serving girls gathered up the pillows and discarded robes as all the ladies prepared to follow us.

"We will speak to the girl alone." The order left them gasping almost in outrage. Nothing so exciting had happened in years. Already they were imagining how to tell the story to other friends. We left them whispering together when the door closed softly behind us.

The palace was more magnificent than anything I could ever have imagined. There were amazing paintings on the walls. Carved furniture with animal feet lined the hall and panels of gold decorated doors that loomed taller than the largest home in Goshen. Everything was polished so it reflected each movement. Light and air came in from windows high up near the ceiling. The bedroom was even more wonderful. I had never seen a bed raised off the floor. This one was carved from the same black wood as many of the doors. A wood headrest at one end would keep the royal head raised even in sleep. Linen curtains enclosed the whole thing to keep insects away at night. A large window opened toward the river and, in the distance, I could see temples and pyramids. A long low table with alabaster jars and bottles on it was against one wall. A huge bronze mirror hung over it.

I was startled to see my reflection. We used still pools of water if we took the time to look at ourselves at all. Curious, I edged closer to the mirror. Looking back at me was a somewhat muddied ten-year-old girl in clothes so faded they looked gray. The tunic was much too short because I was already much too tall. My tiny mother had to tilt her head to look at me if we were standing side by side.

In the mirror I saw for the first time the resemblance to Jochebed that many people claimed to see. There was the same wavy dark brown hair, high cheekbones, and wide brown eyes. My hair, smoothly combed that morning, was now tangled and pieces of plants were sticking out of it. I ineffectively attempted to comb it again with my fingers. My skin was tanned from days in the sun tending the garden and working beside my mother. I vowed to begin using the carefully hoarded herbs and oils my mother mixed to keep her face smooth and light in color. I scrubbed one hand over my cheek trying to remove some of the dirt and sweat from my trek along the river.

The Princess' voice caused me to jump and spin around. She held out a clean linen gown. The rough texture assured me that it was servant's clothing but it was still softer than my wool tunic.

"Here child, the attendant for our royal son must not wear rags." She pointed to an indoor pool just visible behind a carved screen. "Bathe there and put this on."

Hesitantly I entered the water, but soon I was happy to splash it over my body. Washing in the Nile was never so enjoyable. There was always the fear of crocodiles or other beasts.

"Much better." She nodded when I emerged from my ablutions. "Tell us your name."

"Miriam, my lady," I replied with a bow. I liked the feel of the linen sliding on my clean skin. It was so soft and light and cool. My fingers stroked the material, and I kept my head lowered as much to admire my new clothes as out of homage to the royal lady.

"Mir-em," she tried it on her tongue. "And the nurse you know of, what is her name?"

"Jochebed." The answer was accompanied by another bow.

"Yo-ka-bad." The lady frowned as she tried to say the name. "What is the name of this baby?"

I shook my head. We had never named the baby. Mother said, 'God will give him a name.'

When I didn't respond, she mused, "I drew him out of the river." Her eyes were soft as she looked at the baby nestled in her arms, content for now with the sugar tit.

"How would that be said?"

Confused at the question, I tilted my head and replied, "The word for drawing out is *mashah*."

"*Me-she*," her pronunciation was strange. "The Egyptian word for begetting a child is *moshe*," she mused, nibbling her lower lip in concentration. "Moses it shall be," she announced with a smile.

Crossing the room, she struck a bronze gong. Immediately a soldier entered to kneel in homage.

"Our litter," she commanded.

The man saluted and marched briskly from the room. Another bell summoned a maid to assist the princess into her traveling clothes. Other attendants hurried from the room after receiving murmured instructions from the royal lady. My brother was laid in my arms. A commanding nod of her head signaled me to follow. We walked through more halls until we came to the front of the palace.

The steward bowed low as he opened the massive door. I saw a litter with delicate curtains waiting outside. Four muscular Nubians stood at attention ready to lift the burden.

"We go to take our son to the nursemaid," the Princess announced to the man.

His training didn't prevent a brief look of stunned surprise from slipping across his face. It was quickly gone as he bowed again.

"Yes, Great Lady." A snap of his fingers summoned another servant who held a fan over the royal head until she was safely in the litter.

Once settled, the Princess held out her arms for Moses. Keeping my eyes on the baby, I handed him to the Lady. Still, I felt the eyes of soldiers and servants staring at me curiously. I forced myself to not show the fear the crawled up and down my spine.

The Princess ordered me to join her behind the curtains instead of running beside with the servants. She nestled Moses in her arms and gazed down into his sleeping face. Curling into as tiny a space as possible, I reveled in the luxury as the bearers set out a trot.

The captain of the Princess' guard looked astonished at her order to proceed to Goshen. His frown was quickly hidden by a low bow although I heard him order extra vigilance from the soldiers. We arrived sooner than I would have believed. I directed the bearers through the narrow streets to my house.

"Great Lady," the officer tried to reason with his royal mistress, "this is no place for one of your rank."

His lip curled as he looked around at the tiny homes with dusty children now staring in startled bewilderment at the black men and the litter as well as the polished armor of the royal guard. Mothers appeared as if by magic to whisk their precious little ones inside away from the feared swords of the Egyptians.

"Nor is it your place to decide such things, Captain. You may bring the bundles." Her voice was cold, and the man stepped back with a frown and nod.

With a shaking hand, I pushed open the door and bowed the Princess of the Two Lands into my home. In her arms, she held my brother wrapped in a fine linen blanket. He whimpered and squirmed.

Her tone was gentle as she crooned, "Moses, my son, you will have milk soon enough."

My mother stood frozen in the center of the room. The bowl of bread dough in her hands tilted. I snatched it from her and placed it on the rough table. I never noticed how poor our furnishings were. Now I cringed that the royal Princess would see our poverty.

"Bow to the Daughter of the Lord of the Black Land, dog of a slave!" The Captain's sharp words broke her trance.

My poor mother flattened herself to the dirt floor. I know she expected the sword.

"Captain, this woman is in our service and under our protection!" The flash of anger in the black eyes caused the proud Egyptian soldier to join my mother in obeisance on the floor. The Princess tapped one sandal-clad foot for a moment. Another whimper from the baby changed her demeanor. "You may go."

The man bowed himself backward through the low doorway. The bearers set down their bundles and also departed. We three women remained. I quickly dragged out the one seat in the house. It was a rough bench pieced together, like the table, from lumber my father scavenged from old scaffoldings. I draped a clean, if worn, wool blanket over it. With a gracious smile, the Princess seated herself. She seemed entirely at home just as though she was in the tiled halls we had recently left.

"Rise, woman." Her voice was soft as she addressed my frightened mother. "Your name is Yo-ka-bad?"

The question caused my mother to dart an apprehensive glance at me before nodding mutely. I crouched beside the royal lady while she addressed my still kneeling parent.

"The god Hari brought us a gift today." A smile accompanied her words.

When there was no response, she continued, "Hari sent me a son."

Again my mother glanced at me. I smiled happily and nodded.

The Princess added, "We have need of a wet nurse. This girl says you would be willing to act as nursemaid for us until the boy can be weaned."

Hope began to shine in Jochebed's eyes but her answer was meek.

"The Great Lady honors her humble slave."

"You will be under our protection. We have brought you food and clothing for your station." The royal head nodded toward the packs by the door.

The two women stared into each other's eyes, my mother with growing optimism, and the Princess with the poise born of her position. I eyed the pile of leather bags curiously, wondering what delights they contained.

"When the boy is weaned," the young woman spoke, "you will bring him to us. He will be a Prince in the land of Egypt. The finest education will be his. Our son will learn to fight. He will have land and houses, horses and slaves."

Jochebed bowed until her forehead touched the royal feet. "I am yours to command. The Daughter of Pharaoh is merciful and beautiful."

"His name is Moses." Gently the lady rocked the baby one last time.

Softly the smooth hand drew back the linen blanket from my brother's face. She kissed him gently on the forehead before handing him to my mother. With greed the woman gathered her son back into her arms. Baring a breast, she gave him suck. After watching for a moment with a half-smile, the Princess turned to me.

"Mir-em." My name was still difficult for her. "You will help with our son and bring news every week of what he does."

I repeated my mother's words while I knelt to touch my forehead to the floor. "Yes, Great Lady, I am yours to command."

She stood gracefully and walked to the door. I scrambled to pull it open. Quite a crowd had gathered outside. The captain glared around and snarled orders at the guards. He was unable to understand why his royal mistress was in this humblest of houses. The shouted questions from the neighbors wanting to know what was happening in the home of Amram and Jochebed only made him uncomfortable. When the Princess appeared, soldiers and bearers bowed low before hurrying to their places. The crowd also knelt.

"Captain," the royal command echoed in the narrow street. "This house and all inside are under our protection. The Daughter of the King of the Two Lands has spoken. Yo-ka-bad is nurse to our adored and beloved son, Moses, gift of the Nile god Hari to his humble maidservant. Anyone found troubling the peace of this house is to be beaten and dropped in the center of the Nile as an offering to gracious Hari. Our son, granted to us by the benevolent Hari, will be a Prince in Egypt and dedicated to the one who brought him to us."

"Yes, Most Royal Lady and daughter of the Mighty Pharaoh, it will be as you have ordered." A low bow and salute from the Captain proclaimed his obedience. Those who understood the words hastily repeated them for friends.

"Now we will go to the temple to offer thanks to the gods for their favor."

With a smile of farewell to me, the Princess accepted the officer's assistance into her litter. The crowd divided as the bearers moved up the street. Everyone gathered around our door with questions. Anxious to return to my mother and brother, I answered as briefly as I could.

"The most royal Daughter of Pharaoh has honored our house by choosing it as home for her son. As she said, the river brought her the baby." I refused to say anything more and slipped inside.

People continued to speculate and whisper for a long time before gradually returning to their homes. In each tiny house, the story would be told and retold for the men when they returned from the mud pits and brickwork.

My mother demanded a full explanation as we sat on the floor and unpacked the packages. We pulled blankets and linen garments out of one bundle. They were softer than anything I had ever felt. From the other leather bag came dried fruits and sacks of wheat. These were items we rarely had on our table. Our usual fare was bean curd with onions on barley bread. Jochebed sighed contentedly as she looked from her dozing son to the mounds of riches piled around the small room.

I had to repeat the story when my father and Aaron came home. Their looks of amazement made me smile.

"God has saved our son, given him a name and blessed us with royal favor." The ringing proclamation from my mother was greeted with a solemn nod from Amram.

"It is as you said," he stated. "The God of Abraham, Isaac, and Jacob has great things in store for our son."

I was forgotten in the rejoicing. I was happy as I sat in the corner and wondered how to use this event to save my family.

Chapter 2

"We must share this bounty with everyone."

Mother's suggestion was greeted with a nod from my father as he and Aaron left the house. The food and clothing given freely to the community silenced most of the rumors swirling in the street. Still, I felt the curious looks from the women at the well each day. My lips were sealed against their questions.

"Does the baby in your home really belong to the Princess?"

"I think it is Jochebed's child …"

"How could that be? No Egyptian Princess would claim a Hebiru child as her own."

"Where do you go each week?"

The last I could have answered, but I chose not to. Four times in a moon cycle, I went to the crossroads where a chariot and escort awaited me. I was driven swiftly to visit the Princess and tell her all about my brother's growth. She lingered in the northern palace to be close to her son. I was amazed and delighted when she began to give me special lessons.

"Mir-em, you are a bright child." Her comment one spring morning surprised me. "It is a shame that you are daughter of a slave."

The lovely woman sat pondering me for a long time. White teeth nibbled her lower lip as always when she thought deeply.

Then with a decisive nod, she announced, "We will do it."

I had no time to ask what she would do. A clang of the gong summoned her steward. The eunuch was given an order.

"Fetch Patamah, the scribe."

Rising to my feet, I prepared to leave. Despite my excited description of Moses' toddling efforts to walk, the lady had urgent business that did not include me. The Princess would not want me near if she were going to dictate a letter.

"No." A gentle hand stopped me. "You are going to learn to write. Then you can send daily reports to us of everything our son does."

The daughter of the house of Pharaoh clapped her hands in joy, obviously pleased with her idea. My eyes opened in amazement. That I would learn to form the secret symbols into words was beyond my dreams.

"Princess." In delight I threw myself down to kiss her feet. "Thank you. I will diligently write down each thing Moses does."

Patamah was not happy about the arrangement.

"Mighty Princess, the King, your father, will not be pleased that a Hebiru is instructed in the written word."

When my friend did not reply, the man continued, "The word is sacred, as my Lady knows, the very essence of the thing it represents."

"We will have Mir-em learn to write so she can make reports to us." The tone of authority caused the man to prostrate himself.

"Let not the most royal Princess be angered with her humble servant. I dare not teach a slave and foreigner the sacred words of Egypt."

On a low stool at the feet of the Royal One, I listened to the argument.

"You will do as we command." At the angry hiss, the unfortunate teacher flattened himself even lower. "Our father, the Lord of the Two Lands, will hear of your disobedience to our desire."

"Lady," a whisper emerged from the distraught tutor. "If my mistress will permit, I will show this girl how to write in the language of traders."

The Princess tapped her foot for a long time. Narrowed eyes looked at the cringing figure. Then her face cleared.

"Yes, that will be satisfactory." With a nod of approbation, the lady ordered, "she will begin today. We must also learn this writing so we will not have need for your translations."

The lessons were difficult even though the letters were not the complex hieroglyphics but the much simpler Canaanite alphabet. My fingers were stained with the ink and my shoulders ached from bending over the papyrus, but each week I went home with more knowledge in my mind.

Aaron too was reaping benefits from the royal protection. Rather than working on the monuments, he was apprenticed to the goldsmiths. It was a position rarely offered to a Hebiru. He showed an aptitude for working with the soft metal that impressed even the master goldsmith.

With each visit to the palace, I became more positive that the great lady would find me indispensable. In the chariot, I wove grand dreams. Pharaoh's daughter would release me from slavery to be her personal companion. Rather than Patamah, she would ask me to be her scribe. Then I would grandly insist that Aaron, Jochebed, and Amram be included in my newly free status.

"You are such a sweet child." The often spoken words made me glow and reinforced my fantasy.

Before long, I was able to write a short note to the Princess. Each day I carried the small scroll to the guard post. A runner took the note to the palace. Even when the royal entourage moved back to the capital, the Princess heard news of her son. I missed my visits while she was gone and rejoiced when the lady returned after the Inundation.

My life was so wrapped up in the visits to the palace and reports on my brother that I barely noticed when I began to take on the form of a woman. Even my mother was oblivious. She spent every second adoring her special child and dreading the coming separation. I became a woman one morning in the presence of my now beloved mentor. When I reached her rooms, I was almost sobbing from the pain in my belly. Although I tried to conceal the fact, she knew something was wrong.

"Mir-em." The gentle lady held out her hand. "Come sit beside us. You must tell us what is wrong. You are not feeling well."

Her compassion made me begin to sob.

"I think I am dying." The words came out in a rush. "There is pain and I am bleeding."

Soft laughter made me jerk my head up to stare in amazement at her pretty face.

"Surely you know ..." The smile was not mocking but comforting. "You have become a woman this day."

Only then did I remember the instructions my mother had given me years before.

"Then I should not be here. I cannot be outside my house at such a time." Panic stricken, I darted my eyes around trying to figure out how I could return home.

"Hush, child." The lady took my hand. I continued to sob despite her reassurance.

"My women will get you what is needed and you will stay with them for this time. I will send a message to your mother."

So it was that I spent my first week as a woman in the house of Pharaoh. The Princess' servants pampered me and made much of my new status. I learned that for an Egyptian girl this was a much-celebrated time. At home, I knew the occasion would not be nearly as welcome. Too often becoming a woman was the beginning of sorrow for the girls in Goshen. We were ready prey for the guards and overseers.

Jochebed welcomed me home at the end of the week with scolding and tears.

"You should never have gone to the palace in such a condition. Why did you not tell me?"

Vainly I tried to explain, "It came on me suddenly on the way. I didn't expect such a thing."

"Your father will need to find you a husband," she concluded more calmly.

I nodded with resignation. It was what I expected even if not what I desired. None of the young men in Goshen excited my interest. Besides, if I were burdened with a husband, the Princess would be less likely to think of me for her companion. I thought it fortunate that other considerations distracted my parents. Moses was old enough to be weaned. On my next visit to the palace, the Princess mentioned the fact.

"It has been three years since our son went to live in your home."

"Yes, Great Lady," I acknowledged as a lump grew in my throat.

"Then it is time for Moses to take his place here." Softly the words were spoken but the royal eyes had an excited glow.

"Yes, Mighty One." I nodded as my heart sank.

My mother would be heartbroken. The Princess' gown swished softly as she rose to pace up and down the room. She stopped to look out the eastern window.

"You must bring him to us. There is much to be done. A room must be prepared and tutors found." When the lady turned, she was smiling. "Our son will come home in a week. Moses will come with you next time."

Happily, the woman hurried across the room to summon her maids. I heard her whispering his name, "Prince Moses, my son, Moses," as I bowed myself from her presence.

Tears stung my eyes all the way home. Disappointment welled up inside me. The Daughter of Pharaoh had not mentioned me at all. I barely saw the scenery and ran all the way from the crossroads. Jochebed knew what I was going to say when I burst into the house.

"It is time." The resignation in her voice broke my control. We wept together.

Chapter 3

"My son." Through tears my mother held the three-year old boy close to her, despite his protests. "Never forget your people or the God of your fathers. The God of Abraham, Isaac, and Jacob has promised us a homeland and deliverance from this bondage. Learn and be wise, my son, but do not forget your family."

Impressed with the woman's tears and solemn words which he only half understood, my brother stared into her face.

"Yes, mama," he promised. "I love you."

Jochebed drew the boy close to her then and kissed his soft curls. With a final hug and caress, my mother let him go. She turned away as I took his small hand to lead him out the door. I wondered if he realized that he would never again play in the dirt streets or run with the puppies and other children down to the riverside. The unusual bath in the early morning light and the new clothes he wore were of more interest than the farewell of his mother.

"We are going to the palace," I told the boy in an attempt to keep my mind off the separation and my mother's grief. "It is a wonderful place. There are paintings and gold decorations. You will live there with the Princess."

In the chariot, I distracted myself by pointing out ibex and hippos. Moses laughed and joined in my game. His sharp eyes noticed many more animals along the way than I did. We reached the royal complex much too quickly. I led my brother to the garden entrance. It was a shorter way to the Princess' apartments than down the long front corridors filled with officials and petitioners. It was the path the Princess herself used.

"Come on." I took his hand as the boy lagged behind to stare in astonishment at the flowers and trees.

As the time for goodbye approached, I felt a lump building in my throat. The child's eyes were huge when we entered the palace. Paintings and carvings caught his eye. He reached for a giraffe carved from cedar. Eager suddenly to have the parting over, I almost dragged my brother through the halls.

"You'll have time to look later." I jerked his arm sharply. For a moment, I thought he would cry, but another object further on caught his attention. "We must go to the Princess, your mother." My voice broke on the last word. In my mind, I saw again Jochebed's bent head as we left the house.

Familiar guards opened the doors to the royal apartments and the eunuch led the way to her chamber. Sitting alone by the window on a stool, the Princess held needlework in her hands. It fell to the floor when we entered. She held out her arms.

"Moses, my son, I have waited so long for this day!"

The joyful welcome and unexpected words made my brother shrink against me. Jewelry tinkled as the lady rose and moved toward us.

"It is all right." My shove between his shoulders urged the boy forward. "This is your home and the Princess is your mother now."

Like a child, I rubbed my arm across my eyes to stop the tears that brimmed. I would not let anyone see me cry.

"Such a sturdy boy." The woman slid to her knees gracefully and held out her arms.

Her smile brought a tentative response from Moses. Still he clung to my hand.

"Look what I have." She produced a toy cart from the table beside her.

Cautiously, glancing back at me, the boy took the wooden object. Stepping back, he examined the toy. Then like a true boy he began rolling the cart across the shining tile. His delight in the wheels that really turned made the Princess grin at me. I couldn't help but respond. My brother's joy was wonderful to see.

"Mir-em, we would provide a place for you here at our side." The suggestion made me spin around to face her.

For a moment, I was tempted. It was what I dreamed of. Then again, I saw my mother's sorrow. I knew that the royal offer did not include my family. It never would.

"My Lady is most kind and generous," I assured her with a low bow. "I am most honored that the Daughter of the King of the Black Land would so much as consider me." Swallowing very hard, I stated, "My place is with my mother."

Looking into my tear-filled eyes, the lady placed her smooth hands briefly on my shoulder.

"You are a dutiful daughter. Have no fear for your brother. Moses will be great. He is highly favored by the gods. Hari brought him to us. The name of Prince Moses will be known throughout the world."

"Yes, Great Lady," Again I bowed.

The time had come to leave my brother. He belonged to Egypt now.

"Take this for what your family has done for the House of Pharaoh." A pouch was pressed into my hands.

The weight surprised me. I knew it contained gold. A moment's doubt seized me. Was I selling my brother for gold and royal favor? Seeing my sad glance toward the boy happily building a tower from the royal cosmetic boxes, the Princess beamed.

"See how happy he is. We love him as our own. He is our son now. Do not be afraid, he will have the best of the land."

"Royal One, you are most gracious," I spoke past the tears that threatened.

With a final bow, I ran from the room. Moses didn't even notice that I was gone. The chariot waited for my return journey. It would be the last time I would ride in such style. Grateful that I didn't have to walk the miles to Goshen, I sank into the bottom of the vehicle and leaned my head back. Tears slid silently down my cheeks. Desolation settled in my heart. Why had I refused the Princess' offer? I was startled when the movement stopped. We were off the road.

"Do not be sad." The kind words and gentle touch on my cheek were even more surprising.

The Egyptian soldier took a seat at the back of the chariot. He took my hand in one of his. The other hand stroked my hair. For a moment I was comforted. It felt so good to be held and comforted. He encouraged me to touch his smooth cheek, so unlike the bearded faces of the men in Goshen. Odd sensations swirled in me when the big hands possessed my girlish breasts. The man bent forward and captured my mouth with his. Suddenly I knew what we were doing was wrong. I pushed against the muscled chest to no effect. I managed to tear my mouth free by pressing my hand against his throat.

A low chuckle at my struggles. "Don't worry, little one, I will be gentle."

"The Princess will hear of this," my threat was gasped as I fought.

"I know you will not be returning to the royal house." His smug words were accompanied by a smirk. "Do you think the Royal One will want you to compete with her son's attention?"

Strong hands slid up under my tunic. The weight of the man nearly crushed me as he took what he wanted despite my fists and nails. My cries of fear and pain he ignored. Sated, the soldier finally lifted himself off my body. The chariot was driven back onto the highway. I drew myself into the corner of the conveyance wishing I could throw myself from the vehicle. Powerful legs barred my way. At last, the wheels stopped turning.

"Here you are, my lady." Mockingly a hand was offered to help me to the ground. "I hope you enjoyed your trip as much as I did."

The leer on his face made me want to slap him. As proudly as I could, I turned my back and walked away from the representative of Egyptian military might. The man's laughter followed me down the road.

Blindly I entered my house and shut the door. Jochebed sat where I had left her, stroking the blanket used by her son. I longed for her comfort yet feared telling her of my experience. She knew without words.

"My daughter," the keening cry was wrenched from her lips.

I clung to the woman and wept. Then she bathed my body and gave me a horrible tasting herb to drink.

"That will prevent any child," she assured me.

Amram and Aaron were not told that night. I hid my anguish from them as I reported how I left Moses playing with the cart and boxes in the palace. They were amazed at the pouch of gold I produced.

"From the Princess," I explained to my family pouring the gold pieces onto the rough table.

The money was hidden deep in the trunk under all the heavy blankets. We never referred to it again.

My life changed. With Moses gone, I no longer made excursions to the palace. Mother must have told Amram of my rape because he no longer sought a husband for me. I caught him staring at me sadly and wondered if he blamed me. In the silence of the night I wept for the husband and children I would never have. No son of Israel would want a bride soiled by the hand of an Egyptian. The stares and whispers behind their hands told me that the neighbor women all knew of my shame. Proudly, I pretended to not notice or care that my friends thought the attack was my fault.

"I will never speak against another man or woman as long as I live." The vow was made to myself as the knife of the unspoken guilty verdict cut into my soul.

I decided to devote myself to easing life for my parents and friends. With my mother, I dealt with the wounds of the people caused by Pharaoh and his minions. I don't think she minded too much that I would never marry. My ears were a ready audience to her stories and dreams.

Jochebed continued to repeat the history of the Abraham, Isaac, and Jacob to any who would listen. The stony, disbelieving faces of the neighbors didn't deter her. Even in the face of heavier and heavier oppression, she continued to insist that the One God was more powerful than the gods of Haran and Ur and even Egypt.

"Abram the Wanderer heard the voice of the True One and left his home and family. For his faithfulness, God gave him a son and a new name." The recitation was as familiar to me as breathing. Her inevitable conclusion, too, was well known. "The promise that his God gave to Abraham is the same promise we should remember. This is not our home and the God of our fathers will bring us back to the land promised to Abraham, Isaac, and Jacob."

"Do you think that Moses will be as important as Joseph the Honored?" Again and again I asked the question.

"Miriam, that is for the Living God to decide. However, my son was saved from the river for some great purpose." Always her eyes took on a faraway look when she discussed Moses. "Who is to say that he will not be the Deliverer of this people?"

Sometimes I imagined myself finding my brother and reminding him that I was his sister. Then, surely, he would take us all into his home and my parents would no longer be slaves to Pharaoh.

The Princess rarely visited the delta now, except in the heat of the summer. One morning nearly seven years after I left the child in the royal household, I slipped away from my duties to seek him out. From a vantage point among the bulrushes along the levee, I could see into the garden. It looked as I remembered it. The same lush greenery and fragrant flowers lined the paths and climbed the stone walls. A boy wandered along the paths. He was tossing a ball into the air and catching it. Whenever it dropped, a servant hurried to retrieve the object and return it to his master with a low bow. I recognized the tutor walking beside my brother. It was the scribe employed by the Princess to give me simple lessons.

I focused on the boy. Moses was growing tall. He no longer looked like a Hebiru. His shaved head with only the prince's lock on the right side gave him the look of Egypt. Linen loincloths and tunics edged in gold rather than ragged wool ones set him further apart from his kin. The proud, even disdainful, tilt of the princely head as he ordered his servants to do some task was evidence that here was royalty. Sadly, I knew this boy would not acknowledge me as his sister. A wave of jealous anger welled up within me. My brother lived a life of ease while his family suffered.

"God of Abraham, Isaac, and Jacob, you have turned from your people. We die in the heat and slavery of this land," I said bitterly. "If you will not help my family, I will ease their burden myself."

With that oath, I turned my back on the girlish dreams of rescuing my family by royal patronage and set out to ease the burden of Amram and Jochebed single-handedly.

More and more my mother became dependent on me for assistance in mixing the herbs and visiting the sick or injured. Because of our skill, we were excused from service on the buildings. Egyptians as well as our neighbors sought out our poultices and medicines. Together we saw more of the pain and suffering of the children of Israel than most of the community. Broken bodies were brought to us for healing. Infected whip cuts needed to be treated.

The occasional simple cut or scrape was a pleasant diversion from the more serious injuries we saw.

A nagging cough settled in Jochebed's chest one fall and weakened her. I took on more and more of the duties, hurrying home to minister to my mother as often as I could. Daily I became more aware of the brutality around me. My mother had always sought to insulate me from the realities of our bondage. Now, as I went among the workers to tend their injuries, I began to doubt that the God of Abraham, Isaac, and Jacob cared for or even remembered his people.

Overseers, both Egyptian and Hebiru, forced greater and greater efforts from men already straining to achieve all they could. Even children as young as four and five were pressed into service to collect straw and beat it fine enough for the mortar. Women tried to tend their families while carrying water to the parched workers. Wearing veils over our hair and faces didn't protect us from the stench of sweat and dirt or from the grasping hands of the Egyptians.

Each time I stirred the herbs for miscarriage into a young woman's drink, I cried out to the silent God.

"Where are you? Is this how you keep your promises to your people? When will you hear the screams of our women and see the tears of our children?"

The seasons flowed by measured by the great river's rise and fall. Aaron grew taller and stronger with each passing year. Even after the royal patronage was removed, he remained in the service of the goldsmiths learning the intricate ways of the metal. The chief goldsmith himself trained the young man because he was so talented.

In the evenings, my brother entertained us with stories of the magic the priests used to impress the people. Jochebed always pounced on the information as proof that the Nile gods were false. I was not surprised that the myriad gods of the Black Land didn't have any power to ease our burdens either.

Many of our neighbors sought out the local deities. They attended ceremonies at the temples. Sometimes I went with friends to some ceremony, but, remembering what Aaron told me of the secret doors and other strategies, I was not impressed with what seemed like magic. Even the yearly festival when some god would answer questions was trickery. Aaron explained it to me:

"The priests know the history of every person. They use that knowledge to give vague answers that seem to be a reply."

"What of the god's movement?" I asked.

The statues appeared to nod and even gesture toward the interrogator. It was amazing and even frightening because the idol seemed to be alive.

"Manipulation of the 'godly' garments gives the illusion of movement. You know the priest and idol are mostly hidden by the clouds of incense," he explained. "It is all delusion meant to prove that the priests are powerful emissaries of the gods."

Understanding the artifice of the Egyptian priests, I wondered if the God of Abraham, Isaac, and Jacob was a deception too. With each new burden, I raged at the God I believed in less and less as the days passed. I hid the doubts from my mother.

"The day will come, Miriam," the old woman often told me, "when you will need all the skills and all the sacred memory of our people. God will visit the children of Israel." A cough ripped through her and made her gasp for air.

"Rest, Mother," I urged, holding a cup of honeyed tea to her lips.

It eased her spasms. I felt her watching me as I sorted the herbs and bandages.

"You are a great comfort to me." The soft words brought tears to my eyes.

Amram was relegated to mixing the mortar when he grew too old to climb the scaffolds. The old men were put to the task of mixing the fine limestone dust and water. Day in and day out they stood in the vats treading the powder into the water to make it the right consistency. If they died of the exertion or choked on the dust, it was not a hardship for the foremen. More were available to take their place. Young men pulled the blocks into place up the long sand ramps. The biggest stones were floated to the site during the spring Inundation when the Nile rose far above her normal banks. 'Hebiru mules', as we were called, erected the walls. Workmen skillfully covered the surfaces with the plaster. Egyptian artisans completed the painstaking work of adding the colorful paintings depicting Pharaoh and the other gods on the buildings and monuments.

One day late in the year, Amram was carried home.

"He collapsed," Aaron announced, as he lay his father's shaking body on the pallet of blankets.

I hurried to mix a warm draught and steeped some medicinal herbs in the water. Jochebed hobbled to her husband's side. She held the cup to his lips. Most of the liquid trickled into his beard even as he tried to control the shaking. She focused on her beloved, trying to warm his body by adding more blankets and lying beside him.

"God, why have you forgotten us?" My brother's anguish rang in the room. "That a wise, strong man who believed in you should die like a dog…"

Jochebed lifted her head to look at the young man.

"My son, God weeps for our bondage." The rebuke was stern though tears ran down her cheeks.

"Mother, I am sorry." The contrite twenty-three-year-old buried his face in her lap like a boy.

"God of Abraham, Isaac, and Jacob," the gentle, wrinkled hand smoothed the tousled black hair as she prayed, "send us a sign that you haven't forgotten us. My husband is ill. Help my children to find you."

She turned to gaze at the beloved face on the pillow. The herbs had done their work. He rested quietly now with only an occasional shudder. Absently the mother continued to stroke Aaron's hair.

I moved to kneel beside my family. Tears of helplessness and desperation trickled down my own cheeks. There was nothing I could do to heal them. Jochebed continued to plead with her God.

"How long will you delay to fulfill your promises?"

"You do not care," I silently said to the God who seemed too distant to be real. "I will rescue my family without you. Perhaps you are like these Egyptian gods of stone and can really do nothing. What good is your promise of a homeland given to Abraham when we die in bondage?"

When I wasn't too tired, I lay on my pallet and wept to the distant, silent stars. My hope of being able to save my family dwindled gradually into the dust of drudgery and despair.

Chapter 4

Spring came. Daily I watered the herbs that were so necessary to my poultices and mixtures. Father remained an invalid and, although her cough was better, Mother was not strong. Still, they spent time in the warming sun and seemed better. Often the old couple just sat side-by-side holding hands. Their obvious love made my heart ache for what I would never have. The frailty of our parents was more than my brother could bear. Aaron spent more time with the smiths. He was an avid pupil and the men were eager to train him in all the various subtleties of their craft.

So, I cared for both Amram and Jochebed while attending to the needs of the community. There were many in need of my skills. The whips, scaffolds, and bricks took their toll on the men and women of Goshen. I gave up hope of ever seeing freedom. Season followed season in the tedium of plaster, sand, straw, and whips. Then one day I saw my brother.

One of the overseers was a brutal man. He delighted in causing pain. Many times, I had to bandage broken hands or cleanse beaten backs after Omarah had passed by. Joel, a proud young man and friend of Aaron, was his latest victim.

"Miriam, come quickly." The small girl, Elisheva, tugged at my hand when I lingered over the basket of bandages and herbs deciding which to put in. "Joel is hurt."

I added another roll of the ragged strips of cloth that served as my bandages and followed the child. As usual, my veil refused to stay securely on my head as I ran beside the girl. My height made me an easy spectacle to recognize. Long ago, I ceased to listen to the condemnation of the other women for my lack of decorum. Too often, I was rushing to the side of a badly injured brother or husband. We hurried through the streets and along the road toward the river. Each day a steady stream of workers plodded back and forth from the landing to the construction site. Today it was eerily deserted. In the unusual silence, I could hear the thud of whip on flesh.

"In here." I pulled my companion into the bulrushes.

We crept forward until we were close enough to see Omarah standing over the bleeding body. The child and I crouched low, barely breathing. Joel lay in the road. I dared not go to his side until the man left. From the split baskets and broken yoke, I could tell that he had been assigned to bring a load of river clay to the nearby monument site.

"See that you show proper respect for an officer of the King of the Two Lands," the order was snarled. A look of satisfaction crossed the broad face of the Egyptian when Joel tried to raise himself.

"Don't," I begged desperately in my heart.

His pride would get the young man killed. The child at my side was crying. I pressed her face into my shoulder so the sound wouldn't be heard. Tears were running down my cheeks, too. Omarah raised his staff again. Joel was spared by the arrival of a man on horseback.

"What are you doing?"

The voice sounded like my father although the words were Egyptian and Amram never spoke with such authority. Startled, I looked out between the stems of the plants. Mounted on a handsome bay was without a doubt a member of the royal household. From the fine linen edged in gold to the neck collar bearing the wings of Horus the man was a prince.

Omarah dropped to one knee. "Great Prince, the dog of a slave was disobedient."

He groveled more deeply when the man dismounted. The prince bent down and looked at Joel. My friend appeared unconscious. I saw the noble face when he turned to the overseer. The high cheekbones and prominent nose were exactly like Jochebed's. I almost cried out. It was my brother! Prince Moses towered over the cringing Egyptian. There was rage in his voice.

"Who gave you the right to beat a man in such a way?"

"Mighty One." Another low bow accompanied the words. "The dog of a Hebiru was proud and insolent. Great Lord, such attitudes must be crushed. They lead to rebellion." A look of cunning appeared on Omarah's face even as he raised his hands in homage to the prince.

"Surely my Lord Prince would not want it known that he pities the despised slaves of Goshen. The Great King, the Father of all in Egypt, would not be pleased."

The royal brows drew into a frown at the implied threat. "Nor would he be pleased to know that this man will not be able to work for weeks, because of your actions."

Moses bit off the words and moved toward the overseer. He picked up Omarah's staff. The man scuttled backward like a crab trying to stay the prescribed distance from the royal person. I saw my brother weighing the rod in his hand. He glanced again toward Joel.

"You beat him with this?" The question was very calm.

"Great Prince, the Hebiru was most defiant." The man held up his hands pleadingly. Like most bullies, he was fearful now that power had shifted.

Moses looked up and down the road. There was no one in sight except the unconscious Hebiru slave and the cringing Egyptian foreman. For a long silent moment, the prince stared at Joel's body. I held my breath wondering what he was thinking. Then he swung around and struck the overseer with his own staff.

"Now you will know how it feels to be beaten with this club." The words were cold with rage.

The blow caught the man on the side of his head rather than the back. He toppled to one side, twitched, and lay still. Moses dropped the weapon and fell to one knee beside his victim. Even from the distance, I was sure the man was dead. With a curse, my brother dragged the body down to the softer dirt by the river's edge. He hollowed out a shallow grave and rolled Omarah into it. Then he rinsed his hands in the river. They were still shaking when he reached for his horse's reins. The look I glimpsed was that of a desperate man as again he glanced all around. With a last look at Joel, he mounted and raced away. I hurried out of my hiding place.

"Go back and get blankets to carry Joel home," I ordered little Elisheva. "Your big brothers must come help."

"Is he alive?" she asked wide-eyed.

"Yes." My assurance was calm, although it could be days before we knew if the young man would survive his injuries.

"Run quickly." With a light shove, I sent the child on her way.

Joel's wounds were severe. Even in the road, I could tell that he had broken ribs. The young man had lost a lot of blood from a deep gash on one leg. The child and her brothers helped me carry the victim to my house. Jochebed and I worked together with bandages and herbs to staunch the blood. One arm was shattered from a blow. I wasn't sure that the man would ever be able to use it again. Aaron paced outside swearing vengeance until I was afraid the Egyptians would hear and blame him when Omarah's body was found. I went to warn my brother and found my little companion there before me.

"Aaron," she tugged the tall man's hand. When he finally looked down, she motioned for him to stoop down.

"He's already dead," she confided in a tone that she thought was secretive.

It carried beyond us to her brothers still lingering in the street. They turned to stare at their sister. I heard the words and gasped. The child knew too much. She could bring death to us all.

My brother looked confused. "What do you mean?"

"The Prince hit him and he fell down." The statement was out before I could intervene.

Still the man was baffled. "How do you know?" He crouched at her level to look into the innocent brown eyes.

"I saw him." Her calm tone seemed to convince him. "Miriam and I went to help Joel. We were in the bulrushes."

My brother raised a questioning eyebrow in my direction. I had to nod.

He turned back to his informant with one last question. "Which Prince?"

"I don't know," the little girl shrugged.

In the open door behind me, I heard my mother whisper, "Moses."

"Aaron, come inside, we need your help." With an effort I kept my voice steady.

I desperately prayed that no one else had heard Elisheva's conversation. It was too late. She scampered over to accompany her brothers home. I heard many voices ask the little girl what she saw on the road. Carefully I closed the door before facing my mother.

"Moses saved Joel's life!" she stated joyfully.

"He killed a man," I pointed out, "and now everyone knows."

With a gesture toward the closed door, I included all the excited speculation in the street. Jochebed didn't seem to hear me. Her voice was raised in praise.

"Praise to the God of Abraham, Isaac, and Jacob who has raised up a Redeemer for the people!"

Amram added, "Amen."

Aaron frowned in disbelief. "Our brother has forgotten that he is Hebiru. I saw him ride by yesterday," the young man sneered. "He is so proud and haughty, he barely looked at the men toiling to bring a statue into position. Instead the man was content to talk to the Master Foreman and tour the completed temple."

"Now he will see." My father wheezed the words feebly. "He will see the pain of his kin and act."

"Yes." Happily, my mother planned. "He will use his royal influence to ease the lot of the children of Israel. My son will be like Joseph. Moses will rescue the people."

A moan from Joel as he regained consciousness recalled us to our duties. Discussion of Prince Moses was forgotten. I stayed at the young man's side as he fought for his life.

Aaron brought the next news of Moses. He came in, blinking after the glaring sun. Mother and Father dozed on cushions in the corner. Joel was at last resting comfortably. The fever I feared had not set in. Now I noticed that my brother had what looked like blood on his hand and a cut on his forehead.

"Have you been fighting?" I whispered, not wanting to wake any of the patients. "Come outside." I gathered up bandages and followed my brother into the sunlight. Shaking my head, I scolded him. "How could you fight? You know it only brings more trouble."

"I was breaking up a fight," he stated, wincing as I cleaned the wound on his head. "Mother will have to give up her dream of Moses as our deliverer."

Surprised at the words and acid tone, I dropped the bandage.

Looking into my eyes the man continued bitterly, "Our fine royal brother has run away."

"Why?" My heart pounded with fear.

"Morhad and Samal were fighting near the new monument site this morning. I tried to stop them and got this for my trouble."

When he gestured toward his head, I noticed it was again seeping blood. With shaking hands, I fumbled with the bandage.

"Prince Moses rode up. It is easy to be superior and noble on a fine horse." The tone was scathing. "Looking down at us he asked, 'Why do you strike your brothers? Are you not all kin? It would be better if you worked together.' The disdain in his voice ..." Aaron ground his teeth at the memory.

"What happened?" I prodded when he glared angrily away from me.

"Morhad was angry. Foolishly he spoke up." Aaron shook his head at the audacity of his comrade. "He could have lost his life for such rashness."

Impatient now, I shook my brother's arm when he sat silent. "What did he say?"

Aaron's mouth formed a half-smile. "Samal and I were on our knees. Morhad stood there staring up at the Prince. 'If we don't stop, Great Prince, what will you do? Will you kill us as you did Omarah the Overseer yesterday?' I couldn't believe he would say such things."

The gasp that escaped my lips expressed my own shock. My brother sat silent, head bowed.

"And ..." I prodded, crouching beside the man.

"The Prince jerked the reins so sharply that his horse shied. I don't think I'll ever forget the look on his face. In that moment, Morhad did look at his own death. Moses bent from the horse with his whip raised. We all cringed away from the rage in the man's eyes. Then without a word or any punishment, our brother whirled the horse and raced off toward the east. When I last saw Prince Moses, it was just a puff of dust disappearing on the horizon."

I sat stunned by the turn of events. Rather than a hero, my baby brother was a coward. My mother's dreams, like mine, had turned to dust.

Before sunrise the next day, Egyptian soldiers were searching the village and riverbanks. We were all questioned about seeing Prince Moses. Omarah's body was found but there was no sign of my brother. Late in the afternoon, the Princess' personal guards summoned me. I recognized the captain and wondered if he remembered as clearly as I did our last meeting. Two decades had passed since that terrifying morning. He made no move to touch me, for which I was both grateful and oddly affronted. The palace looked the same and even the Princess had not changed much. She was plumper but her skin was still as smooth and soft as only the finest of lotions and cosmetics could make it.

"Leave us." The order was swiftly obeyed. "Mir-em, I sent for you because my son is gone."

She paced in agitation, wringing her hands. The bracelets on her wrists were set to tinkling by the urgency of her movements. The woman turned hope filled eyes toward me.

"Has Moses returned to your, uh, his, uh, family?"

I wished I could reply in the affirmative and ease her anguish. My low bow didn't ease the despair in her attitude.

"No, Great Lady," I had to answer truthfully.

"Have you seen him?" From the far side of the room she turned to ask the question.

I opened my mouth and then shut it. How could I tell this gentle, sheltered woman that her son, my brother, had killed a man and fled for his own life? She saw my hesitation and hurried to take my hand.

"You have," eagerly she insisted. "Tell me."

This was not royalty demanding but a mother's pleading for her child.

"Kind Princess." Looking into her eager face, I hedged while my mind sought a way to tell the truth without hurting her. "Moses did not see me."

"You did see him! When?"

Imperiously she lifted her chin. The command in her look forced my response.

"Two days ago." I bent my head hoping vainly that she would ask nothing more.

"Where?" She tightened her grip on my hands.

"On the river road near Piton."

"He was alone?" The question came swiftly.

"There were no attendants," I confirmed.

"How is it that you saw him but he didn't see you?" The lady pounced on the one thing I wished she would ignore.

"I was in the bulrushes beside the road waiting ..." My sentence trailed off because I didn't know how to confess my brother's crime.

The Princess stood up, angry now. "Why were you hiding and waiting at the side of the road for the Prince to ride by?"

Terrified, I fell at her feet. Now the words tumbled out. "Mighty Princess, I did not know that Prince Moses would come. The overseer was beating a man. I have skills in healing. The child brought me to help Joel."

Without lifting my head from the floor, I could hear the gold sandal tapping as she considered my blurted explanation.

"Then tell us." The voice was slightly kinder but still regal. "What did you see?"

Without moving from my prone position, I told the woman of the confrontation between Omarah and Moses.

"My son killed an Egyptian in defense of a Hebiru?" The Princess was stunned and I risked raising my head. Head bowed into her hands, the royal lady sat dejected. "Impetuous, foolish boy," she sighed.

"It was an accident." I felt the need to plead my brother's case.

"That will not matter to my father's advisors." Again the sad sigh. "They have always sought an excuse to get rid of my son. He could have done so much good..."

A single tear ran down her cheek. My heart tightened when I realized that even as a prince my brother was not safe.

"Where is Moses now?" The lady rose, prepared to do battle.

"He has fled." I was glad I could tell the truth.

"Girl, do not lie to me." Surprisingly strong hands pulled me to my feet.

"Great Lady, it is true. The deed became known in Goshen."

At her raised eyebrows, I admitted, "Mine were not the only eyes."

"Where did he go?" The hands released my arms. The Princess moved slowly toward her chair.

"That, Noble One, I do not know. He was seen riding to the east, toward the desert."

Sinking into the seat, the woman buried her face in her hands. "My son, my son."

She pushed away my comforting hand. I slipped out of the room to find her maids. Then I hurried back to my home. For the next few days, any sudden noise startled me but no soldiers came to drag me away to prison. We heard that the Princess was in disgrace because it was believed her son was the murderer of Omarah, Overseer to the King of the Black Land. Moses' flight was taken to be an admission of his guilt.

"There are no eyewitnesses to be found." Sadly, my brother explained the facts to Jochebed and Amram. "The soldiers have spread the rumors heard among the workmen. Pharaoh's advisors eagerly believe them. It seems that Prince Moses was not as well liked in palace circles as we thought. His horse was found wandering along the desert highway. The man has disappeared into the sands to the east or has been killed by bandits. Should he return he would be an outcast. His name has been erased from all official records. His *ka* will be forced to wander the wastelands forever."

"God will preserve my son," confidently both Mother and Father continued to insist. "Moses was not saved from the river to die in the desert."

I marveled at their faith and wondered what it would feel like to believe as deeply and surely as they did in a God that really cared for the children of Israel or anyone.

Chapter 5

Joel slowly healed. A love blossomed between us that I never dreamed I would find. We sat together in the warm sun as his ribs knit. I rejoiced in the company and conversation of the young man. He was ten years older than Aaron. My brother spent long hours following his hero when we were children. Even then, few men possessed Joel's skill of leveling the huge bricks. He could strike a block of limestone at just the right point for it to split neatly. Of all the men in Goshen, Joel was the only one I dreamed of marrying, but I put away those hopes years earlier. He was one of the few residents taller than me. Joel didn't make me feel like an awkward giantess. Now it was delightful to sit in the spring sun with my spinning and listen to his stories of work on the monuments. It was enough that we were together and I could watch his expressive face as he talked. I suppressed the occasional longing to run my fingers through the man's straight black hair.

"From the tops of the buildings you can see the sea," he told me. "As I work, I can watch the sails on the ships arriving in the delta or leaving for foreign lands. I think about the sights the sailors see and the adventures they have. Do you ever wonder what life is like outside of Goshen?"

"I have been to the palace," I confessed, "but I would like to see other places. Egypt is such a narrow strip of land along the Nile. I wonder what other countries are like."

"Across the delta to the west are cliffs and then sand as far as the eye can see." With a shake of his head Joel informed me, "If that is where the *ka* of a person goes after death, I don't want to die. To wander such a wasteland must be like living as an invalid ..."

The words trailed off and the man tried to flex his injured arm. A frown crossed the once handsome face now marred by a jagged scar across one cheek. As I feared, the muscles refused to gain strength despite my daily massaging with herbs and Joel's impatient attempts at forcing the limb to bend. I dropped my spinning whorl and began to massage the muscles almost desperately. Each squeeze of my hand was a prayer to God for healing. I didn't expect a miracle though. Anger flashed through me and I silently raged at heaven.

"What is to the east?" I asked as much to divert the suddenly dark turn of conversation as out of curiosity.

After a moment, the man responded, "To the east is the King's Highway along the Great Sea. The delta stretches for miles until it merges with the estuary called the Sea of Reeds. I have watched caravans camp for days before the tide lowers enough to allow a safe crossing. Beyond that, somewhere, is the land of our fathers." A dreamy note entered his voice and brown eyes stared into the distance. "Far away is Canaan, the land that Jacob and his sons came from."

"Someday we will return to that land." My mother's voice surprised me. She leaned on the bent limb I found as a cane for her. Eyes bright with hope stared to the east. "God will send a Deliverer to lead the children of Israel out of bondage."

Her oft-repeated belief no longer stirred me. Looking at the wounded man beside me, I wondered how a compassionate God could allow strong young men to be beaten so that they could no longer work.

I was surprised when my companion took my hand one evening as the sun disappeared into the western desert.

"Miriam." His tentative tone alerted me to a change in the conversation. "Miriam."

The caressing tone made my heart begin to pound. My breath came in short gasps. I wanted to let him continue to stroke my palm but I didn't dare allow myself to hope that he cared for me. When one strong arm slipped around my shoulders and drew me close to the man, I stiffened.

"Don't be afraid," Joel whispered, "I will not harm you. I owe you my life, Miriam of the healing hands and beautiful face."

I couldn't believe the words.

"Joel, you should not say such things. Someone will hear you."

"That would not be a problem," he insisted. "Don't you understand that I love you, sweet Miriam?"

"You cannot." I pulled myself free, appalled that I had allowed the young man to think that I was marriageable.

Joel retained my hand.

"Miriam." His voice was deep with emotion. "I know that you think no one can desire you."

Tears rose to my eyes. With an effort, I drew myself back from the young man. The last rays of the sun glanced off the gold of the temples and monuments and lit the sky with an unusual glow. In that light, I saw tenderness and love in the brown eyes.

"You cannot. You don't understand ..." My voice was choked and to my dismay tears started rolling down my cheeks.

I caught my breath when a gentle thumb brushed the drops from my face. My heart urged me to accept the offered love however fleeting it might be. Pride and the memory of my secret shame kept me from throwing myself into the man's arms.

"Miriam." Again my name was on his lips. "I do understand. You think that you are an outcast because of something you had no control over."

Startled, I pulled back. "How?" My question came out as a croak.

A fresh wave of grief washed over me at the thought that everyone in Goshen, even this man, knew of my secret childhood shame.

"I asked Aaron years ago." A tug on my arm brought me into the Joel's lap. He wrapped his strong arm around me and held me securely against his shoulder. "Amram refused to consider my request for your hand. I had to know why I was not good enough to marry my friend's sister."

Twisting in the embrace, I tried to see the face bent over me.

"You ... you ... wanted to ... to ... m-marry m-me?" Amazement made me stammer.

"I still do." The deep words had a ring of sincerity. His arm tightened around my waist and drew me closer. "What will prevent us?"

"I ... I ..." My mind refused to cooperate and find a rational excuse.

A thousand answers raced in my head. My shame, our slavery, facing the gossip, all the reasons were lost when persuasive lips covered mine. I responded with all the longing stored in my heart. Eventually we drew apart slightly.

"My beloved Miriam." I began to cry again at the caring in my lover's voice.

That was how Jochebed found us. I was sobbing in Joel's arms while he stroked my hair. Wisely, the woman said nothing. Later Amram and Joel talked long into the night. I never asked what arguments were used, content to have my father's blessing to be Joel's bride. After his initial surprise, Aaron was delighted.

"Congratulations, my friend." A slap on his friend's shoulder signaled approval. "My sister will make you a fine wife."

I was amazed at the genuine joy in the community when the announcement was made public. My mother washed and combed my waist-length hair until it was as smooth as silk. From deep within the leather trunk she drew out the dress she wore years earlier to her own marriage feast. We added a new layer to the skirt so that the gown was long enough for my height. After I was dressed, we stood side by side in front of my father and brother.

"My wife, in our daughter I see my bride again." Amram's choked words made tears rise to my eyes. "You are a lovely jewel, my child," he added with a kiss on my forehead.

"Joel is fortunate indeed to marry my lovely sister," Aaron surprised me by stating with a hug.

Our wedding was a grand celebration of food and dancing. There was even wine obtained by Aaron. I didn't ask where he got it.

As the feast continued, I began to feel very nervous. From beneath my veil, I shot glances at Joel. He seemed unconcerned with the coming night. The bridesmaids led me to my home, decorated with special flowers for fertility. Even the bridal bed was strewn with lotus blossoms. The whole house was scented with the rich fragrance. Feeling very young, I sat on the soft blankets to await my husband. He was not long in arriving. Hearty congratulations and the sound of clanging instruments signaled the groom's arrival at the door. By the flickering light of the one oil lamp, I saw the tall figure enter the room. My hands began to shake and I felt tears of hysteria rising in my throat.

"Joel, I cannot." I wasn't even sure if I spoke aloud.

The man crossed the small room in two strides to kneel beside me. He took my trembling hands in his warm grasp. Then he brushed my hair off my forehead to kiss me where my brows met in a pucker.

"My wife, there is no need to hurry."

When he spoke, a tremor ran through me. It was a shiver of desire not fear.

"God has given us this night and all nights for our love."

His lips traced the curve of my face with little kisses until he reached my lips. Dread gone, I offered my lips to my husband. Confidently I responded to his desire. My hands began to explore his body as the man ran his hands down my figure. I had seen and bandaged the broad chest but it was different in the magic of the night and the scented bridal bed. I forgot my doubts and my shame in the ecstasy of the night. Never again would nightmares and memories of the Egyptian captain trouble me.

Morning light found us dozing in the tumbled blankets. Joel roused to bend over me. His loving and passionate kiss awakened me. Joyfully I welcomed my lover again.

For a week, we were allowed the privacy of the house. Because of my parents were ill, Joel agreed to live in my home rather than taking me to his father's home. After the bridal week, we all resumed the normal day-to-day existence. I went to the well and market each morning. Sometimes Jochebed helped me as I tended the sick and injured.

Aaron left each morning with Joel for the work site. It sickened me to know that my husband was forced to work in the mud pits. He had no strength to swing the hammer to split the rocks and, with his ruined arm, he could no longer climb the scaffoldings. Instead, he was ordered into the pits with the old men. Each night he returned covered with evidence of the bondage of the children of Israel.

Privately I raged at God. It surprised me to learn that Joel firmly believed in the God of Abraham, Isaac, and Jacob. One night I bitterly confronted my husband.

"How can you continue to trust a God who would allow you to be humiliated day after day? Because God turned his face away," I rubbed the man's useless arm, "you are condemned to tramp in the mud all day like an animal."

"Miriam, just because God seems to be silent does not mean that he is absent." His answer was patient.

"Why will God not act to rescue us then? Are we so evil that God has turned his back?" The question nagged me.

"Was I evil so that I was beaten?" Joel's argument surprised me.

"Of course not," my answer was heated. "It was Omarah's viciousness that made him beat you."

"It is the same with our bondage. The children of Israel are not being punished. God will act in the time ordained."

"When is that?" I demanded.

My father's persistent cough barked into the room. I saw my mother push herself to her feet despite her own frailty and bring her husband a soothing drink.

With tears I whispered, "All who trust in God will all be dead before we are delivered."

Joel reached out and drew me into his lap. Gentle kisses on my cheek emphasized the words.

"Miriam, who can know the mind of the Living God? I suppose many would say I have a right to be bitter. The Egyptian left me with a scarred face and useless arm, but I have a greater treasure because of that. What does it matter that I stamp mud all day if I can hold you all night?"

The argument ended with kisses and caresses. I began to understand that my husband saw God's hand even in the tragedy of his beating. For many days, I pondered this idea. Still I could not see that God cared for the children of Israel. Each season brought harder work and stricter taskmasters.

I had a brief interval of expectant joy. My faith was renewed as I felt the new life growing in me. For nearly five months I carried Joel's child under my heart. Then my body rebelled.

"I am cursed," I sobbed in heartbroken grief to Jochebed. "Even this greatest of a woman's joy has been denied me."

Joel held me. He let me weep and rage. I knew he was saddened but he never spoke a word of blame although I almost wished he would. It would have eased the guilt I felt. Each evening the man made me walk outside because I refused to be seen during the day. The sympathetic words and looks from the other women were too much to bear.

"It is because of the Egyptian," I told my husband one night as we stood near the river.

"No, Beloved," sternly the man spoke. "You must never think that. God has a plan for you. Think of the promise that the One God gave to Abraham."

Dully I recited, "God said, 'You will have descendants as the stars.' Abraham only had one son," I argued obstinately.

"Abraham's children are all around you here in Goshen and as far away as Midian where the family of Esau settled." My husband kissed me. "You are one of Abraham's offspring. Whether you see it or not, you are part of the fulfillment of the covenant with our father Abraham."

"I wanted to give you a son," I wailed, clinging to the gentle lover at my side.

"Do not grieve for what might have been." Joel caressed my back until I stopped sobbing. "We have to trust even when we don't understand the ways of God."

My nights were spent in Joel's arms and my days were devoted to caring for my parents and the other sick and injured among the people. I even became reconciled to the lack of a child. Moses was only a distant memory. Occasionally I wondered if my brother had survived in the desert when he fled from Egypt. Thoughts of freedom seemed as remote as the Great Sea to the north.

As the weeks passed, I let my husband heal the sorrow in my heart. I grew to depend on his deep faith. I could almost believe that God had plan for my life as wife of Joel. I was sure my life would continue in the steady routine until I died. There was no way I could rescue my parents from the death that grew closer with each cough. Still I found a kind of contentment.

Then God struck me at the depths of my heart.

"Miriam, come quickly." I heard the urgent shout even before the speaker was in sight. "There has been an accident."

Hastily I gathered my supplies and hurried after the young man. My heart clenched when I saw the crowd. This must indeed be a disaster to draw such a mob. The people moved aside when they saw me. Abel led the way. A huge stone block had rolled off the transport logs. It lay tilted at an awkward angle near the pit.

"Here, Miriam." Stout Seth motioned me closer. Several men lay bleeding on the straw at the edge of the mud hole. I set to work and didn't even notice the awkward silence for several minutes. When I had bandaged the bleeding, I looked around.

"Are there more injuries?"

The question was met with sidelong glances and shuffling feet.

"None that you can help," at last Seth responded.

I followed his slowly turning head. The sound that came from my throat was animal-like. Joel lay beneath the edge of the stone. Strong hands prevented me from throwing myself on his body. I struggled against the men until I collapsed into hysteria.

"He pushed several others out of the way." Seth tried to comfort me with the information. "There are men who will live because of your husband."

The news was no solace. I crawled across the muddy ground to take my lover's hand. Already it was as cold as the stone that took his life. Sobs shook my body and I wailed like a lost child. Aaron finally arrived and carried me home. Jochebed was unable to stop my keening until she mixed some herbs that made me sleep.

From the moment we buried Joel, I shut myself off from God and my kin. My challenge was thrown into the sky night after night.

"How dare you steal the only happiness I have known? It is not enough that you withhold the answer to my mother's prayers and turn your back on your people. Now you have killed my love."

Jochebed tried to reason with me. "God did not kill Joel. It was an accident. Other men, both Hebiru and Egyptian, were killed and injured."

"If your God truly cared about us, the stone would only have killed Egyptians. You say God will deliver the children of Israel. That is the delusion of a fool."

I didn't care that my harsh words made the old woman wince. Inflicting agony on others was the only way to ease my pain. Eventually my rage subsided to a dull uncaring ache. I resumed my work as healer to the community. There seemed to be no feeling left in me. In my heart, I nursed a secret contempt toward the God of Abraham, Isaac, and Jacob.

"Prove to me that you are real," I defied my silent opponent. "If you can prove that you exist, then perhaps I will believe in God again."

Chapter 6

The long years stretched out and receded in sameness. Aaron and I mourned the death of first Jochebed and then Amram. They died within a few months of each other. The gold from the Princess was used to purchase the services of the embalmer and a small tomb. My parents would not lie in the desert sand to be ravaged by wild beasts.

I never saw the princess again. A few years after Moses disappeared, the royal barge brought her body to be buried beneath the small monument that bore her name. A year later the old Pharaoh died. Grand ceremonies were held at the temple that bore his name and was inscribed with his exploits. Then his embalmed, wrapped, and sanctified body was taken to the secret burial place of Kings. When alive, each Pharaoh was Horus, son of Osiris. In death, the king became Osiris, in charge of all life in Egypt. It was very important that the *ka* of the King remain undisturbed even after death. The silent pyramids and their attendant monuments and mortuary temples all paid tribute to attempts to keep past rulers undisturbed.

The new Pharaoh was a harsh, proud man. I saw him from a distance once. He insisted on more marvelous feats of building and statuary in the Treasure City called by his name, Raamses. Men pushed beyond endurance died in the heat and dust.

I wept angrily to the One God. "Don't you see us? Can't you save us?" The faith of my parents seemed futile and foolish. With each year of God's silence, I became more and more convinced that the God of Israel was helpless. The songs my mother had sung seemed empty memories of a hopeless people.

There was joy, too. Aaron finally married. He chose little Elisheva. The little girl had matured into a sweet, softly rounded young woman. Unlike me, she was careful to keep her face covered with a veil as soon as she was old enough to wear one. From the day she saw Moses kill the overseer, Aaron had been her protector and champion. I was not too surprised when he announced that he spoke to her father. The wedding was a simple matter of the girl's father binding the couple's wrists together with a scarf and calling down a blessing on their union. We had a small feast but the oppression of the increased workload made it a muted and shortened affair. He brought her to our small house. I envied his joy and remembered my lost love. Many nights I cried for Joel and ached for his touch and comfort. In the silent loneliness of the darkness, I tried to remember what my husband believed.

"God is present, even in the darkest times." I could almost hear his voice. "The hand of the God of our fathers is not against us. Instead, God wants to give us all that has been promised. When we turn to God we'll find he has been near all along."

My heart refused to believe that Joel was right, even though I desperately wanted to be comforted. The daily sight of our bondage and the shouts of the overseers drowned the beckoning whisper of God.

In quick succession, I became the aunt of Nadah, Abihu, Eleazar, and Ithamar. Somehow, the children's eagerness and joy inspired hope in me. My grief eased when I held the small bodies in my arms and told them stories. I began to recite the saga of Abraham the Wanderer, Isaac the Shepherd and, most of all, Jacob and his sons. Like me, the youngsters loved the story of how Joseph the Honored came to power under Pharaoh.

"It could happen again," I told the boys.

Gradually, I began to almost hope that it *was* possible for God to intervene in the lives of his people. By telling the stories of the patriarchs, I began to find faith.

My heart cried out, "Surely now is the time for you to act. The people cannot bear your silence."

Oddly, the more Pharaoh sought to crush our spirit; the more I began to believe in the God of my mother and father. Despite the harsh cruelty of the Lord of the Two Lands, the children of Israel prospered. Couples found love with each other and bore strong sons and daughters. Our children played secure in the love of their parents. The royal shepherds complained that the flocks of the slaves were more vigorous than the animals they tended. Fields tended by our youngsters produced bountifully so we were never hungry.

"You are a Mighty God," I confessed one night looking up at the stars that hung in the black night sky. "I see that you are making of us a great nation, just as you promised Abraham. Won't you share your plan with your servants so that we may not lose hope and follow the gods of Egypt?"

One night Aaron stopped me as I returned from washing old Ethamar for burial. It was a sad task and I was glad of the interruption.

"Miriam." My brother's voice was a hoarse whisper. "I have to talk to you."

"Are you sick?"

Surprise at his tone gave way to concern as I saw his odd look. I gripped the man's wrist and pulled him aside.

"Miriam," he repeated my name in the same desperate whisper.

"Aaron, what is wrong? What has happened?"

Heart pounding in apprehension, I felt his forehead, but he didn't seem to have a fever. Fear crossed my mind. Surely this brother had not also murdered. The man caught my hands in a tight grasp.

"I think I am going crazy," he gasped out.

Then he released me and sank down against the well. Holding his head in his hands the forty-five year old man rocked like a frightened child. Truly concerned, I knelt in front of him.

Gently I asked, "Why do you say that?"

"I have been hearing things," he answered, still rocking and shaking his head.

"What things?" Carefully I kept my voice calm even as my heart pounded.

Aaron moaned deep in his throat. He stared past me.

"A voice that says, '*Go into the desert toward Midian. Meet my Servant. You will speak for him to Pharaoh*'."

I sat back on my heels wondering if God had suddenly started answering prayers.

When I didn't say anything, he added, "Every day for a week these words have drummed in my head. I hear them in my dreams, *'Go into the desert'*. The pounding of the hammers intensifies the words. *'Meet my Servant'*. Am I going mad, Sister? Give me some herb to stop the voice." My brother dropped his hands and stared at me in desperation. There were tears in his voice as he pleaded for relief.

I never knew how, but I understood. Leaning forward, I assured the man. "It is God calling you."

The words shocked me as I spoke them. Who was I to claim to know what the One God did? Yet, a great confidence grew inside me. The God I raged against was putting words into my mouth that I would never have spoken. Aaron shook his head in denial and opened his mouth to speak.

I continued to declare the path. "The Living God has chosen a Deliverer for his people. You will be the one who proclaims the Redeemer." I stood up and looked down at my unhappy brother. "You must obey God and go into the desert. The God of Abraham, Isaac, and Jacob will be with you and direct you."

"How can I go?" The man argued. "I cannot just walk out of town and go to the desert."

"You have to," I repeated. "Isn't there a caravan leaving for the east to trade for camels and horses with the nomads?"

The solution presented itself and I smiled complacently. In my mind, I saw Aaron meeting a shadowy figure and heard rejoicing in the streets of Goshen.

"I am not a trader. I am a goldsmith. I will not be allowed to go." Aaron shook his head.

"You will go." I nodded my head firmly.

Still my brother argued. His eyes were narrow with annoyance as he stared at me. I was not moved from my newfound belief that, indeed, God was calling to Aaron bar Amram, goldsmith in the land of Egypt. Finally, I sent him to his wife and sons.

"Tell your family that you are going with the traders," I suggested.

Shaking his head, the man shook my shoulder. "Miriam, sister, there is no way I can go to Midian. Even if you are right and this voice is from God, I cannot obey."

Watching my brother plod away with head bowed, I understood his doubt. There was no rational way one of Pharaoh's Hebiru goldsmiths would be allowed to leave the land. However, my heart insisted that God would fulfill what he ordained. I pondered the conviction that clung to me. Just as Joel had said, when I looked around, God was present. Now the One who met Abraham and wrestled with Jacob was urging my brother into the desert to meet the Deliverer. For the first time in years, I found myself humming. My imagination painted a grand picture. Together Aaron and I would join this Deliverer and lead the people from bondage.

I wasn't too surprised to look up from drawing water in the morning and see Aaron hurrying up the street. Anxiously I ran to him, leaving my water jar at the well and ignoring the curious questions. When I caught up with the man, he glanced at me.

"I am being sent with the caravan."

The words, half-expected, still made me gasp, "How? Why?"

Eagerly I trotted beside my brother as he strode toward home.

"A commemorative plaque for the outpost beyond Pi Hahiroth, near the Brook of Egypt, needs special care with the installation. I am being sent to do it. A troop of Pharaoh's soldiers will accompany us for safety."

We reached the house. Elisheva looked up in surprise from her kneading as her husband rushed in.

"I am being sent to install a gold plaque." The brief explanation was all the man said.

Rapidly he folded a blanket and one of Amram's desert robes into a bundle. They would be needed in the open air of the desert and against the chill evening breezes from the sea. Hastily I added some bread and dried fruits because Elisheva stood stunned and silent in the middle of the room. The bread dough hung limply from her hands. A water bottle completed the packing.

"It will be all right, Wife," tenderly the man assured his wife with a quick hug. "I will return in less than a moon cycle. Miriam will explain it all to you." After a quick kiss on her forehead, he hurried out the door. I followed although I had to run to keep pace.

"At least the voices have stopped," he remarked after stowing his bundles in one of the carts.

"Aaron, don't you see? That piece of gold is just an excuse." I waved my hand to a nearby cart guarded by four alert soldiers. "God has made use of Pharaoh's business to get you into the desert to meet the Deliverer."

My brother smiled at me. "Miriam, you place too much weight on this trip. Amroth, the Egyptian who was to go, fell sick in the night. That's the only reason I am being sent."

Stubbornly I shook my head. With confidence I repeated, "You will meet the man the One God has prepared for the deliverance of the children of Israel."

Aaron clapped his hand over my mouth and looked around guiltily to see if anyone overheard my ecstatic words. Seeing that each person was busy with loading, he relaxed.

"Do not say such a thing! Would you bring death to us all?" The words were an angry whisper. "The one thing the King fears is freedom for the Hebiru slaves. The hint of such a thing will bring down his wrath in a massacre."

Angrily I twisted away from my brother's restraining hand.

"If the God of Abraham, Isaac, and Jacob desires our freedom, it will be accomplished!" I hissed the words in a low whisper.

The statement surprised me. It was something Jochebed would have said. Never would I have expected my own tongue to utter such words. Aaron turned his back but I followed.

"You are part of that plan, Brother," I warned. "God has shown you the part you are to play. You will speak for God's messenger."

Silently we stared at each other. Disbelief was plainly written on his face. Shouts and the movement of camels and wagons prevented further conversation. The man glanced over his shoulder and started to leave. Impulsively I threw my arms around my brother's neck.

"May the One God of our Fathers bless you and bring you home safely."

Aaron relented enough to give me a quick hard hug in response. I was left standing in the settling dust. Shading my eyes with my hand, I watched the caravan move off into the morning sun. When the wagons were only a cloud of dust in the distance I turned back to the well. All the other women had long since taken their full jars and returned to their homes or gone to take water to the men sweating in the sun.

"God of Abraham, Isaac, and Jacob, be with Aaron; he is afraid and confused." I prayed to the God who suddenly seemed very near and almost *too* real. "Help me prepare for your Deliverer. Tell me what you want me to do," I begged.

Unlike my brother, I didn't hear any voices. The first step seemed to be explaining to Elisheva why Aaron was on his way to Midian. She was doubtful of my interpretation of the journey.

"Miriam, my husband cannot be chosen by the God of our Fathers," she insisted. "He has turned his back on God because the people suffer in bondage."

"I too have raged at the Living One," I admitted. "Day after day I have asked why the chosen people are enslaved. However, I have noticed that even in our bondage, we are blessed with families and children and flocks. Perhaps now is the time for our freedom."

"Perhaps," the young woman was still skeptical. "If it happens, then I will believe."

A crying child interrupted us and I soon wandered over to stare out the window. My heart was filled with a longing for assurance. When I spoke to Aaron, I knew my words were true. Now, with night coming on, I was not so sure. The bright stars rose in a moonless sky and I remembered again the promise of God to Abraham.

"We are a great people now," I mused. "Have you waited until now to fulfill the covenant?" The question was asked of the silent sky. There was no answer. I fell asleep still seated at the window staring at the stars.

Chapter 7

When I saw my brother again, he was a changed man. The moon was new when he left and almost new again when I saw him. Aaron came to me as soon as the caravan returned. I was deep in my thoughts and meal preparations when I heard the door open and then close. Expecting an injured neighbor, I turned to greet my visitor. The man looked different somehow. The confusion was gone from his eyes. It was replaced by a calm purpose that I didn't remember ever seeing on my brother's face.

"Did you meet God's Messenger?" I strained to look behind the man, hoping to see the Deliverer.

Aaron startled me by gripping my arms. His voice resonated in the room. It held the same confidence I saw in the brown eyes looking at me.

"Miriam, you were right. The command came from the God of Abraham, Isaac, and Jacob. I did meet the one chosen by the Living God." He shook his head and confessed, "I still do not understand why this man was picked, nor does he."

"Let me meet him." Eagerly I opened the door.

A bearded stranger stood looking toward the pounding hammers. Occasionally the crack of a whip or cry of pain drifted into town. I barely heard the sound of our bondage any longer. The man at my door winced with each sound.

"Sir, won't you come inside?" Shyly, I spoke to the man the One True God had sent to free us.

The simply woven wool robe and shepherd's staff in his hand marked him as a visitor to Egypt. I stared up at the stranger. He had streaks of gray in the hair above his ears and in his beard. Strong tanned hands held the staff. Honestly, I was disappointed as I held open the door in invitation. The man didn't appear different from any other wandering shepherd. Sometimes nomads brought their flocks from the desert for sale or when grazing was poor. Then the owners begged space in our fields for their animals.

"Don't you recognize me?" The voice was almost familiar. I tilted my head to see the tall man's face. The smile that accompanied the words was sad. "Has it been so long?"

It was that smile, my father's smile, that made my eyes widen. I took a step backward.

"Moses ..." The name was barely a whisper.

One hand caught me as I stumbled. As he stooped to enter the house, I saw his eyes. Deep within the brown depths gleamed conviction and boldness. I gasped at the enormity of the task before this man. Aaron chuckled as he pulled me inside and closed the door.

"It is not often our sister is at a loss for words," he remarked, motioning our younger sibling to take a seat.

Staring from one brother to the other, I stammered, "Why? What? How can this be? We thought you dead." My mind whirled with the realization that a fugitive sat in my home claiming to be the Deliverer from God.

"You are the one who insisted that the God of our Fathers is greater than the gods of the Nile," Aaron reminded me.

I stood in the middle of the room, suddenly aware of how small and dusty the house was.

"This isn't what you are used to," I apologized, finding relief in focusing on the simple task of pouring barley beer into cups for the two men.

A deep laugh startled me. I slopped the liquid onto my hand.

"No, sister." Moses was grinning. "I am more used to stars or a hide tent for covering than four walls of mud brick."

"But you are a Prince of Egypt," I reminded the man.

Hesitantly, I presented the drink to my brother, unsure if I should bow. He took it from me before I could decide.

"I've been a shepherd longer than I was a prince." The words were spoken quietly. "Now I am the servant of the One Living God." The ring of conviction amazed me. "He has sent me to bring the children of Israel out of Egypt."

My heart began pounding so hard I found it hard to breathe. One of my hands went to my throat.

Unbidden the words came, "God of Abraham, Isaac, and Jacob, my mother was right. She said that her son would be the Deliverer sent from God." I addressed the man sitting humbly in my home. "Jochebed believed that you were saved from the river and death for this purpose. Even in your name she saw the hand of the One God. 'He will draw the people out of Egypt'," I quoted.

"Miriam." The man rose to cross the room. He touched my cheek and brushed away the tears I wasn't even aware of. "You and my mother tried to teach me that the One God of our fathers was the only God. I lost that in Pharaoh's house. God had to take me into the desert to teach me …"

A faraway look appeared as my brother remembered his encounter with God. In the silence that followed, I looked at Aaron. He was gazing at his younger brother with a mixture of awe and misgiving.

Returning to the present, Moses looked at me. "I see that you still doubt. You wonder how God could have chosen *me* to free this people from the oppression of the King of Upper and Lower Egypt."

Surprised that he saw through me, I could barely nod.

"My brother has fears also," the stranger asserted, glancing at seated man.

I saw the look the men exchanged. Aaron looked away with a sigh almost like relief. Moses took my hand and led me to a seat beside my brother. Looking from one face to the other the man crouched in front of us to plead his case.

"I understand your uncertainty. Why should I be the one sent to be God's messenger? I have done nothing in my life worth bragging about." A grim smile creased the face. "As a child I hid behind a woman's skirts and denied my heritage and family. Nothing but curiosity led me to visit Goshen. I was only on the river road that morning because I wanted to avoid going through this town."

The shame on my brother's face caused me to reach out a hand. Lost in the memory of that terrible morning, he didn't see me. When he continued, my hand fell into my lap.

"Something erupted in me when I saw the overseer bent over that helpless man." Tanned fingers racked through the dark hair knocking his turban to the floor. "I didn't mean to kill a man. The Egyptian died when I struck him with the rod he was beating the Hebiru with."

Agony rode the confession. Staring beyond us, I knew Moses saw again the crumpled figure of Omarah. I too remembered that morning. I realized that my brother didn't know that I was a witness to the scene. My mouth opened to tell him. The anguish was too much for one man to bear alone. Seeking absolution, he looked at me and then at Aaron.

"I didn't mean to kill the man." The words were a hoarse whisper. "But I did. Then, in terror, I fled from Egypt. Being an adopted prince would not have saved me from the punishment for murder." His face softened with a bleak smile. "There were plenty at court who would have seen to that."

"Brother." I was amazed at such an admission and sought to ease the torment. "You saved Joel's life."

"Miriam," he responded, "I killed a man. That truth remains."

"It was an accident. You didn't know that he would move just as you swung the rod. Omarah lifted his head. That is why …" My voice trailed off when the man bent forward and gripped my arms.

"What do you mean?" Brown eyes searched my face for an answer.

"I was in the bulrushes." The words made the man's hand tighten convulsively and I gasped.

Moses released me. He bent forward waiting for my explanation.

"A child brought word that Omarah was beating another person. I went to take bandages. When I got to the river road, I thought Joel was dead. He lay so still." I shuddered remembering the broken body. "Then he moved and the overseer prepared to beat him again. That's when you arrived." I leaned forward to lay my hand over my brother's clenched fists. "It was good to see our tormentor afraid for a change."

Understanding cleared the frown from the man's face. "Now I know how the men at the monument knew of the deed the next day."

"A little girl was with me," I explained. "She told Aaron and the conversation was overheard."

"It was Elisheva," Aaron remarked defiantly. "The girl is now my wife."

Moses' answer eased our fears. "The hand of God was in it all. Will you listen to what happened to me in the years I have been gone? The God of Abraham, Isaac, and Jacob met me in the desert. I have been changed." Humbly the man asked permission. "Will you let me tell you the story?"

Eagerly I nodded.

Aaron too moved his head in hesitant agreement. "Yes, I would like to hear how you came to be at the Brook of Egypt. We haven't had time to talk."

Glancing at the sun drooping low in the western sky, I suggested, "Go, wash. Elisheva and I will prepare a meal. We will eat and hear our brother's story."

When the men returned, a woman with an infant and a tall son walked with them. Gracefully my new sister-in-law inclined her head. Flowing raven locks were just visible under her veil. She came up to my shoulder when we embraced. I offered water to wash hands and face. Elisheva put the finishing touches on the trays of meat. I was glad for her contribution of vegetables from the market.

"In this same way the tribes of the desert greet their guests," the tall man mused. "Our mother maintained the traditions of our ancestors, even here in Egypt. She told the stories of Abraham, Isaac, and Jacob too. Sometimes I remember bits of them." Then he introduced the woman at his side. "My wife Zipporah," proudly he laid his hand on the boy at her side. "This is Gershom." He gestured to the baby in my sister-in-law's arms. "And Eleazar, my sons. They waited with the caravan while I came here."

My heart was touched by the loneliness evident in the name he gave the older boy. Gershom meant, 'I am an alien in a foreign land.' My brother must have missed Egypt terribly in his exile. Still I wondered at the transformation from honored Prince of Egypt to a despised shepherd and landless nomad who claimed to be God's messenger. I noticed Zipporah's adoration when she looked at her husband. In this woman of the desert, my brother had found a treasure, it seemed. I looked forward to getting to know her.

Chapter 8

I mulled over my brother's confession even as my hands served the bread, vegetables, and bean curd.

"Not grand food," I apologized as we sat down together.

Moses surprised me by taking a piece of the bread and offering thanks. "Blessed be the God of Abraham, Isaac, and Jacob, who gives us bread for our nourishment. May the hands that made it and the lips that taste it be made strong for your service." The words rang out in the small room and I felt the presence of God.

We ate in silence, a family group, each busy with private thoughts. Zipporah sat close beside her husband. I wondered if she believed in Moses' call as he did. Aaron and Elisheva dipped into the bean curd together and I saw a smile of love pass between them. For a moment, the deeply buried knife of grief twisted in me. Never again, for me, would a man's eyes soften with affection. I would not hold a child of my own body. Firmly, I set aside my sadness when my brother spoke.

"You are all impatient to hear what I have to say," he began with a smile. "As you know I fled from Egypt in fear of my life. No doubt you believed that was the last you would ever see of me."

The grin was directed at Aaron. A grunt was all the acknowledgment given. Avoiding the wanderer's eyes, the man bit into his bread.

Eagerly I leaned forward. "Tell us, Moses. What has happened to you?"

"I had no idea where to go." Staring over my head, my brother began his saga. "I let my horse go as soon as I passed the border outpost. A beast like that would get me killed in the desert."

"The horse was found," I remarked, remembering Aaron's acid words of years earlier.

"I'm glad," the stranger at my table smiled, "he was a good animal. The Way of the Philistines was not an option. It is too well patrolled and, since I discarded my royal trappings along with the horse, no one would have believed I was anything except an escaped slave." His amused look encompassed first me and then Aaron. "Which I was."

Surprised and frowning my brother objected, "You were a Prince of Egypt." His voice rose in anger. Half rising Aaron challenged, "What do you know of the daily toil of dirt and straw? Have you felt the whips of slavery? Why would you claim slavery as your heritage?"

Gently my youngest brother laid one hand on the angry man's shoulder. The other hand was held out to me. Hesitantly I took it.

"I was born into this house. Like you I am the son of Amram and Jochebed of the line of Levi." The words were firm but they held an astonishing humility. "Does not that make me a slave, even if I grew up in Pharaoh's courts?"

Still Aaron shook his head, although the rage was gone.

"When did you remember?" The question slipped out.

"The day I met Omarah the Overseer beating that man." Shamefaced the man sighed. "I rode out of the royal house to observe the Hebiru at work. I was raised to believe that my kin were less than human. 'Hebiru dogs' was the kindest term used in the palace. You left me with the Princess when I was three, Miriam." Brown eyes sought understanding from me. "She made every effort to convince me that I was a gift of the Nile gods. Any question about you or my family she deflected. The stories of my mother were forgotten. Every day she insisted, 'My son you must never forget that the river god Hari adopted you and brought you to me so that you could be my son. You are a Prince in the Black Land. To you belongs the heritage of the joined crowns of Upper and Lower Egypt.' For years, I was content to believe her. The image of Hari adorned all the walls. We made offerings regularly to that strange god with the breasts of a woman and body of a man. The Princess saw to it that I had excellent tutors and spent the proper amount of time learning the temple procedures. I began to doubt the gods of the Nile when I saw the magic arts and skillful strategies used by the priests."

"Yes," Aaron agreed, "I too have seen the way statues are made to speak and move. Mirrors and shadows are used to fool the faithful."

"I was sure there was trickery even before Aaron explained it," I couldn't help inserting.

"My sister is wiser than many in Egypt to understand that wood and stone cannot speak or move," the Shepherd smiled. "As a temple acolyte I was sworn to secrecy. The priests of Hari left no doubt of the fate of anyone disclosing the hidden things of the worship. The god might even demand the life of a rash prince, or so I was told."

Again, Aaron nodded. "I have seen the punishment. It is not unusual for a boy to be thrown into the river for any small infraction. Whether he lives or dies is at the god's behest."

Moses met his brother's eyes. "Someone even suspected of sharing a temple secret will be thrown to the crocodiles. I watched and learned of the gods of the royal family, but somewhere deep inside I seemed to hear a woman's voice telling of One God who needed no image. He would be a God whose promise was goodness and love for the dispossessed. I didn't entirely forget what our mother taught me."

Lost in thought, the man was silent. Zipporah laid a hand on her husband's arm. She answered my unspoken question.

"My father knows the same God. He calls him the God of Sinai."

Moses returned from his memories with a start. He squeezed the work rough hand.

"True, my love, and his teachings reawakened the stories learned in this very house." The dark eyes looked around at the dirt walls. Then he resumed his tale. "I roamed the wilderness for weeks. The heat during the day was only made worse by the bitter cold of the nights. Silent stars stared down at me as mile after mile of sand separated me from Egypt. A weary nomad replaced the proud prince. I learned to live in the desert and to find water in the low-lying areas. Finally, I settled with Jethro, priest of Midian. From my father-in-law I learned how the One True God brought prosperity to Esau, twin brother of our father Jacob. He too became a strong nation. The children of Esau settled in Midian. I began to understand that no people chosen of God is ever lost."

Aaron opened his mouth to object, "We are…"

My youngest brother lifted one hand. "I remembered too well my kin in bondage. Seared in my mind were the memories. They tormented me with thoughts of the beaten man on the road, the crack of the whips and the sight of men and women being beasts of burden." A tanned hand ran through the graying hair. Shamefully and sadly he admitted, "I required an answer from the Living One to ease my own guilt."

There was no answer I could offer to ease the remorse plainly written on Moses' face. The man reached for the plain pottery pitcher that held beer. It was empty. I took the jug from my brother to refill it. Aaron stared silently at the man who rose to take his sleeping son from Zipporah. Gently he laid the boy on the mat in the corner. Gershom followed drowsily to curl beside his brother.

Elisheva picked up the basket. Confusion showed as she folded the soft cloth that had wrapped the bread.

"I don't understand. How is Moses your brother? He is son of the Princess."

I was reminded that the woman was too young to have heard the rumors about Moses. He had gone to live in the palace before she was born. Her only memory of the man was seeing the Prince kill Omarah.

Patting her on the shoulder, I soothed, "He is brother to Aaron and to me. Although raised as royalty, he was born in this house."

My own thoughts were in turmoil as I poured the weak beer into the jug from the skin it was stored in. Moses, my brother, born to Jochebed and raised a prince, claimed to be the Deliverer promised by the patriarch Jacob. Yet he bent over the mat tending his son like any normal father.

Zipporah brought the empty food trays and came to stand beside me.

Softly she admitted, "I feared for my husband. He raged against God. Day and night I heard him demanding an answer. 'Why have you left your people to die as slaves in Egypt? Generations have passed but still you ignore the children of

Abraham, Isaac, and Jacob. Are you too weak to save them?' They were not prayers as much as confrontations. Often I begged him not to tempt God's wrath. When our grazing took us near to Sinai, I saw him staring at the mountain. Each day we moved closer with our flocks." With a glance at the man now rubbing her shoulders, she shook her head. "He would not listen to my fears. One day, from the tent, I saw him suddenly turn away from the flock and start up the rocks. I was terrified. Gripping the tent pole, I watched until he disappeared behind an outcropping. The bleating of the sheep reminded me that they needed a shepherd. Calling Gershom and the servants, we went to tend the flock. I was sure I would never see my husband again."

When she stopped speaking, I realized that I was holding my breath. Awed, I looked at Moses. My brother had dared to confront the Living God. He looked almost embarrassed by Zipporah's words. Impatient to hear the rest of the story, I carried the beer back to the table and trimmed the lamp wick so the light flared more brightly.

When my brother didn't speak, the question burst out, "What happened?"

"As you see I was not struck dead." My brother grinned almost playfully.

"Well?" I prodded when again he looked away.

The harsh lines on his face seemed to soften and his eyes glowed when they turned to look at me.

"Miriam, the One I met on Sinai *is* God."

Leaning forward, I stared expectantly into his face.

Looking into the past, my brother explained, "As Zipporah told you, I raged against God for ignoring and deserting his people. Despite her fears and Jethro's warnings, I knew I had to climb the mountain. Early one morning, I stared at the hillside half in dread and half in antagonism. Then I saw something." His voice trailed off at the memory.

"What?" My hands were gripped together in anticipation.

Moses spoke so calmly that I wasn't sure what to expect. When he continued it seemed anticlimactic.

"A bush was burning. I told myself that I didn't want the fire to spread. It was an excuse," he admitted glancing out the corner of his eye guiltily, like a little boy caught red-handed in some trick. "Climbing was harder than I anticipated. It took me several minutes to scramble close to the bush. I kept my eyes focused on it as I climbed. The fire never spread to the nearby scrub. Neither did it get any larger or smaller." Amazement was reflected on the man's face. "At last I was level with the plant. Close up the flames seemed to dance on the ends of the branches while at the same time the entire bush seemed to be of flames, not wood."

Moses paused and I tried to picture a bush of fire not branches.

"I stepped forward with my hand held out to touch the odd fire," my brother's tone changed. Remembered awe deepened and softened the words. "I heard my name. The sound seemed to come from the bush. Still I looked up and down the mountain seeking the person who spoke. Except where I stood, there wasn't a level place large enough for a bush or rock to hide anyone. I didn't see any caves, either. You see," he inserted, "I remembered too well how the Egyptian priests could make objects seem to talk by means of hidden tunnels and special tubes. All around I searched. Still the bush flamed but didn't change size. Then I heard my name again. *'Moses, take off your sandals. You are standing on holy ground.'* The order was not angry but I hurried to slip off my shoes. The very tone convinced me that I was in the presence of the One God of Abraham, Isaac, and Jacob."

"What did God sound like?" The question burst out when my brother paused for a sip of the weak beer.

Aaron frowned at the interruption but Moses was not offended.

"I'm not sure my ears heard a sound. The voice spoke to my heart and I knew..."

The man was silent. No one spoke. I yearned for such a voice to speak to me, ease my confusion, and answer my questions. A wild dog barked in the distance and was answered by a nearby hound. Moses seemed to come back from far away.

With an apologetic smile, he cleared his throat. "Where was I?"

"'Take off your sandals'." Aaron's tone was normal as he repeated the order.

"Then God spoke to the anger and despair in my soul. *'I have heard the cries of my children in Egypt. I will bring them out with a mighty hand.'*"

I gulped in air realizing I was holding my breath again.

"Mother was right. She swore that ours would be the generation to leave this land."

Eagerly I looked at Aaron. He nodded in confirmation of my words. Still he was holding himself almost aloof from the group. I wondered how he could doubt his own voices now that Moses was among us.

My brother continued, "I couldn't believe what the voice of God told me so I argued with God."

My mouth dropped open. Face to face, he dared to dispute the Holy One of Israel.

"Yes, Miriam." The man chuckled at my expression. "When God told me that I was to return to the Black Land and lead the people, I had many excuses." Ruefully the chosen leader laughed. "I begged God to change His mind. 'How can I go? I am a fugitive. The people will not listen to me. I was their master and enemy. You need an orator to go before Pharaoh and I am slow of speech. My life is here with Zipporah and Jethro and my son.' Finally I cried out, 'Send someone else!' There was no answer to my complaints and evasions. When my words ran out, God repeated, '*Moses, you will speak to the King of Egypt. You will say 'Let my people go.'*'"

Moses rose to his feet. Memory of intense emotions drove him to movement. He paced around the small room. My brother's concerns were all true. They were the thoughts that had crossed my mind as soon as I saw the Deliverer at my door.

The man threw up his head and continued. "I fell on my face before the bush begging God to reconsider. 'No one will believe me. I am a hated upstart and murderer. You are sending me to my death. Send someone else who can convince Pharaoh. I don't even know Your name.'"

Pausing to stare out the tiny slit of a window, Moses gripped the edges of the opening. Through the same window, Jochebed had prayed for deliverance. Day after day and year after year her petitions had risen from the house. The Deliverer now stood gazing toward the east where freedom was promised. After a long moment, he turned back. Coming to me, the man dropped to one knee and took my hand.

"My sister, God spoke to me again." Intense brown eyes glowed with passion. "The words still ring in my heart. '*I AM that I AM. If anyone asks who sent you, your answer will be I AM has sent me.*' God is *HAYAH*, the word that means BEING. From *I AM* comes all that is or will be."

"*I AM that I AM,*" I repeated.

The name settled comfortably around my heart. There could be no other name for the One True God, ever creating and redeeming.

"*HAYAH* is All Being," I whispered. "Now the God of Abraham, Isaac, and Jacob, *I AM* of all things, has sent you back to free the children of Israel from the King of Egypt. Blessed be the Living God who remembers his promises from generation to generation. Truly you are the Chosen One of God." Of their own accord, my hands rested on his head. "Moses, you were drawn out of the Nile to draw forth a nation from slavery. The God of our Fathers is mighty, holy be the name of *I AM.*"

In my ecstasy I forgot the others in the room until Zipporah added her voice to my praise.

"The God of Sinai will show wonders to the people. With a mighty hand and outstretched arm the family of Jacob will be freed."

Aaron rose to place a hand on his brother's shoulder.

"I was sent to meet you, Moses and to bring you to Pharaoh. Despite my hesitancy, the Living God has acted. Truly I see that we will be slaves no longer." Dropping to his knees he sobbed, "Forgive my doubts and my jealously. I did not understand that you are the chosen instrument of God. Miriam has spoken truly, you were saved from the river to rescue the children of Israel." Brother faced brother when Moses raised Aaron from the dirt floor.

"You are the confirming sign that God gave me. '*Your brother Aaron is coming to meet you. He will speak for you. I will give you the words and Aaron will recite them to Pharaoh.*' Until I saw your face I was almost convinced that I was going mad." The smile so like my father's lit the younger man's face. "When I came down from the mountain, Zipporah was waiting."

"I was in a fever of fear," the woman admitted. "For an entire day Moses was on the mountain. The evening meal was prepared before he came back."

She reached out a hand to touch her husband as if to convince herself that he was indeed standing beside her. A look of love passed between the pair.

"I couldn't believe that we were supposed to leave the flocks where they were with just the servants to watch them. He barely waited to pack before we set out. All Moses said was 'I must go to Egypt. God has sent me.'" Black hair flowed softly around her face when she shook her head. "I didn't understand. Even now, I cannot imagine how so many people will be delivered."

"The hand of God," confidently my brother spoke.

"It must be so," she admitted. "Your brother met us as you were told. Now we are here," a graceful hand gestured to the house and beyond.

Again words of praise rose to my lips. "The One True God is great and wonderful. My eyes rejoice to see this day. To Abraham and his seed are given descendants as the stars. To Israel a homeland is given and to Jacob return to the land of promise. By you, my brother, God will free the slaves from Pharaoh's rod!"

Even Aaron smiled and relaxed. Zipporah clung to her husband. She knew, like I did, that the task ahead would not be easy. Yet, in that moment, I knew that *I AM* would prevail over the gods of the Nile.

"The falcon of Egypt will fall from the sky," I exalted. "The lion of Judah will be triumphant."

Chapter 9

Moses seemed almost shy the next evening when Aaron brought the tribal leaders to my door. Looking at their antagonistic faces, I understood his hesitancy. Before he stepped from the house, I saw him bow his head. Lips moved in a brief prayer. Then he lifted his chin and crossed the threshold to stand beside his brother. The two brothers were equally tall and I was only slightly shorter. We all took our height from Amram. His imposing presence had made him well known throughout Goshen until he became ill. Now the sight of Aaron standing beside the striking stranger silenced the crowd.

"My brethren," Aaron announced, "our father Jacob foresaw that we would remain in Egypt four hundred years. Joseph the Honored, on his deathbed, prophesied that the One God would bring the children of Israel back to the land of Canaan. He ordered that his bones be carried out of Egypt and buried in the hills he knew as a boy."

Dramatically the man placed a hand on Moses' shoulder.

"Now is the time of deliverance," he stated. "The God of Abraham, Isaac, and Jacob has heard our pleas. He has sent his Messenger to lead us out of Egypt."

Simon of the house of Reuben spat on the ground. "You expect us to believe that this murdering former Prince was sent by God to bring us out of bondage?" He nudged Jonah son of Barachiah. "This 'Deliverer' won't last through one interview with Pharaoh."

"If he gets that far," another voice taunted. "A wanted fugitive is fair game for any of the King's soldiers. He'll be dead before he can even get to the court."

Derisive laughter came from the crowd and some turned to leave.

Aaron bristled and opened his mouth to answer. Moses silenced him with a lifted hand. The crowd gasped and took a step backward. I saw the reason. My brother's hand was covered with leprosy. Without saying a word, the man placed his hand inside his robe. When he drew it out there was no sign of the disease. My mouth gaped open in amazement. Murmurs of astonishment came from the crowd. Only Aaron seemed unaffected by the display. He still stared angrily at the neighbors gathered by our door. My youngest brother stepped forward into the mob. The men parted before him.

"Sons of Israel," he addressed them. "I am indeed, as Simon has said, the fugitive ex-prince of this land. Few of you know that I was born in this village. My mother was Jochebed and my father Amram of the tribe of Levi."

The statement caused a stir of interest and many whispers. Standing silent in the midst of the throng, my brother faced Simon's sneer.

"The God of Abraham, Isaac, and Jacob saved me from the swords of Pharaoh's soldiers as an infant and placed me in the royal court. In my youth and pride I rode out to see the work of the Hebiru dogs." Purposely he used the term of derision applied by the Egyptians to the children of Israel. "When I saw the overseer beating Joel I was overcome with rage." The tall man lowered his head in shame. "I killed the man and fled for my life. God led me through the desert. There I came to know the God of our fathers."

Moses looked around at the watchful men. Most of the faces were still hostile.

"In my exile, I railed at God. I demanded to know why he didn't keep his promises."

There were murmurs and nods at this admission. Few in Goshen had not asked the same question, whether they still believed in the One God or worshipped at the temples of Egypt.

"At the mountain of God I ..." The man paused and his face again softened and changed as he remembered the meeting. "God spoke to me out of a bush that burned but was not burnt."

Brows drew together at such a claim. Simon thrust a half-raised fist toward Moses.

"You expect us to believe that the God of our fathers spoke to you?" The angry man spat in his rage, "Pah! You are nothing!" Scornfully he pointed, "Behold Moses, outcast of the house of Pharaoh and of the house of Israel."

Next to me, Aaron drew an angry breath.

"If you really spoke to God," Jonah now spoke up in challenge, "tell us the name of the God of Abraham, Isaac, and Jacob. Our father Jacob wrestled with God at Jabok. Even then God did not reveal his name." Turning to my brother he threatened, "Tell us if you can, Moses bar Amram, what is the name of God?" The mood of the men was growing ugly. Fists were clenched and I sensed danger in the narrowed eyes and bated breathing.

"His name is *I AM that I AM.*"

Moses didn't seem to hear the derision or see the fists. He calmly faced the encircling crowd. For a moment they had seemed like a pack of dogs ready to attack. His calm demeanor defused the potential assault. Fury changed to respect as my brother continued to speak.

"The God of Israel has heard your cries for freedom. The Living God will bring you out of this land to your homeland. As in the days of our father Jacob, you will herd your own flocks and till your own fields. What you grow will be yours to store or to sell. The bricks you make will be used for your own homes. Your children will play on your doorstep without fear."

The assurance with which the shepherd spoke had nearly all the men nodding and smiling. A feeling of hope swept through the gathering. Moses walked back to stand beside Aaron.

"Tomorrow, Aaron and I will go to Pharaoh. We will say to him, 'The Lord says, let my people go.' If the King refuses, God will show his power."

Each man turned to his neighbor with questions and exclamations.

"How can a shepherd see Pharaoh?"

"It is too good to be true."

"How can Moses be sure?"

"I'll believe we're free when I leave Egypt behind."

"Do you trust Moses? He could be tricking us."

"Remember he's a criminal."

"He seems so sure."

"What sign will you have for the court?"

The last question was addressed to my brother. It silenced the discussion. Eager faces turned toward the stranger in their midst. Everyone in Egypt knew that the Lord of the Two Lands surrounded himself with magicians and prophets because he believed the gods directed him by the auguries of the priests. He would only act when all his advisors agreed on the interpretation of a portent.

Moses raised his shepherd's staff. "Behold the sign from the God whose name is *I AM*."

He cast the rod onto the ground. I watched in horror the transformation from shepherd's tool to dreaded cobra. The gnarled branch seemed to ripple when it touched the ground. From dull brown, the color changed to glossy black. A snake's head appeared where a moment earlier the broad end of the staff lay. An audible hiss issued from the open mouth as the creature coiled its body and spread the menacing hood. Men scrambled backward with curses and shouts of alarm. I cried out in fear when my brother stepped toward the reptile. Calmly he took the serpent by the tail. Suddenly it was a piece of wood, which he tapped on the ground. A reassuring hollow thump echoed in the sudden silence. Surely Pharaoh would pay attention to such an omen. That the Shepherd could produce and control the cobra, symbol of Pharaoh himself, would strike the heart of all Egypt.

Garbled words came from frightened throats.

"A cobra!"

"Moses produced a cobra!"

"Even the priests dare not use such deadly snakes!"

"Surely it was a trick!"

"I saw the creature with my own eyes!"

"Get rid of any foreign gods in your households." The instruction came from Aaron. "Trust in the One God, the God of Moses, and we will be free."

"Not the God of Moses," the younger man turned with a gentle rebuke. "The One whose name is *I AM* is God of all creation. The children of Israel are his chosen people. I am only his Messenger to the Lord of the Two Lands."

Joy flooded through me. A song of praise burst from my lips.

> "Praise to the God of Israel.
> *I AM that I AM* has heard our cries.
> Sing to the One God for He will redeem His people.
> A chosen and holy nation is born.
> Glory to the God of Abraham, Isaac, and Jacob."

A cheer greeted my song. The next sound was a grim reminder that we were not yet free. The thud of marching feet and the clink of weapons dispersed the crowd. Before the Egyptians soldiers appeared, the street was empty. I stood alone. Aaron had dragged Moses inside.

"Woman, what is the noise?" a burly sergeant confronted me.

"I was singing to my God," was the honest reply.

"Where is the mob?" Hand on sword hilt the officer loomed over me.

"There is no crowd." Again I spoke the truth for the street was empty. Not even a dog stirred.

"A riot was reported," the man insisted.

"I have seen no riot," I replied calmly, "and I have been here all evening."

Frustrated and muttering to himself, the soldier ordered his men back to their posts. The tramp of feet receded but I remained for a long time staring at the stars rising in the night sky. I felt a serenity and assurance that I finally identified as faith. A tiny voice tried to convince me that the freeing and moving of so many people was impossible. I silenced the doubts by reminding myself that God had brought my brother home. The God of Abraham, Isaac, and Jacob was forever active in the lives of his people.

"It will not be easy," I acknowledged to the stars. "We will have to learn to trust You."

It was late when I finally sought my bed. Moses snored beside Zipporah. My nephews curled together like puppies on their mat. Aaron held Elisheva and his sons dozed beside their new cousins. Quietly I slipped beneath the blankets. The sun awakened me in the morning.

Chapter 10

Moses and Aaron left to see Pharaoh, confident in God's power and proud of their mission. I watched them go, a little hurt that I was not asked to go with the men.

"Of course," I rationalized, "the presence of a slave woman would not help our cause."

They returned humbled and doubting.

"What happened?" I barely restrained myself from shaking the men's shoulders.

Moses greeted Zipporah and his sons absently. Wearily he dropped onto the floor and bowed his head into his hands.

"I have failed God," he groaned. "My misuse of his signs leads to greater hardship and not freedom for the people."

Staring from Aaron to Moses, I waited for an explanation. Aaron refused to meet my eyes. Moses rocked back and forth in agony. Zipporah knelt beside her husband, trying of offer comfort.

"God forgive me," he sobbed. "I am not the man for this task."

I poured a gourd of water. Lifting his head with one hand, I offered the drink to my brother.

"Tell me," I ordered in a tone usually reserved for wayward children.

The man stared at the liquid and would have set it aside but Zipporah urged him to drink. Then he leaned back against the wall.

"Pharaoh will not let the children of Israel go," he stated in a dead tone. "He is so angry that he has ordered the bricks be made without straw." Another groan of sorrow. "I have harmed the people I was sent to help. 'Everyone will have to work to gather straw in the fields'," he quoted. "The tally will not be less."

I couldn't suppress my gasp at his words. Aaron bowed his head in resignation. Zipporah stroked Moses hair in sympathy. The silence held hopelessness. My brothers looked like whipped puppies rather than messengers of the Living God. Anger helped me find my voice.

"Are you going to let one setback discourage you? Do you plan to quit after one attempt?"

"These are not things a woman understands." Aaron's voice was harsh and arrogant.

Hands on my hips, I faced my brothers. "If a woman gave up after one attempt at birthing a child, children would have ceased to be long ago. Women know more about perseverance than any man." I turned to my youngest brother. "You are birthing a nation. It will not be easy. Do you think that the God who has preserved you this far will abandon you now?"

"My sister." Moses looked at me, desolation in his eyes. "I threw down my staff as God commanded. At first, the cobra frightened Pharaoh. Then the priests used their drugged snakes to do the same thing. The King and all the court laughed. Pharaoh asked if I had other magic tricks to show him."

"So you have given up because of a little derision? The laughter of men is more important than the will of God? The Living One said you would do great things, and that He would bring the people out with mighty wonders. Surely the God of Abraham, Isaac, and Jacob is stronger than the Nile gods, even Pharaoh."

Bending, I took hold of the staff. It lay where Moses had dropped it. Both my brothers stared at me. I stood in the center of the small house with the staff planted in front of me. Tossing my hair out of my face, I drew myself up to my full height.

My voice rang through the room, "Moses, God will not fail you. See that you do not fail God." I held out the rod to the man. "Trust in the power of *I AM* and you will see great things." Moses looked up at me for a long silent moment. Then the Deliverer stood up to place his hand over mine on the staff.

"I was embarrassed by the taunts and laughter," he admitted. "I lost sight of what God sent me to do. Miriam, thank you for reminding me."

He kissed my forehead and took the rod. For the first time since he came in, the man smiled.

"God's cobra devoured the snakes produced by the priests of Egypt..." The memory made him lift his chin confidently. "Just so will *I AM* overpower the gods of Egypt. The God of our Fathers *will* free the chosen people!" Aaron looked at his brother in amazement.

"You will try again? How will you get back into Pharaoh presence?"

"God will provide a way," the man responded with old confidence. Squaring his shoulders, he announced, "I must tell the people that God will prevail."

It was not easy to persuade the men and women filling the street. Hope had been replaced with angry alarm and visible consternation. Clods of dirt as well as accusations were hurled at my brother as soon as he appeared. Calmly the man accepted their rage.

"You are not sent from God. Pharaoh has sent you to kill us."

"We were better off before you decided to help us."

"Some Deliverer you are, Moses."

"Will you help us gather the chaff in the fields every night?"

"Go back to the desert and free the cobras."

Moses let the men rant until old Azariah stepped forward. The crowd parted for the ancient rabbi. I had not seen my father-in-law since Joel was buried.

"Let the man who saved the life of my son speak," he urged.

The crowd became silent. It was a hostile silence, heavy with antagonism and disbelief.

"The God of our Fathers has heard your cries," my brother repeated the promise.

"If God is so powerful, why must we make bricks without straw?"

I was not surprised to hear the question from Jonah.

"Pharaoh is stubborn. He must see mighty signs from the Living God. Only then will he know that there is only one true God. The God of Abraham, Isaac, and Jacob will triumph over the gods of Egypt."

It was not the answer anyone wanted to hear, and murmurs of anger started up again.

"Will you make snakes multiply?" The taunt came from Simon. "That doesn't seem to impress the King. Perhaps next you can pull a falcon from your sleeve."

The sally produced laughter. My brother remained unmoved by the confrontation. There was sorrow on his face as he looked around at the men he expected to be eager supporters. I heard the man sigh. When he spoke it was a warning.

"You too will see the signs that the God of Abraham, Isaac, and Jacob will do in the land. *I AM* will do what is necessary to create a faithful people ready to enter the Promised Land." Moses' next words were a stern order. "Tonight fill all your containers with water. Every jar and basket that you can find must be filled with fresh water. Tomorrow God will strike the waters of the Egypt. No one will have water unless they draw it tonight."

In a swirl of desert robes, my brother entered the house. The crowd still milled in the street. Zipporah and I hurried to gather all the jars and water baskets we could find. At the well we found only a few women.

"Tell everyone to do as Moses said," we urged. "Tomorrow there will be no clean water."

They nodded but didn't meet our eyes. Even when we knocked on doors to repeat the warning, we were met with disbelief.

"Go away, your brother is a troublemaker."

"It would have been better if he stayed away."

"Pharaoh is stronger than Moses."

"Tomorrow your brother will get what he deserves."

Sadly, my sister-in-law and I returned to the house.

"They don't believe you," the woman reported through tears.

Moses gathered her into his arms. "Dearest Zipporah, my faithful wife, do not blame the people. To these men and women I am a fugitive prince masquerading as a prophet. How can they be expected to understand what the hand of the Living God can do?"

Eventually she was comforted.

I slept restlessly, awakening at the slightest sound. It was still dark when my brother sat up. A touch of his hand awakened Aaron. In the dark silence, he put on his shepherd's robe and picked up the staff. When the men quietly opened the door and stepped out into the darkness of the predawn, I rapidly grabbed my own woolen shawl. The warm material covered my head and wrapped cozily around my body. Softly I trailed after my brothers. We left the town behind and headed down the river road. I wondered if Moses was thinking about what happened on this same road years earlier. A journey begun with murder long ago brought him here as God's servant.

The two men turned onto the levee beside the river. Without a pause they walked briskly south toward the royal palace. My mind raced backward to my visits to the great house with news of my baby brother. *Ra*, the sun god, was beginning to turn the horizon gray when Moses stopped. I sank into the bulrushes and grasses beside the path to wait.

Soon the tall ebony-wood doors swung open silently. Pharaoh and the priests came out to call on the gods to bless the Nile and bring another day to Egypt. Every morning Pharaoh became the god Horus when he performed the ritual ablutions. First came royal guards who took up positions along the steps leading to the river. The apprentice priests entered next, sweeping the marble. Dancing girls with flower petals and musicians who played a solemn tune on drums and pipes followed them. The priest of the day appeared carrying aloft the bowl of water for the purification of the King and the river. More priests, each in the regalia of the god he served, marched through the doors. The stately movements of the priests were impressive. With the ease of daily practice they formed an avenue for the Great One of Upper and Lower Egypt. At the foot of the stairs, near the river, a priest waited with the bronze basin of water.

Finally, Pharaoh himself appeared. Slaves held a fan and umbrella over him. He did not wear the massive crown on his head or the breastplate of Horus on his chest. I was astonished to see that all the ruler of Egypt wore was a pure white linen loincloth. He was not a majestic figure. Flabby muscles drooped over the golden waistband. Thin legs like the river ibis protruded from beneath the garment. I almost giggled at the sight.

I saw Moses bow his head over the staff. I couldn't hear his words but I knew he prayed for courage and strength.

My own lips moved in a prayer, "God of Abraham, Isaac, and Jacob help your servant. You know how much he wants to please you. God, whose name is *I AM*, work in my brother."

Pharaoh had nearly reached the river before Moses and Aaron stepped forward. A buzz of irritation ran through the assembled priests. The chief priest whispered to the King who turned to look at my brothers as though they were vermin.

"So the Shepherd has returned. Perhaps we did not make ourself clear yesterday." There was a sneer in the voice and the royal lip curled in derision. "The Hebiru dogs are ours. We will not let them leave. Slaves have no need of a god. If they must worship, let them worship the gods of Egypt who have nurtured them since they came to this land."

With that, the man turned his back on Moses. The priest knelt and presented the bowl of water to Pharaoh. Two young apprentices came forward to dip small alabaster jars into the water. The King held his hands out and the water was poured over them. A second pair of young priests stepped out of line to dip lotus blossoms in the water. The moistened flowers were used to sprinkle the chest and back of the man who stood with arms held out parallel to the river. A gold pitcher was handed to the figure that represented the life of the land.

Although mesmerized by the actions of King and priests, I saw my brother move forward until he was standing on the riverbank. Aaron followed. When Pharaoh began the morning incantation, Moses lifted the staff and brought it down with a thud.

"Pharaoh, King of Egypt, hear what the God of the children of Israel says. *'Let my people go so that they may worship me in the wilderness.'* You did not listen to the words or heed the sign given. Hear and obey now."

Priests and King stood still. Pharaoh's brows drew together in outrage at the interruption. Some of the priest exchanged concerned glances with one another as they looked at the brightening sky. The ritual needed to be completed before the sun topped the horizon.

My brother stepped into the water. The staff was raised aloft and extended to Aaron.

"Thus says the Lord, '*By this you will know that* **I AM** *is the One True God.*' Pharaoh, King of Egypt." The man repeated the title. "God will strike the water of the Nile. It will turn to blood. The fish will die and the river will stink. Everyone in the Black Land will thirst, for there will be no water in all of Egypt."

Aaron took the rod from Moses and thrust it into the river. My gasp was covered by exclamations and cries of horror from the assembled priests and soldiers. Pharaoh dropped the gold pitcher as he leapt backward from the blood red water lapping at his sandals. Cries of dismay ran through the worshipers.

"Surely this is an evil omen!"

"Hari, god with the power of the Nile, bleeds!"

"Great One, save us!"

Without another word, Moses and Aaron returned to the levee and began to walk home. They passed my hiding place. I saw Aaron glance back as if expecting pursuit. The guards milled in fear and confusion while Pharaoh shouted at the priests, demanding an explanation. Desperately the religious leaders huddled for consultation, longstanding rivalries forgotten. I saw them gesturing toward the river. The crimson liquid now ran into the fields through the canals dug from the river to water the crops. At last a young priest raced away. He returned in a few minutes with a bowl and a bag. The eldest priest took the items. Astonished, I saw the magicians turn the clean water in the bowl as red as the river. Pharaoh made a contemptuous gesture that took in the spreading color in the fields before dashing the bowl from the servant's hand and storming into the palace.

When everyone was gone, I raced back to Goshen to tell my brothers. The water in the fields was as red as the river now. Crocodiles and hippos crawled out of the river and fish began to float in the current. Animals were refusing to drink from their troughs because that water, too, was tainted. As I entered Goshen, I heard cries of dismay from the direction of the well. By the time I reached my house, there were women gathering at the corner. When they saw me they rushed forward.

"Miriam, the well water looks like blood."

"What will we drink?"

"How can we clean and…"

The complaints stopped briefly when Moses appeared. He laid a hand on my shoulder. I wasn't sure if it was to give me support or silence an angry response.

"Pharaoh has refused to hear the word of the One God. Therefore, all Egypt will see the signs of the Living One. The King of the Black Land will let us go when he has seen the wonders of the *I AM*." My brother spoke with assurance.

"Meanwhile we die of thirst," grumbled the assembled women.

I had to bite my tongue to keep from reminding them that we had been warned. Moses hand tightened on my shoulder and I heard him sigh.

"When Pharaoh sees the thirst of his people he will send for me." With these words, Moses ended the conversation and led me into the house.

I hoped my brother was right, but no summons came from the palace. One evening Moses invited me to walk with him as the sun was setting. It hurt to see mothers hurrying their children inside away from my brother. The people refused to listen to Moses any longer. Even when we shared our water with everyone in the town, they complained that there was not enough and that the country stank of dead fish.

We strolled toward the river. The man looked down at the steadily flowing Nile. It had been nearly a week and the waters of the great river were almost clear enough to drink.

"Pharaoh is stubborn," he stated. "The children of Israel doubt the promise of freedom. It is easier to grumble about slavery than to fight for liberty."

"This is the only life they remember."

Even as I weakly defended my friends, I wondered why I bothered. My presence was barely tolerated and Zipporah was shunned as an outsider. The neighbors sullenly ignored both my brothers. Everyone blamed Moses rather than seeing the hand of God.

"God does not want anyone to be in bondage." My brother looked down at me. His voice was firm but sad. "In the beginning *I AM* created man and woman with freedom. Even when they chose to defy Him, God provided food and clothing. The promise of a homeland was given to Abraham and renewed in Jacob. The people have forgotten the mighty acts of the God of Abraham, Isaac, and Jacob."

In silence, the man looked across the river. On the far shore the last rays of light glistened off the gold ornamented temples.

"The gods of Egypt are stone moved by trickery. The God of our Fathers is truth and freedom. All Egypt and all Israel will see the greatness of the Living God." Moses' assertion rang out in the air like a challenge.

Was it a trick of the setting sun or did his face take on that strange exalted brightness I had seen when he spoke of meeting God? Now he turned from the water. His step seemed to have renewed vigor. I had to trot to keep pace with him as we returned to the house.

Chapter 11

With confidence, the Deliverer strode past the muttering neighbors. He ignored their comments or perhaps didn't even hear them. His mind seemed to be on something else.

"Aaron," he told his brother, "in the morning we will visit Pharaoh."

In the gray dawn, Moses turned to me; "My sister, warn all the women to cover their grain and wrap their food or it will be ruined by frogs."

I know I looked puzzled.

"Frogs?" I repeated somewhat stupidly.

"Do as I say." He smiled with a pat on the shoulder.

Shaking my head in confusion, I watched the two men walk up the street. I told Zipporah what her husband said. Immediately she began wrapping and covering the bread and flour. With a sigh, I went out to give Moses' command to the rest of Goshen. Although not everyone complied, I noticed that many of the women hurried home to do as my brother said.

"More of them believed the warning this time," I told my sister-in-law with a smile when I returned.

Those who tarried or scoffed soon regretted their hesitation. By midmorning when Moses and Aaron returned from their audience with the king, frogs were already appearing. From the river and then from every steam and puddle of water came a croaking mass of green, goggle-eyed amphibians. They were hopping everywhere. The slightest crack or open door was an invitation. Frogs sat on beds and tables. Their protruding eyes peered from bowls and baskets. At the well, you often had to fish the horrid things out of the water in the bucket.

We shared our stored and sealed grain with the families who didn't prepare. The only ones who enjoyed the infestation were the children. They laughed as they chased and caught the creatures. After only a short time, even that entertainment paled.

Midweek brought a message from Pharaoh. A squad of the royal guardsmen summoned Moses to the palace. I laughed at his description of the scene when he returned.

"There sat Pharaoh, King of Egypt, Lord of the Two Lands." He grinned at the memory. "All around, like small courtiers, sat and hopped and croaked frogs. They were on the arms of the throne. Brave ones leapt to the top of the falcon wings that form the back of the royal chair. Frogs peered from under the footstool and perched on the statues of the gods. Wherever you looked or stepped was a croaking reminder of the power of the One God. Of course no one dared to kill one of the creatures." Moses chuckled at the irony. "Frogs are sacred to Heka, the goddess of procreation and resurrection. To kill a frog is to sentence yourself to death."

"What did he say?" I asked the question eagerly.

"'You have caused this plague. We demand that you make it cease.'" My brother imitated Pharaoh's high-pitched voice. "My response was to ask, 'Tell me, my Lord King, when you want this plague to end.' I thought the man would explode with rage. His face became red and he half rose from the throne. Then a frog jumped up and struck him on the royal neck-plate. Right in the center of the symbol of his kinship with the gods." My brother chortled at the humor of the situation.

I had to laugh too. The picture in my mind was so clear. I could almost see the frog striking the pompous chest of the King. Zipporah giggled, too. She was relieved to have her husband safe. All morning she had feared for his life.

"Then?" she asked.

Smiling down at his love, Moses replied, "Pharaoh commanded me 'Remove the frogs tomorrow. We will let the people go.'"

I clapped my hands in delight. "He really said that?"

Aaron muttered, "He won't keep his word."

Moses looked from Aaron to me. His voice grew serious.

"Tomorrow the plague of frogs will cease. There will only be frogs in the Nile. Aaron, you are right." He turned to his brother. "Pharaoh will not let the children of Israel go, yet."

My brothers were right. The King of the Black Land never issued the order. Zipporah and I wept when the leaders harangued Moses.

"What have you done, Prophet?"

"Pharaoh's officers mock us as they load us with greater tasks."

"Perhaps Moses will use his tricks to do the work."

When Aaron would have responded, my younger brother silenced him. Eventually the crowd grew quiet. Then the man spoke.

"The God of our Fathers has promised to bring you out of this land. *I AM that I AM* is his name. He will keep his word. Our father Abraham was promised descendants as the stars. Look around." My brother gestured. "Hasn't that promise been fulfilled?"

A few heads slowly nodded. Men were looking at each other with renewed hope.

"Abraham's covenant with the One God included a homeland also," Moses spoke firmly. "The great patriarch Jacob fought with the Living God at the Jabok. For his perseverance he was given the renewal of that promise. God gave him the name of Israel for his faithfulness. He knew that his descendants would return to their own homeland." The man leaned forward slightly to inform the crowd. "Now the time is fulfilled."

Frowns were still visible. The Prophet continued patiently, as though teaching a lesson. "Joseph the Honored, son of Jacob, God raised up to be governor in this land to save the lives of his brothers. He too knew this day would come. His sarcophagus will go with us to be buried in the land of his birth."

The man took a step forward. He was an imposing figure facing the sullen men without fear. Some of the faces showed less hostility, but all still held doubt.

"The God of Abraham, Isaac, and Jacob is the God who will accomplish your redemption with a mighty hand." Moses raised his voice so that it carried to the ends of the street. "You will see the power of the True God and know that *I AM* is the One Living God."

The bold words hung in the air. Silenced, men glanced at one another from the corners of their eyes. Moses' assurance took them by surprise. My brother's words reminded them of history that was all but forgotten in the dim recesses of the past. The mummified body of Joseph resided in the small mortuary temple not far away. The suggestion that the body would actually be carried from Egypt convinced me that Moses had regained his faith and courage. The group dispersed to talk in small groups. I followed my brothers into the house.

Zipporah hurried to her husband. "Surely the people will believe now."

He bent his head to kiss her hair. "If only it was so simple to convince the hearts of men."

I added, "It is not only Pharaoh who is stubborn and needs proof."

The man sighed deeply. "The children of Israel doubt the God of their fathers. They fear the chance to be free."

I knew it was true. The talk at the well and in the market was full of fear of the unknown. My imaginings had not prepared me for the hesitancy of the people. In every daydream I ever had, the entire community rose up in joy at the promise of freedom. That was not what was happening.

"Yes." Zipporah sadly stroked her lover's hand. Whenever she could, my sister-in-law touched the man, as though seeking to convince herself that he was still alive and still human. "I have heard the complaints. How can you continue to have patience with such people?"

"They are my people, just as you are my wife." The words held a reprimand. "God has put their welfare on my heart. I can only do what *I AM* commands."

"This generation has never known freedom," I inserted a weak excuse. "It is easier to accept the hardship that is known than to step out in faith into the unknown."

I was rewarded by a smile from Moses. It warmed my heart. Later when everyone was in bed, I saw my brother slip from the warmth of his blankets to kneel by the window. My heart joined his as he sought strength to face not only Pharaoh's contempt but also the doubt of his own brethren. Morning finally came. We had both dozed in our vigil. The rays of morning light on his face awakened my brother.

"Aaron and I will go again to Pharaoh," he stated, barely taking time to swallow a piece of bread and some barley beer.

Chapter 12

The cycle of broken promises continued. I was saddened by the refusal of even our closest friends to believe that God could free the children of Israel. When I refused to join in the gossip and accusation, I too was mocked.

Again, Moses had to face the crowds by my door. They buzzed almost like the incessant gnats that plagued all of Egypt. I saw my brother lift his head and square his shoulders before he opened the door. Murmuring stilled at his appearance.

"God has heard your grumbling." The statement was not said in anger but with compassion. "Your burdens have been made worse. With all of Egypt you have been tormented by lack of water, by frogs and by these gnats."

Nods and a low dangerous growl were the response from the listening men and women. I feared the mob would begin to stone my brother and prepared to drag him inside. Moses calmly stared into Naham's eyes when the burly workman stepped forward. After a moment, the big man stepped back.

"You will learn that the God of our fathers is greater than the gods of this land, which are only images of wood and stone carved by human hands." Over the heads of the crowd the man pointed at the temples across the river. I was reminded that many of the neighbors worshipped those same gods. "You will no longer be troubled by the plagues that will come on Egypt."

Simon could no longer contain himself. "Are you a god yourself that you can promise such things?" A hum of agreement and hisses of derision from others in the group encouraged the man to add sarcastically, "Perhaps the prince has not forgotten that the royal family is kin to the gods."

Calmly, Moses waited until the chuckles ceased. "God has set apart the land of Goshen. He will protect the children of Israel from the swarms of flies that will cover the rest of the Black Land."

My brother paused to look around. There was compassion in his voice and tenderness in his expression

"Thus says the Lord." The man spread his arms wide as though to embrace the assemblage. "'*I will preserve an inheritance and gather my people. I will bring them from bondage in Egypt to the land of promise. This is a land flowing with milk and honey. The world will see and know that you are a chosen people.*' Return now to your homes." The voice was gentle. "The Living God has not forsaken you. Pharaoh will learn that there is a God in the land."

When Moses entered the house, Zipporah ran to him. Looking up at her husband's glowing face, she sighed. Except for a brief hug, the man ignored his wife. I saw tears brim in her eyes. He spoke to Aaron.

"My brother, in the morning we will go to the King of the Land. Again we will tell him that the One God says, '*Let my people go that they may worship me.*' I know that still the Lord of the Black Land will not obey."

"Will he ever?" Zipporah's discouraged question was mirrored in Aaron's downcast face.

Before Moses could speak, I answered, "No man can stand against the power of the God of Abraham, Isaac, and Jacob. Pharaoh may believe that he is a god, but he is only a man. We will indeed live in the land of promise." I wasn't sure where the conviction came from as I continued. "All who obey the word of God will find peace and freedom."

Later Zipporah questioned me. "How can you be so sure that Pharaoh will let your families leave?"

"God has not forsaken the children of Israel or the descendants of Esau," I reminded my sister-in-law.

Proudly she lifted her chin. "The land of Midian has never been under foreign rule. Each tribe is an independent entity. We find our own grazing and are not dependent on anyone."

"Perhaps the sons of Jacob learned a different way of life." I heard the tension in my voice as I tried to refrain from raging at my brother's wife. "In the time of famine each man learned to value the assistance of his brother."

"And became slaves to their own brother in Egypt." The vehemence surprised me. I wondered why the woman was so angry. "Now my husband is forced to grovel to the King and endure the hatred of the very people he is trying to help." Her words explained the passion.

"Moses believes that is what *I AM* wants him to do. Would you have him defy the Living God?" I tried to reason with Zipporah.

"God doesn't need Moses," she cried. "I need him and so do his sons." Tears brimmed in her dark eyes. "We might as well be in Midian for all the attention he pays to us."

"My sister." Gently I tried to draw the woman into my arms.

She refused to be comforted and pulled away. It was true that my brothers were entirely consumed with freedom for the nation. There was nothing I could say to assuage her longing.

"I do understand your frustration." My own words held the anguish of my secret dreams now dashed by events beyond my control. "Neither Aaron nor Moses consult me. They barely notice that I am here except to put food on the table. Didn't I encourage my brothers time and again when they faltered? I prayed for deliverance for years and offered myself as the instrument of redemption. Yet I am not even included in the visits to the palace."

The woman looked amazed at my outburst. In sympathy, we held each other. I was not surprised when she announced that she wanted to return to her father's tents in Midian.

Moses looked forlorn as he watched his wife bundle together the few items that she would take with her. Gershom and Eleazar clung to their father until Zipporah took the baby. Aaron had arranged for a caravan to take them to Midian.

"It is time to go." With a last sad glance at her husband, the woman walked out the door.

"You can go after her," I urged when my brother leaned his head against the door after his family disappeared from sight.

"God has called me to remain here." The agony in the man's tones told of the shattered emotions he struggled with. "Why will the King not listen to God?"

Pharaoh and his advisors seemed to delight in raising the hopes of all in Goshen. When the swarms of flies covered the country in a black sheet, the King announced that we could leave to worship. As soon as the insects left, the man canceled the order. Then the horses and flocks and herds of Egypt died. Even in Goshen, where neither a hide nor hoof was touched, we heard of Pharaoh's rage at the priests. Word traveled through the ranks of the royal guard to the overseers. Women bringing water to the workers heard the story and gleefully told it at the well.

"Did you hear what Pharaoh said to the priests? 'Surely the gods of the Nile can protect the animals of the King! Why can't Apis defend the sacred bulls at On? They die with the rest of the cattle. Are you priests good for nothing but fattening yourselves on temple grain? Offer sacrifices and learn how to defeat this single desert god for we will not let the Hebirus go!' What does that mean?"

"Pharaoh is afraid," I responded. "He does not want to believe that the God of our fathers is the One True God. The gods of Egypt have been shown to be weak and at the command of Moses. Geb and Khepfi allowed the gnats and flies to infest the land. Apis and Hathor could not prevent the animals from dying." I smiled. "If our 'desert god' is God, then Pharaoh is only a man. I doubt he enjoys that revelation."

The women giggled as they agreed.

Across the river, from the temples, we could hear the petitions of the priests and see the smoke from the incense and unusual number of sacrifices. The Egyptian overseers, however, became almost laughable in their attempts to keep the construction progressing for the King and not antagonizing the workmen. Moses especially elicited fear. There was not an Egyptian in Goshen who would look my brother in the eye. They became servile in their manner when he approached.

"Great Master," they pleaded, "do not turn your staff against us. We see that you have more power than even the priests of Ra and Horus." The words were whispered, "Can you protect us from the curses you send on the land?"

I knew Moses was tortured by the death and devastation in Egypt. After the livestock died, the people developed awful blisters on their skin. The priests would not even leave the palace except for the morning offering and then only under concealing scarves.

"We must go to Pharaoh again," wearily Moses spoke to Aaron. "Even the sickness and misery of his people has not convinced the King." I saw tears in the man's eyes. "Why can't he have pity on his own country? He will bring about such sorrow in the land."

I didn't understand his compassion. It seemed only just that the Egyptians were made to suffer for our generations of bondage.

"Send for the chief overseers," my brother ordered.

Obediently I sent word by my nephews. When the foremen came, groveling, to the door, my brother went to them.

"The King of the Black Land has not listened to the God of Abraham, Isaac, and Jacob. Still Pharaoh refuses to let the children of Israel worship in the wilderness as we are commanded. This is a warning for those who will hear." The seriousness of his voice made the men glance at each other and risk a look at Moses. "Tomorrow I will go again to your King. Then next day will be a storm of deadly hail and lightning. If you want to save yourselves and your slaves and your animals," the man looked at the frightened faces and his voice softened, "see that they are safely inside on that day."

When my brothers returned from the court, I knew that my youngest brother was burdened. Looking to the south, I could see towering clouds that shot lightning. Beneath the gray clouds a sheet of hail poured down onto the land. The barley and flax in the fields would be pounded flat. For the first time, I felt sorrow for the people of Egypt. Like us, they were beaten under the pride of the King of the Black Land. Without the barley and flaxseed, there would be no food for the poor of the land. The wealthy ate the wheat that was not yet sprouted. Pharaoh and his counselors would not suffer because of this plague. I wondered if the priests believed that this was punishment from Isis and Seth, who gave life and protected the crops.

"Miriam." For the first time in days, Moses spoke directly to me. "The King of Egypt continues to refuse to obey God."

"Yes," I nodded, wondering why the man spoke to me.

Both brothers usually ignored my suggestions until I quit offering counsel. Aaron especially seemed haughty in his role of spokesperson for the Deliverer. He spurned me when I warned him that Elisheva missed his company.

"My brother, like Zipporah, your wife and sons want you to spend some time with them. Be careful or Elisheva will grow to despise you."

"She is only a woman and cannot understand the great responsibility I bear with my brother." The haughty words caused me to choke on a response.

Now, today, Moses was seeking me out. My brother's torment was palpable.

"Pharaoh is entrusted with the crook as a symbol that he is the Shepherd of the people. He is allowing the nation to be in misery because of his stubbornness. After tomorrow, the crops will be ruined and the people will starve this year." A distracted hand raked through his graying hair. I realized that there was more white in the dark waves than when he arrived only months before.

"Why does the God of my fathers have to destroy this land?" My brother faced me and stated, "I grew up Prince to these people. My heart aches for them. I hear their cries of fear and despair."

The man groaned and gripped his ears as though to drive out the voices of misery. I touched his arm wanting to ease the despair.

"Surely God also hears their cries, just as our pleas have been heard." I struggled to explain my thoughts; "It is not your fault. The King has a choice. Because Pharaoh does not listen to your requests for mercy and justice, his own people suffer."

"The people of Egypt have to endure hardship because the King is a proud and stiff-necked man who believes that he can challenge the One True God." My brother was angry but it evaporated on a sigh of grief. "He is only a man, not a god, but he will not admit that truth. The nation is destroyed. The arrogance of one man may bring down the dynasty."

"God is God," I offered. "Who are we to question His ways? You have said yourself that the children of Israel need these signs, too. They will not believe in the power of the One God. Many are still afraid to leave Egypt."

Moses bowed his head. Anguish filled the deep voice. "The land will be desolate when we at last leave it. The people of Egypt, the very ones I was taught to care for as a prince, will be destroyed before Pharaoh will let go of his pride. In his conceit, he believes that he can keep us in his grasp. Only by the mighty hand of death will he learn humility and let the children of Israel leave."

Later, I wondered if, even then, my brother knew how far the One God would go to bring us to the land of promise.

Chapter 13

When Moses returned to the court to speak to the Lord of the Two Lands, I begged to go along. Despite Aaron's frown, he agreed.

"Our sister has been faithful," the shepherd told his brother. "She encouraged me when I doubted. Miriam has not wavered in her belief in the One God and the fulfillment of the promise made to our fathers." I opened my mouth to confess. Neither man noticed.

"She taught a boy the stories of God's works," Moses reminded his brother. "It is fitting that she sees how the ruler of Egypt mocks the God of Abraham, Isaac, and Jacob. She will tell the saga of the way the Living God overcomes even the pride of a mighty nation so that the people can be free."

So I walked between my brothers through the palace. I remembered the tiled halls and murals on the walls. The new paintings were more spectacular with scenes of the reigning monarch as Horus and Ra on many panels. The throne room itself was ornamented with gold figures of the gods. My eyes were wide and I realized my mouth hung open as I stared at the fabulous decorations. Behind the King's chair a huge falcon rose up. I recognized the symbol of Horus and was not too surprised to see Pharaoh's face on the carving.

"Are you a fool or only mad?" From the throne the Ruler of the Black Land spoke. I was surprised to see how small he looked, even seated on the dais above the assembled nobles and officials.

Moses stepped forward, "Thus says the Lord, the God of the Hebiru who you despise, '*How long will you refuse to hear and obey? Let my people go so they may worship me.*'" My brother waited for a response. The King looked at his fingernails in boredom. "If you refuse, tomorrow a storm of locusts will cover your land." The Deliverer continued when there was no response. "The countryside will be black indeed. It will be black with locusts. They will devour anything left by the hail. You will find them in your palaces and in the homes of your officials."

Turning, the Prophet looked around at the assemblage. I saw priests and officials whispering to each other.

Moses addressed them. "All of Egypt will be filled with locusts from the Cataracts to the Sea. Anubis will not be able to prevent the destruction of the fields. Nor will Isis or Seth protect the wheat and smelt that are just coming up." Lifting his head, my brother stared long at the man on the throne. "Only in Goshen will there be no locusts."

I saw the little man on the throne begin to puff up to respond. My brother didn't wait. We turned and started out of the audience chamber. The royal advisors gathered around the throne to plead.

"Great Lord of the Nile, Egypt will be ruined."

"The wheat is barely sprouting. The hail didn't harm it, but locusts ..."

"Mighty King, locusts will devour anything green."

"The new grain and even the leaves on the trees will be gone."

"You want us to give in to this insane fool?" As the doors closed behind us, I heard the petulant whine.

The counselors must have prevailed because we had barely left the palace when a contingent of royal officers came after us.

"Halt!" I heard the shouted command and glanced over my shoulder.

Leather helmeted soldiers were bearing down on us. My heart leapt into my throat. I grabbed Aaron's arm. Moses seemed unafraid. He turned to face the guards.

"You shall return with us," the captain ordered. He seemed unsure whether to salute or arrest my brother.

With a smile, the Prophet nodded. We marched back into the King's presence. He was alone except for a scribe, his fan bearer, and a couple of top officials. I saw at least three priests lurking behind the curtain on the side of the room.

"Our advisors, it seems, do not trust in the gods of Egypt to preserve her against your threat," Pharaoh drawled the words scornfully. "They counsel us to let you all go and worship this god."

The sneer in his tone was offensive. I bristled. Aaron gripped my arm and I relaxed. Moses stood silent, waiting for the King to continue.

With an angry glance at the hovering counselors, the man asked, "How many will go for this festival?"

Planting the staff of God firmly, my brother looked straight at the man who believed he was a god incarnate. "We will go with our children and our parents and our wives. Our flocks and our herds must go so we can hold a feast to the True God. The children, both sons and daughters, need to go to see the day of the Lord's redemption of Israel."

The man on the throne turned almost purple in his rage. He leapt from the seat and shrilled, "Get out of our sight, Troubler of Egypt! We are Pharaoh, King of Egypt from the Cataracts to the Great Sea. We alone hold the power of freedom for the slaves in Goshen." A look of cunning narrowed his eyes. "Your men may go to worship this desert god, but the rest of the people will remain in Egypt. You will not so easily plan evil against our throne."

Moses shook his head. Calmly he watched the Lord of the Black Land. I was shaking from fear. The guard's spears looked very sharp. Aaron looked like he wanted to disappear from the room. The King and my brother stared at each other for a long time.

"We gave you your chance," Pharaoh announced turning his back to end the confrontation. "If we ever let your children and herds leave with you, then you will know that your god is great." The threat in the low tone was more frightening than the wrath had been. Suddenly the man swung around, arm outstretched to order, "Leave us!"

With curses and blows, the soldiers shoved us through the doors and down the hall.

As we left the city, Moses pointed his staff to the east. A wind began to blow from that direction. On the wind came the sound of devastation. In the morning, the workmen on the monuments reported that the countryside was covered with a moving mass of black. Where they passed only brown remained. No hint of green was left.

"It is the locusts." The word was whispered from household to household at the well and across the mud pits.

From the tops of the obelisks where the most skilled of metal workers applied gold plating came word that the moving black carpet stopped at the edge of Goshen. Our fields remained green with the new growth.

I was not surprised that Moses was summoned back to the palace. We went together. I felt myself shiver in disgust and waved my shawl in a vain attempt to keep the insects from hopping against me as we walked. They were everywhere. Indeed the very floor of the throne room was covered with locusts. Slaves were kept busy beating them and sweeping the carcasses into piles. I could hear the shrieks from the harem women as their quarters and clothing were invaded.

Surrounded by his officials and priests, Pharaoh assumed an expression of humility.

"We have sinned against your god," he announced. "Pray that these hordes of insects be removed from our land and from our palace."

Moses waited for the man to continue. He did not move from his position in the center of the room. I tried to keep from shuddering when one of the locusts flew into my hair. Calmly my brother plucked it off and dropped it to the floor.

"Remove the locusts," at last the King spoke, "and you may take your families to worship this god."

Moses inclined his head to the King and we turned to leave.

"He has promised that we may go," I whispered ecstatically.

Pharaoh was not truly humble.

With pride and scorn the royal voice addressed his officials; "We are the Morning and Evening Star. We are Horus, son of the gods. It is our word that starts the day." I felt the scorn as the man continued, "Behold even the god of this Moses the Shepherd, Troubler of Egypt, has obeyed us. Eight time the plagues have been removed at our order."

"Mighty King, take care," one of the priests gasped, even as Aaron jerked to a stop.

Before he could turn and speak, Moses gripped his elbow. We heard the man on the throne sneer.

"Are you priests so fearful that weather and insects make you grovel? You are fortunate that we, Shepherd and Judge of this Land are not so easily fooled."

Outside in the sunlight, I watched Moses face west. He raised the staff high with both arms and bowed his head. Even as we walked along the road toward Goshen, a gale began to blow. It gathered up the locusts. In great clouds they were blown toward the desert and sea to the north and east of Egypt.

Aaron confronted his brother, "How can you remove the locusts? You heard what Pharaoh said. He has no intention of letting anyone leave Egypt."

"The word of God is true," the servant of the Living One replied. "The King will bow to our God."

Still Aaron sputtered as he walked behind. I was confused but didn't dare ask any questions. My mind still heard the contempt in Pharaoh's voice when he spoke of the God of Abraham, Isaac, and Jacob.

"Why doesn't God strike Pharaoh dead?" I turned the question over and over in my mind.

My brother spent the night in prayer. I lay on my mat listening to the man. He begged for God's mercy not only on the children of Israel but also for the suffering people of Egypt. Clutching the staff, he faced out the window to the east.

"Lord God, you met me at the burning bush and ordered me to go to Pharaoh." The whispered words were forlorn. "You promised that I would free your people. I have returned again and again to the King. Each time he answers more harshly. The nation suffers and still Pharaoh is not humbled."

For a long time, there was silence. I almost dozed off. Then the plea resumed.

"How long, my God, will this continue? Do you not see the agony of the Egyptians as well as your chosen people? Have pity on the land. Pharaoh must let the children of Israel go."

Moses was quiet again for a long time. I thought that the man was asleep. Then I saw him open his hands in surrender. The staff tilted forward to rest on the windowsill when he fell to his knees. My brother bowed his head to the ground.

"*I AM that I AM.*" I heard the name of God pass his lips. "Forgive me, I am your servant. You alone will bring about the redemption of your people."

I drifted to sleep while Moses still worshipped God. The sun was up when my brother rolled out of his blankets. The man stretched and looked for a long time toward the rising sun to the east.

"Pharaoh has mocked the God of our fathers by claiming that he alone causes the sun to rise in Egypt. There will come darkness over all the land for three days. Only in Goshen will there be light. All the King's magicians will not prevail against the dark. Then Egypt will understand that there is a God greater than the gods of the Nile. A God who is greater than the man who claims kinship with the gods."

He turned to eat the morning meal. Elisheva was still shy with her new brother-in-law. With shaking hands, she offered him a cup of fresh goat milk and a sweet cake instead of the usual flatbread. It was a special treat because it was Ithamar's birthday. Almost since she could bake, she had become famous for the tender morsels made with honey, dried fruit, and nuts and barely a hint of dough. Her round face shone when the guest accepted her offering.

After one bite, he exclaimed, "This is delicious! It is no wonder I have heard of your skills in baking. You could put Pharaoh's chefs to scorn."

We left Elisheva blushing with pleasure. With my brothers, I walked toward the construction site where I had not been since Moses returned to Goshen. My heart was saddened by the sight of beaten backs and bowed shoulders. How long would it be before we were free? I wished, as always, that I could ease the burdens. Instead, I found myself trotting behind my brother. At the appearance of Moses, workmen dropped their tools and followed us. Curious Egyptian guards and foremen also gathered around when he stopped in front of an obelisk depicting Pharaoh as Ra. With his staff, my brother pointed to the elaborately colored carving.

"Pharaoh has mocked the One True and Living God of Israel by claiming to be a god. He has said that he alone makes the sun rise in Egypt. Behold a darkness such as has never been seen, will cover the land. For three days there will be no light anywhere except Goshen."

The man raised the Shepherd's staff toward the sky and faced south. The entire gathering turned. Gasps of surprise and screams of terror rang out when like a huge blanket, blackness dropped over the horizon. Around us was light, but to the south there was nothing. Egypt had disappeared into night in the middle of the day.

Curses burst from Egyptian lips and they gathered together in confused groups. Strong soldiers were reduced to babbling fools by the sight. Finally, one captain drew himself together and snapped an order. Two guards set off at a trot to report to the King what had happened. My friends and neighbors surrounded Moses and Aaron.

"Now Pharaoh will have to let us go," I heard Aaron proclaim.

"With a mighty hand the Lord will bring us out of this land," Moses repeated the promise. "The King of Egypt will learn that it is God who has the power of life and death over all people."

Chapter 14

I expected Moses to confirm Aaron's words and tell everyone to pack and prepare to leave. Like my brother, I was sure that Pharaoh couldn't refuse our release after seeing how his prayers or the incantations of the priests did not move the darkness.

Moses was finally summoned to Pharaoh. Word spread throughout Goshen. I was not alone in rolling up blankets and stacking baskets. Food supplies were readied for travel.

"When do we leave?" My eager question greeted the man on his return.

"Only after the heart of the King is humbled," he replied sadly, shaking his head at my preparations. "God will tell us when we will leave."

"But..." I tried to argue.

"Trust God." Implacably, the Prophet gave the order. "God will bring us out of this place in his time."

I had to be content with that. There was grumbling in the streets though. Moses spoke calmly to the crowd.

"Pharaoh will not allow us to take our flocks and our herds," he told the people.

"We should go now if he is willing to let us leave," insisted Naham from his position at the front of the mob.

Simon stepped forward. "We can get new flocks once we are out of Egypt."

Murmurs of agreement sounded. The grumbling stopped when my brother raised his hand.

"Wait only a little longer and the God of Jacob will lead us from this land of bondage. We will go with our children and our parents. All the men and women will be free. Our flocks and our herds will provide food and sacrifice in the desert."

Something about his assurance quieted even the most vocal of his opponents. The ring of conviction carried to the extreme ends of the town.

"The people of Egypt will heap gifts of gold and silver into your hands before we leave."

Excited chatter greeted the last statement. They were still discussing the news when my brother walked away from town with stooped shoulders. I wondered why the man was sad. Everyone else was elated at the possibility of becoming rich at the expense of the hated Egyptians.

"Moses." I caught up with my brother as he walked along one of the levees between the river and the land. "Tell me what is troubling you."

"Miriam, my sister." The eyes that looked into mine were bleak.

He glanced back toward the mud brick houses in the town. The sound of excited discussion drifted to us. His head was bowed.

"They are rejoicing," he sighed.

"Of course they are, freedom is within their grasp," I confirmed, still not understanding the grief that gripped my brother.

Restlessly he paced toward the river and stopped at the water's edge. "God of Abraham, Isaac, and Jacob will you not have mercy on the people of the land? Why did you call me to be the cause of the destruction of Egypt? It would have been better if I had died here in this river." An agonized cry rose from the man as he raised face and hands to the sky. "God, the cost is too much to bear!"

Dropping to his knees my brother ignored the lapping water. I knelt beside him.

"You are God's chosen Prophet," I stated, trying to penetrate the despair.

Moses stared across the river. "As a prince, I learned the tricks and magic of the priests to use against them in God's service. It is far beyond that now. These plagues are not a trick or illusion." He looked south at the sand where fertile fields usually stood. After a moment the man continued. "Even though I was born a Hebiru slave, I was taught the ways of a prince. Royalty learns that caring for the people should not be taken lightly. In the name of my God, I

have ruined the land of my birth. The final judgment on Egypt…"
With a groan, my brother buried his face in his hands. When he
lifted his head to look at me, there was grim misery in the brown
eyes. The statement was a tortured whisper. "There will be a great
cry of grief throughout the land. The firstborn in every house will
die."

"Moses." His name was all I could say.

Tears gathered in my eyes, as I understood his despair and
sorrow. His obedience to his God and the love for the people of
Egypt tore at his soul. My heart went out to the mothers who would
be bereft. I remembered my desolation when my child miscarried.
From my childhood came the memories of the mothers in Goshen
whose sons were slaughtered by Pharaoh's edict. Through my mind
flashed a vision of every man I had prepared for burial after an
untimely death on the monuments. Joel's crushed body was among
them. For a long time I could not speak. Silently I held my brother's
hand feeling his heartache and seeking words to offer comfort.

"It is Pharaoh's stubborn pride that has brought this judgment."
My softly spoken words didn't ease my brother's anguish. I tried
again. "How many of our sons were killed by the decrees of the
King of the Black Land? Who can number the men lost to the
quarries and mud pits? Our mothers have wept for their children.
Perhaps the hand of God is simply making redress. The priests of
those temples would say that *maat*, order, must be preserved."

Still the strange man who was my brother stared silently across
the water. A scene from the distant past came to my mind, of my
mother kneeling over a basket in prayer.

"Moses." I tried a different approach. "I was with our mother
when she put you in the river. In her prayer she gave you to the God
of our fathers." Taking his chin in my hand, I turned the man to
face me. "Nothing has ever separated you from God. Jochebed
always believed that the Living God had destined you as the one to
deliver the children of Israel from this land."

"What of the people of Egypt?" My brother's brows were
drawn together almost in anger. The question was a cry of
desperation. "Pharaoh cares nothing for them. God has stricken the
land on our behalf. Who cares for the people?"

"You say that *I AM* is everywhere." Still I held Moses face between my hands. "No matter where you have roamed, God has protected you. Certainly he saved you from swords and river crocodiles to bring you to Pharaoh's daughter. As a prince, you had favor with nobles and priests so you could learn the arts of the temple. When you killed to save Joel's life, God was with you. You came safe to Midian where the Living One gave you a family. Jethro taught you of the God of Jacob and Esau, so you recognized his voice in the bush. Has not the hand of the God of Abraham, Isaac, and Jacob been on you for protection from the wrath of the King? Can you doubt that the One God will bring the children of Israel out of Egypt?" Still the mournful eyes stared at me. With an assurance I barely understood, I stated, "Surely God will be with all of the Egyptians, too. Joel always told me that God cares for everyone. The True God is God not only of Israel but of Egypt and all of creation."

I finished my statement to find Moses staring at me. Gone was the look of despair. He lifted his chin and stood up, drawing me to my feet.

"Yes, Miriam, you are right to remind me of all that God has done and promised. Indeed the Living One is Lord of all creation. It is true that *I AM* is not stopped by the obstinacy of one man. Nor," in humility my brother lowered his head, "by the doubts of his messenger."

The man remained silent for a minute. I felt him gathering himself together. When he raised his head there was confidence in his demeanor.

"We must tell the people how to prepare for this night," he scrambled to his feet, drawing me with him and started back to town. I had to run to keep up with my brother. People still talked in small groups. Everyone began to follow Moses, calling questions.

"When will we leave?"

"Where is the Promised Land?"

"What about food in the desert?"

"Do you know the way?"

The Shepherd stopped in front of the mortuary temple of Joseph the Honored. He mounted the steps to the entrance. Standing between the huge statues of the favorite son of Jacob, the man remembered in Egypt as the Lord Governor, Zaphenath-Paneah, Interpreter to the King and Preserver of the Land, my brother turned to face the crowd.

"You are the chosen people of the One God, the God of Abraham, Isaac, and Jacob. Since he called our father Abraham from Ur, he has been with your fathers and with you. Look around and see what a great nation the children of Israel have become. Joseph, the son of Jacob, came to this land four hundred years ago a slave like us."

He indicated the paintings on the wall behind him. The dimming colors told the story in a series of murals that ran around the building. On one side of the massive door was depicted a young Hebiru, bound and kneeling. Emblazoned on the opposite side was the governor of Egypt, imposing in his regalia as he welcomed his family to the land.

"Our father Jacob came here with only seventy men. Look around." The man gestured to the multitude of men, women, and children listening to his words. "The Living God has blessed you and made you strong. Even as slaves Pharaoh fears the strength of the sons of Abraham."

Cheers from somewhere in the back of the crowd interrupted the speech. The applause swelled and subsided. My brother raised his hand to forestall further acclamation.

"On this night the God of Abraham, Isaac, and Jacob will create a free people. Pharaoh will send us out of the Black Land in fear. Dread of *I AM that I AM* will finally convince the King that God is God."

The words were confident. Not even the doubters scoffed.

"Each of you must borrow gold and silver ornaments and ceremonial dishes from your Egyptian neighbors for the feast we will hold in the wilderness. Tomorrow we will leave this place." Pointing the staff toward the sun descending in the west, Moses stated; "This is the first of all nights, this month the beginning of months. When the sun sinks below the horizon and the full moon rises, it is the beginning of the free nation of the children of Israel. No longer will we be known as Hebiru, but as Israel!"

I caught my breath with pride at the new name. It was fitting that we take the name given to Jacob after he wrestled with God himself.

"The leaders of each of the tribes of Israel must come with me. I will explain what our God commands this night." The Prophet strode through the crowd, a path formed.

Twelve tribal patriarchs followed my brother. Aaron led the way as representative of the house of Levi. I hurried through the back alleys and reached my home before the men. Hastily I tossed bread and dried fruit on wood trays polished by sand and use and brought out jars of barley beer. By the time the council arrived, everything was in order. I sat back in a dark corner to listen. The men squatted on the floor. Moses calmly looked around at the faces. Most were curious; a couple had some hostility and doubt in their eyes.

"This is the first of all nights," my brother repeated his earlier statement. "On this night, God will act to bring the chosen people out of bondage."

"How can you be sure?" Malac from the house of Zebulon challenged.

"We have heard the promise of freedom from you before," Abrim spoke up for the sons of Dan.

Simon of Reuben's line leaned forward with his fist clenched, "What proof do you offer now, Prophet?" The tone was scornful. Aaron frowned at the speakers, but Moses didn't seem affronted. Instead, he nodded and lowered his head humbly.

"My brothers, I understand your doubts. That is why our God is making a new covenant with you this night."

He took a moment to look at every man. Each pair of eyes lowered before the speaker. The next words had such deep anguish that I nearly cried out.

"The Angel of Death will pass through the land of Egypt and gather up the firstborn of every house."

Before he could continue, pandemonium broke out. Several men jumped to their feet gesturing angrily.

"What kind of covenant is this?" Barak bar Judah shouted, looming over my brother.

I gripped my hands together in fear. Moses stood up. He was a tall man. Everyone stepped back from the confidence and faith that created an almost visible shield around the servant of God.

"Brothers," his voice rang over the chaos, "be seated and hear the covenant of the Living God."

Awed by his commanding presence, the group subsided again to stare with hostile and frightened eyes toward the man standing patiently in the middle of the room. In his hand he held the staff of God.

"*I AM* has shown you all his power again and again." My brother began the recital in a soothing voice. "The Nile ran red, fish died and frogs came out of the water. The hand of the God of Abraham, Isaac, and Jacob has protected you from the insect plagues and the boils and the darkness. Here in Goshen you have been safe while all of Egypt has been destroyed." A tightening of the man's lips showed that he still ached for the devastation of the land. "How can you doubt that the same God will continue to protect you?"

Torn between sorrow and anger my brother again stared at each of the elders in turn. One by one, they lowered their eyes and unclenched their fists.

"What is the covenant?" Aaron finally asked the question when Moses didn't continue.

As though returning from far away, the Prophet looked at his brother. Then he squatted in the circle with the men of Goshen.

"This night will be a memorial for all generations. You will tell it to your children and children's children. This month will be counted as the first of all months. On this, the fourteenth day, you will take a yearling lamb. It must be pure and unblemished," he ordered. "The animal will be killed at sunset. Roast the meat whole. With it you will eat unleavened bread and bitter herbs. As you eat, you will have your sandals on your feet and your staff in your hand ready to leave this land." After a pause, the man added. "This is the night of the new covenant. God will pass through the land of Egypt. Every first born of the nation will die." Just for a moment, the shadow of sorrow crossed my brother's face again. "If you obey the word of God and do as he commands, you and your children will live. The Angel of Death will pass your homes."

"What must we do?" Simon humbly asked the question on everyone's mind.

"Take the unblemished lamb and kill it at sunset," Moses replied. "Dip a bunch of hyssop in the blood. Mark the lintel and doorposts with the lamb's blood. By the blood of the lamb, the Angel of Death will know to pass by your home. Eat the meat roasted, do not break any of the bones. If anything is left, burn it in the fire. You must leave nothing until tomorrow."

Moses leaned forward to pick up a piece of the flatbread from the platter. He held it up for all to see.

"You will eat the meat with newly made unleavened bread. There is no time to bake leavened bread before the sun goes down. Eat the meal with herbs to remind you of the bitterness you are leaving behind." The Prophet looked intently around the circle. "Perform this covenant so *I AM* may be with you to bless you and your households through the coming generations."

In awed silence, the twelve men looked at each other. Like them, I felt the presence of something holy and beyond my comprehension in the words of my brother. When no one spoke, the Prophet of God stood up.

"Go," he urged, "choose a lamb for the sacrifice. Tell every family of this covenant and help them carry out the word of our God. Small families must join with larger ones so that the food will not be wasted and so that no one will lack."

Subdued and respectful, the twelve men scrambled to their feet. They shuffled to the door with heads lowered.

Moses spoke again, "Rejoice, my brothers, on this night a nation is born. No longer are you Hebiru dogs, slaves of Pharaoh, King of Egypt. Tell everyone the price that God requires of Egypt and recite to all generations how he redeems a free people to serve *I AM*."

Still silent, but with less dejection, the tribal leaders began to leave. With a few words and strong handclasp, my brother answered each man's unspoken concerns.

"Malac, do not be afraid, God's promises are true." Moses gripped the man by the shoulder.

"Abrim, you will see freedom this night." The assurance brought a smile to the man's lips.

"Simon, God is not mocked." Still the heavy brows drew together in doubt. "He will humble even Pharaoh on his throne."

"We will see," the heir of Reuben's line growled as he left.

When the house was empty, Moses turned to Aaron. "My brother, we too must have a lamb. God will act as I have said."

"It is a fearful thing," the older man responded.

"Aaron, you have seen each sign to Pharaoh. How can you doubt now?" I spoke up as I came forward.

The two men looked at me.

Angrily Aaron snarled, "Woman, don't you see? If Pharaoh doesn't let us leave Egypt tonight, all of Goshen will rise up and stone us."

Proudly I tilted my chin and glared up at the man. "If the One God fails in his word, it would be better to die." Looking at Moses I added, "Elisheva and I will prepare the meal."

"Miriam, our family will keep this covenant meal together," approved the man.

Aaron was left to sputter impotently when I turned to my task.

"Come, my brother." Moses put an arm around the resistant man. "Let us get a lamb."

I was left to my thoughts when the men closed the door behind them. Hastily I gathered the barley meal and began to mix the bread. "God of Abraham, Isaac, and Jacob, may your hand be on your people this night." I sent the brief prayer heavenward as I headed for the well.

Chapter 15

Other women scurried to and fro making preparations for this unexpected event. I saw a few carrying gold dishes and realized that they had borrowed from the Egyptians just as Moses urged. At the well, I was confronted by many of the women of Goshen. Their chatter stopped when I appeared. Immediately, they all turned to me with questions.

"Miriam, will my baby be safe?"

"Are we really leaving tomorrow?"

"What about my new table? Ezra just made it for me."

"How much can we take?"

"Esther's baby is due soon. How will she travel?"

"Can your brother be sure that Pharaoh will let us leave?"

Patiently, I answered each concern. My calm surprised even me. "Prepare the covenant meal as Moses has told us. Be ready to leave in the morning. We must take what we need, but," looking around at the anxious faces, I added, "some things will have to be left. Only what we can carry on our backs and our beasts will be taken. The few wagons and carts we have will be used for the elderly and the sick. We will load extra jars of water in them, too."

The babble of discussion began again.

Before I left the women, I stated, "The One Living God of Abraham, Isaac, and Jacob will visit Egypt this night. Even Pharaoh on his throne will be humbled." Unconsciously I imitated Moses intonation. "Trust in God and follow his command this night so you and your families will be spared. This is the price for our freedom. The lives of all the firstborn sons of the land are our ransom. It is a high price indeed." My voice broke on the last words and I felt tears of sorrow rise for the grief coming on Egypt.

"It serves them right," old Huldah spoke. "Were not our sons sacrificed to the Nile a generation ago? Have not our men died in the mud pits and quarries building Pharaoh's monuments?"

Sounds of assent caused me to turn back to the women.

"Then pity the mothers of the Black Land. It was not the women who ordered these things," I reminded the frowning faces. "It was the King and his officials. Now the people bear the burden for the royal obstinacy. Go now and prepare the covenant meal so the Angel of Death will pass your homes and families."

Elisheva stood in the doorway. Her welcome was nearly hysterical and tears streamed down her face.

"Tell me it is not true. The firstborn sons will not all die, will they?"

My nephew, Nadah, looked rebellious and I heard him complain; "Mother, I should be with Father and Uncle Moses. All the other men are preparing a lamb for this night."

"We have the promise of God. A new covenant is enacted this night. The firstborn of the obedient of Israel shall not die. Your son will be safe."

I smiled at my nephew who pulled free from his mother's relaxed arms.

With all the pride of his twelve years, the boy announced, "I told you, Mother, that I would be fine."

He looked so much like his father for a moment that I was taken back three decades. Just so had Aaron looked, when he told Amram and Jochebed that he was selected by the goldsmiths to continue as apprentice to the Master Smith himself. Aaron's boyish arrogance had burst through his manly self-esteem.

"Come, Elisheva, we have much to do before the men return with the lamb." I pulled the woman through the door.

Dark eyes watched her son run from the house to find his father and uncle. Fingernails dug into my arm as the mother sought reassurance.

"He will not be harmed?"

"We will fulfill the commandments of God. Everyone in this house will be safe from the Angel of Death." I took the young woman by the shoulders. "Tonight is the beginning of our freedom. Do not be afraid."

Tears stood in her eyes as Elisheva confessed, "I don't have the faith of you and your brothers."

Taking the small figure into my arms I shook her gently, "Then believe in what they say because they speak for God. Tonight is a night of change. A new people and a new dream are born this evening. No longer are we Hebiru slaves of Egypt but free children of Israel on the way to the Promised Land. Let us prepare for this feast."

I felt a hesitant nod against my shoulder. Elisheva wiped her eyes and together we set to work. When Moses and Aaron returned, Nadah was with them. They carried the carcass of a lamb. The boy carried a basin with the lamb's blood in it with pride. We all watched as Moses took the hyssop branch and marked the sides and top of the door. All along the street, other men were doing the same thing. A solemn silence hung over the town.

"The children of Israel have obeyed you, Moses," Aaron stated, inclining his head toward the town.

I stood beside my brothers. The sky itself was blood red in the sunset but the splotches of lamb's blood stood out dark against the varying shades of mud brick along the street.

"Lord God, behold, your people have heard your word. Do not forsake them but hold them safe this night. Bring your chosen nation to freedom. You alone are the True God who blesses and redeems all creation." My words came from a heart filled with hope and reverence.

"Lord of the Universe," Moses took up the prayer, "spare the innocent of Egypt, if it is possible. *I AM that I AM* have mercy on the people." My brother bowed his head briefly. When he looked up the glow of the setting sun was reflected in his face. "God of Abraham, Isaac, and Jacob, your will be done. Deliver your chosen ones by the strength of your hand. Behold, we are your servants."

The man gripped my hand and Aaron's. I felt a consecration in my soul for the task ahead. It was a deep peace. We stood together until the sun disappeared into the western desert.

Each man entered his home to eat with his family. I wondered how many shared my sister-in-law's fears that a son would die in the night. Several times during the evening, I saw her look at Nadah and reach out toward him. His cloak lay in her lap and she pretended to be mending a small tear. I knew it was a pretext for holding something of his.

Despite my brave words to Aaron and Elisheva, I was in a fever of impatience for the night to end. Watching my nephews sleeping together as the night stretched out, I sent a prayer to God for their safety. The death wails from nearby Egyptian houses made me start and glance around.

"My sister," Moses took my hand. He seemed to have read my mind. "You spoke to me of God's love even of the Egyptians. Are you doubting now?" He stared sadly past me, "It is true that many mother's arms will be empty in Egypt from Pharaoh's house to the maidservant in the field. This punishment comes to the King because he would not listen to the One God. All Egypt and the world will know that Pharaoh is a man, not a god."

"Couldn't we have warned Pharaoh?" I asked, gripping the man's arm.

"The King has heard," Moses voice was stern. "Still he will not humble himself before God. Tomorrow we will leave Goshen. Our route will take us toward Succoth. From there God will show us the direction to go." He paused, and then added, "We will not travel beside the Great Sea. The Philistines are a warring people."

The death wails continued to increase from the Egyptian homes. I prayed for each mother who lost a child. Night was moving toward dawn when the rumble of chariot wheels and pounding on the door roused me from the restless doze I finally drifted into. Springing to my feet, I was beside Moses and Aaron when the door slammed open.

"Pharaoh will see you," the soldier ordered. I noticed that he wore the insignia of captain in the royal guard. "All of you," he added, pushing me into the vehicle behind my brothers.

In the far corner of the room, Elisheva stifled her sobs of terror with a blanket. My last sight of her was of frightened eyes darting from her still sleeping sons to her husband as we were hustled out the door.

I walked between my brothers into the palace and down the tiled halls. Guards marched in front and behind us. Sobbing and wails could be heard all around. I shivered and felt my youngest brother's hand rest on my shoulder. We were not taken to the throne room but to a smaller anti-chamber. The King of Upper and Lower Egypt, Lord of the Nile and god of the land, was slumped in a leather and wood chair. He wore no royal regalia. The shaved head bowed over the carved arm of his seat. Haggard eyes looked at us when we were shoved forward.

"Bow to your master, Hebiru dogs," the captain's words were harsh.

Following Moses' lead, I remained standing even when the flat of a sword stung my back.

"Go."

Pharaoh spoke only one word. Our guards left. The man repeated the word. His voice was hoarse.

"Go."

Still we stood before the broken figure. The Great One of Egypt did not look at us. He stared at a spot somewhere to the left of our feet. At last, the empty eyes lifted to stare at Moses.

"Take your flocks and your herds, your children and your old women. Get out of Egypt. Your God is too strong." The rasped acknowledgment hurt worse than our freedom. The man lowered his head into his hands in an admission of defeat. "Your curse has left us bereft. Our son is dead."

The words were a low growl filled with misery.

"We will go, as the King of Egypt has said," my brother replied. "May your grief be eased, Great One."

I gasped when Moses dared to place a hand on Pharaoh's shoulder in sympathy. The man reared back from the touch.

"Do not mock us!" he shouted. "Leave us! Do not try to return."

In rage and anguish the incarnation of Ra turned his back on the messenger of *I AM*.

Moses turned to the door. Aaron and I followed him out of the palace. On the walk back to Goshen no one spoke. I saw my brother's lips moving and knew he was praying although I couldn't hear the words. Cries of mourning accompanied our journey. I was glad to get back to the house. Elisheva threw herself into Aaron's arms. He stroked her back until the sobs ceased.

"Aaron, summon the leaders," Moses ordered. "We will gather with the dawn."

In an astonishingly short time, the people had assembled.

"The God of our fathers, the One whose name is *I AM* has set us free. The God of Abraham, Isaac, and Jacob is the Lord we will follow and serve," Moses announced. "No more will the Children of the Promise serve the King of Egypt. We have Pharaoh's permission to leave the Black Land."

A cheer greeted the words. My brother raised his hand.

"Bring what you have packed. We will gather between the pillars of Ra to begin our journey to the land of Canaan. The Living God fulfills the covenant made with our fathers."

The answering shout of joy made my skin prickle with anticipation. Looking at the excited mob, I sent a prayer to their God and mine.

"God of Abraham, Isaac, and Jacob, Great *I AM*, you have humbled Pharaoh on his throne. Bring us safely to the land you have promised. Don't let the people become discouraged and falter in the way."

Before the sun was even halfway up the sky, the community was assembled and ready to leave. The hostile eyes of the Egyptian soldiers and overseers watched our preparations. Some of the priests joined the throng observing our preparations. Their mocking words drifted to me as I loaded extra blankets and bandages into the wagon designated for the sick and aged. I had to grit my teeth to prevent myself from responding with rage.

"This rabble will give up before they have gotten to the border."

"The gods have lured the fools into the desert to kill them for daring to confront Pharaoh."

"It's not as easy as you think to escape from the eyes of Ra."

"The Hebiru will turn back. Slaves have no stamina for a journey even soldiers find difficult."

I saw anxious glances being darted toward the taunts and knew that I was not the only one hearing the scornful predictions. A voice I recognized as my own began a chant of praise.

"Blessed be the God of Abraham, Isaac, and Jacob.
    By a mighty hand he frees the slave.
God's power triumphs over the man who is not a god.
    The pride of Egypt lies in the grave.
I AM is the name of the only True and Living Lord.
    Israel follows the One who does save."

I heard other voices joining me when I began again, "Blessed be the God of Abraham, Isaac, and Jacob."

Moses stood beside me. Aaron and Elisheva were beside the water wagon. With my nephews, they began to chant with me. Gradually more and more of the people began to repeat the words. Our song drowned out the mockery of the watchful Egyptians. I noticed the priests crossed their arms across their chests and glared at us as we finished the loading. As one, we faced the east.

Chapter 16

With the entire community assembled, Aaron and I waited for Moses to give the signal to start. My brother surveyed the mass of humanity seething at the edge of the town. Men, women, and children carried huge bundles of possessions on their backs. Unnecessary things like chairs and stools teetered unsteadily on the very top of many packs. Some of the travelers were almost bent double under the load of the items they couldn't or wouldn't leave behind. Flocks of ducks and chickens wandered among the waiting group followed by their young attendants. Herds of sheep and goats milled around just beyond the people. Shepherds with their own bundles of clothing and household items kept the animals from straying far. An occasional curse was heard when something toppled from an overloaded bundle.

Toward the front of the group stood the guardians of the body of Joseph the Honored. A lump rose in my throat when I saw the young men standing in formation around the ornate sarcophagus that held the bones of Rachel's firstborn son. Each of the bearers was a descendent of either Manasseh or Ephraim. When the man known in Egypt as the Lord Governor, Zaphenath-Paneah, died, his sons had been charged with care of their father's remains. The family maintained a perpetual watch at the mortuary temple and now bore the body home to Canaan. 'God will visit the children of Israel and bring them out of Egypt.' The dreamer's promise was being fulfilled after four centuries of bondage.

A feeling of hopeful expectation not unmixed with anxiety filled the air. All eyes were fixed on the man who spoke for God. The trumpeters and the men holding the tribal banners waited for the signal to start the procession. I smiled at the ingenuity shown in the transformation of the standards used to designate a work site into symbols of pride and kinship. Each panel of wool now bore a different emblem. On his deathbed, Jacob bar Isaac had blessed each of his sons by their resemblance to a totem animal. That figure now led his descendants from bondage.

Moses looked at me. His eyes held uncertainty. "The people are so many." The whispered words sounded unsure and almost fearful. "How can I lead them? Where will I find food and water for so many? They will turn on me. I cannot do this."

"My brother." I gripped the man's arms. "You were a prince in this land, but it is not your strength that will lead these people." When he still looked confused and unsure I spoke sternly to God's messenger.

"The True and Living God has brought freedom to the chosen children of Israel. Surely *I AM* will not abandon them now. You are only the servant of God." My tone was sharp with the reminder.

The man gazed into my eyes for a long time. When he finally took my hands, the faltering look was gone.

"Miriam, you are wise and God has reprimanded me through your words." The graying head lowered until his chin touched his chest. "May God forgive me for doubting, again, that he is in charge."

After a moment of silence, the man gave me a quick hug. We looked up as Aaron approached with a worried look on his face.

"The people grow restless." A hand waved in the general direction of the murmuring company.

Moses clapped his brother on the shoulder and strode forward as though he never had any qualms about the journey.

"Come, we will leave Egypt. Today we journey toward Succoth."

A cheer greeted our arrival. When the man raised the staff of God the crowd fell silent.

"Give praise to God," Moses the Shepherd of Israel shouted. "It is God's hand that brings your freedom. *I AM* will lead us on the way."

Turning to the southeast the man squared his shoulders and stepped out.

That first day seemed like a party. Everyone laughed and sang as we walked. No one had any idea where we were going, but it didn't matter. I saw some of the young men making rude gestures at the Egyptians we passed.

When Moses called a halt at a water hole, he spoke sternly, "The people of Egypt have endured much for our freedom. The land is bereft on our behalf. Do not mock them. It is their King who has brought disaster on the land, but it is the innocent who suffer."

His words caused contrite looks to be exchanged. I noticed that several families took the reprimand to heart when we camped at an oasis. As darkness descended, I saw them divide their meal with a group of Egyptian travelers. A feeling of peace filled my heart watching the exchange.

A few large tents were set up. In the meager shelter, all the women and children slept together. The men bedded down under the stars. It felt odd to have thin animal skins rather than four solid mud brick walls to keep out the evening chill. The hides didn't keep out the night sounds. I heard wild dogs and other animals calling in the darkness. The odd rustles in the sandy ground under my blankets made me nervous. Ra was barely on the rim of the world when the ram's horn awakened me from the fitful sleep I had finally drifted into.

"We should reach Succoth today," I heard Moses tell Aaron.

It was a hard trek to the outpost on the edge of the desert. Night had fallen when the city at last came into view. We camped outside the gates. All afternoon I listened to complaints.

"My feet hurt and my back aches from this load."

"Does Moses think we are animals?"

"I hoped to sleep in a bed in Succoth tonight."

"Where are we going?"

I couldn't answer except to say, "Wherever the God of Abraham, Isaac, and Jacob has promised will be our new home."

Exhaustion made it easier to fall asleep on the hard ground. The morning trumpet, signaling the opening of the city gates, jolted me from my dreams. Moses and Aaron were already waiting between the pylons while the elders were summoned. I wondered if my brothers ever slept. The leaders spent a long time talking and gesturing from camp to city and back again. As I assisted with the morning meal, I wondered what was being discussed. My eyes were not the only ones straying toward the group. I heard fearful whispers.

"Will soldiers be summoned to return us to Goshen?"

"What is taking so long?"

"Aren't there Hebrews living in Succoth, too?"

"Does Moses expect them to join us too?"

"They haven't suffered as we have. Why do they need freedom?"

"We won't have enough food."

I wanted to reassure everyone, but, as the conversation stretched out, I became concerned, too. Eventually, Moses drew an official scroll from his robe. At the royal seal, the elders became obsequious. They began to nod vigorously rather than shaking their heads. Aaron returned to camp while my youngest brother accompanied the leaders of Succoth into the city.

"We will fill our water skins here. The people of Succoth will provide us with more food." He had to pause when cheers interrupted the speech. "Any children of Israel living here may join us. Moses has gone to talk to the people."

I saw a few frowns at the mention of more travelers. However, the gifts of food and water seemed to have appeased most of the grumblers. Women and children hurried off to gather all the empty water skins. Men hitched a pair of oxen to a cart for the water jars.

Seeing my brother's worried look, I confronted the man. "What is wrong?"

"We should make haste to leave Egypt. This trip to Succoth wasn't necessary. Two days have been wasted. By now we could have been out of the Black Land." With a heavy sigh, Aaron confessed his fear, "What if Pharaoh changes his mind? We will be trapped."

A vague gesture indicated the outposts of royal power just visible in the shimmering distance.

"We cannot leave our brethren in slavery while we go free," I argued.

"You sound like Moses," the man snapped. "If God wanted them free, he would have sent a deliverer to them, too."

"He sent our brother to all the nation," I asserted gently.

Stubbornly Aaron shook his head. "These people will not go. They are comfortable here in this trade outpost. Rich and settled instead of beaten and cursed, these men have no reason to want to leave Egypt. The elders didn't even want to give us any assistance and they are of the tribe of Gad." A venomous look was directed at the city. "Besides, the people here have forgotten the God of Jacob. Look at the temples in Succoth. You can see the obelisks from here. This place is more Egyptian than Hebrew."

The tall pillars he indicated were visible above the walls and through the gateway. I wondered which gods they honored. My mind sought a reply. It was not needed. Moses strode from Succoth. He swerved toward us when I waved.

"Well?" Aaron's one word was full of rancor.

"Some will join us." The man looked discouraged. "There has been no one to remind them of the God of our fathers. In the delta, Jochebed and Miriam kept the story alive."

I bent my head in humility at my brother's approving smile. A sad sigh made me long to comfort the Prophet.

"The gods of Egypt are the only gods these people know." Moses was explaining the reluctance of the residents. "They would rather remain here serving shadows than risk an encounter with the Living God. The priests here have explained all the plagues as punishment from the various local deities." Tears stood in my brother's eyes as he looked at the city. He lowered his head, shaking the shaggy beard sprinkled with gray. "They do not understand that each sign has been the hand of God acting for our freedom. Too easily people reject the True God. I have failed."

"No, my brother." I took the callused hand of a shepherd. "It is their choice. God does not force obedience. Look." I tugged the hand I held. "Here come some families to join us now."

It was a paltry group of mostly disgruntled men and women who joined us at Succoth. I saw Moses go alone to pray as the sun was setting. My heart went with him even as I worked with the women to prepare the evening meal. The newcomers were eventually settled according to their families of origin. Each tribe welcomed the new kin, even if reluctantly.

Unable to sleep, I sat staring at the stars. Behind me in the tents, women and children dozed. The men snored on their blankets spread around the campsite. I envied their ability to forget the worries of the day.

"God of Abraham, Isaac, and Jacob, you are the God my brother follows. Give him the wisdom to lead this great people you are bringing out of bondage. Send Moses wise assistants on the journey." As an afterthought I added, "Living One, thank you for Joshua."

The young man was a devoted aide to my brother. The only son of Nun had been a water boy to Pharaoh's troops at Raamses. That city was heavily guarded because already the king had begun amassing treasure into the completed buildings that would be his memorial in the afterlife. Now barely twenty, Joshua used his experience gained watching the soldiers to organize our ragtag company of refugees. Early the second day, he divided the people into tribal groups. Each elder followed the designated standard and maintained a set position in the march. I had been amazed at the difference such a simple order made in the efficiency of travel. Even now, so near the city of Succoth, Joshua had insisted that a type of watch be set against thieves and marauding dogs. Despite some complaints, Moses had agreed. A few boys watched the herds and a couple of men patrolled the outline of the camp.

My disjointed prayers and reflections were interrupted by a commotion close to the walls. I saw Joshua sit up, immediately alert with his hand on the short sword he habitually wore. He strode toward the voices to return a moment later holding a ragged boy by the arm. Quietly he roused my brother. Curious, I followed the men away from the sleeping camp. The words I heard chilled my blood.

"My stepfather sent a runner to the guard post when you arrived," the boy panted. "He just received a scroll from the lieutenant. Pharaoh is sending troops to intercept you if you continue toward Lake Timnah."

"You saw this scroll?" Joshua crouched to gaze into the boy's eyes.

"I heard my father read it to the other elders." A steady look was returned. "They want to keep you all here with excuses until the troops arrive."

"Why did you come to us, lad?" Moses' question was gentle as he laid a hand on the curly head.

"My mother believed in the One True God." There was a proud lift to the young head. "She taught me about Abraham, Isaac, and Jacob before she died. She knew that God would deliver the people and we would return to Canaan."

Tears welled in my eyes and I yearned to clutch this boy child to my breast. My child would have been only slightly older than this lad.

"Bravely said, my son." I heard the smile in my brother's voice.

"I want to come with you," the messenger continued, tilting his head to look up at the man. In an eager tone, he offered, "I can fetch and carry and run errands."

Joshua and Moses exchanged glances. Impulsively, I stepped out of the shadows. Three pairs of eyes stared at me wondering what I was doing listening to their conversation.

"Yes, the boy should come. Anyone who seeks the Living God must be welcomed. This boy will be an asset." I didn't question my words, even as I spoke. "He will be a leader of the people."

My brother inclined his head and then nodded.

"Miriam speaks as a prophet. The boy has been sent by God to warn us of Pharaoh's plans. The hand of *I AM* is upon him." Again, the big hand rested on the child's head. "He may stay with us."

"What of his father?" Joshua voiced concern.

"Tabed is my stepfather," scornfully the boy spoke. "He does not care or even notice if I am around."

"Go with Miriam, my son." Moses gave a shove in my direction. "What is your name?"

"Caleb, son of Zephunneh of the house of Judah," he answered proudly avoiding my outstretched hand. "This day I am thirteen. No longer do I stay in the tents of the women."

Joshua chuckled, "Then go and sleep among the men," he ordered pointing to the snoring bodies not far away.

I turned back to my own bed when the pair moved further out of camp to discuss the news. Now exhausted, I slipped into a dreamless sleep to be roused by the trumpets from city and camp.

In the early light Moses announced, "We will turn south." Shouted questions were firmly answered, "The way is not safe to north or east. It is the route we will take."

Tabed and the other elders did try to delay our departure with many excuses.

"Offerings to the gods must be made for your journey."

"Let the women and children rest another day."

"We will prepare a great feast this night to honor you."

Moses calmly refused every offer. "The God of Abraham, Isaac, and Jacob is our shield. You have been most kind in your hospitality. *I AM* calls us to move, we must obey."

Joshua marshaled the people. We set out at a steady pace toward Etham near the Red Sea. I wondered if anyone else noticed that we were traveling faster than before. Caleb didn't appear until we were out of sight of Succoth.

I heard Joshua greet the boy and saw him proudly fall into step beside the broad shouldered young man. My eyes followed the child as he strutted happily beside his heroes. It seemed he never grew tired of running from one end of the long column to the other to bring messages from Moses and Joshua to the tribal leaders.

The trek to Enath was swift. We covered the distance in just over two days. There were complaints from the shepherds that the flocks couldn't sustain such a pace.

"At Enath we may rest a day," Moses announced. "There is grazing and water."

There was grass and water but no welcome from the inhabitants of the city. The elders rebuffed my brother. The gates were shut firmly against us. Aaron was very angry.

"They act as though we were thieves and not fellow residents of Egypt," he raged.

"We aren't Egyptian any longer," I reminded the man. "We are exiles seeking to escape from the land."

My brother had no response.

Moses looked discouraged when he came from meeting with the tribal leaders.

"What is it?" I hurried to walk beside this moody man who God had called to be his messenger.

He didn't respond immediately and I wondered if he would answer. The deep voice was heavy with regret when at last he spoke. A big hand rubbed across his forehead.

"I have failed my God. Already some of the people want to turn back. They are afraid of Pharaoh and do not trust the Living God." The man heaved a sigh; "I have been listening to complaints about the food and the distance and the speed of travel. Why am I burdened with such ungrateful people?"

I tugged my brother's arm until he sat beside me under a palm tree. My hand indicated the hundreds of men, women, and children milling about the camp. Pointing out a few, I reminded the Deliverer of the past.

"Look at all you have done. A week ago, that child was gathering straw in the fields. The rough stalks no longer chafe his arms. Two moon cycles past that man fell from scaffolding. He will never have to risk his life again. That woman was one of the many victims of the lust of the overseers. Now she can live without fear of rape." I crouched in front of the man. "You have given all these people a chance for a new life."

"They hate me," he announced in the same dejected tone.

"No." I tilted my head considering a reply. "It is the newness they are afraid of. No one is accustomed to the nomadic life yet. Soon we will learn to travel as swiftly as you do." My hand gripped Moses' wrist. "Be patient. Your God is with you."

"I wish I had a sign." Another sigh accompanied the words.

Looking over my brother's shoulder, I saw something that took my breath away. At first, I thought a gigantic dust cloud was approaching. Then I noticed that this swirling pillar didn't actually touch the ground. It was not made of dust but of light.

"God has heard you and sent you a sign." I gasped out the statement.

A shaking hand pointed to the wonder. The man looked over his shoulder.

"Lord God, forgive me." Moses flattened himself to the dirt.

I dropped to my belly beside him. The cloud continued to move forward. There were no stinging grains of desert sand even when the pillar paused in front of us. I heard nothing, but Moses must have, because he spoke.

"Behold your servant."

They were only three words spoken in homage and humility. My heart swelled at the tone. There was no fear, simply devotion to *I AM*.

The pillar moved away to the north of Enath. Moses scrambled to his feet. Cries of fear were heard as first the children and then the adults saw the motionless towering pillar.

"It is the *Shekinah*, the Glory and Spirit of God, sent to guide us," Moses declared. His face glowed with reverence and conviction. "The God of Abraham, Isaac, and Jacob will lead us in the way we should go. Prepare to leave this place."

With many an awestruck glance at the unmoving column, the community took down the tents and loaded water jars into the wagons. In a very short time, we were heading north. Ra moved down the sky in the west. The cloud took on a warm glow that stayed even after the sun had set. We didn't need torches to see our way because the pillar gave light to the whole caravan. All through that night, we walked almost in a daze, following the glowing pillar. Dawn's light found us at a small oasis. The morning meal was eaten in near silence. Then we moved on, following the manifestation of the True and Living God.

Chapter 17

Day by day the pillar led us. We skirted the Bitter Lakes in the south before turning north. Lake Timnah lay to our west as we passed it. On the seventh day, we came within sight of the Great Sea. Sailors from other lands came across the water to Egypt but few ships ventured from the Black Land. Children were told stories of water monsters, more terrible than the Nile crocodiles, which roamed the waters ready to destroy any who ventured away from the safety of the river. Even before we arrived, I felt the difference in the breezes and saw the sea birds circling overhead. The land reminded me of the delta where I had lived all my life. The animals, too, seemed happy to find a little more grazing than had been available along the desert tracks. Moses called a halt when the column of God's presence stopped.

"We are not far from the Way of the Philistines," my brother stated.

I stood with Aaron and Joshua. Caleb, as usual, hovered nearby. His nearly black hair was neatly combed now and the thin face was beginning to fill out from regular meals. The boy had become my friend and often walked with me when he wasn't helping the men. Every night he assisted with the setting up of my tent. He came to me the first camp we made north of Etham and took the ropes from me.

"You have no husband or son to do this for you. I will be proud to help the sister of the Deliverer."

The words made me want to hug the young man. Instead, I contented myself with calling him 'son' in my heart.

Now everyone listened intently as Moses continued to explain.

"We will cross out of Egypt south of the highway. I know the way," a wry smile tilted the mouth above the beard. "It's how I escaped from Egypt last time. The water flows into a swamp known as the Reed Sea from all the plants growing in the water. It looks impassable but really is shallow enough to wade through. We dare not risk the main route even though it is only a day's journey further north. God is blocking our advance."

The man gestured to the pillar that stood between the camp and the trade route. It was now taking on the warm glow of the evening light. We had grown used to the phenomenon although I still caught my breath at the beauty of the glowing column each night.

In the morning, I accompanied my brothers and Joshua to the place called the Reed Sea. Several of the leaders followed when they saw Moses leave the camp.

"It looks deep," I whispered to Caleb.

The boy nodded. The heads of the plants were barely visible above the water. Moses and Joshua waded out into the lake. Almost immediately the water was up to their waists. I couldn't hear the words but by Joshua's gestures, I understood that the water became even deeper. Aaron turned to face the men now gathering on the shore. There were growls of discontent.

"This is where we are to cross?"

"Are we fish to swim out of Egypt?"

"Might as well just wade through the Great Sea itself."

My brother responded, "We will camp here for a day or two until the water recedes. Then there will be no difficulty in crossing." Moses waded to shore. The wet robe hung heavily around his legs. "The estuary is flooded from storms," he admitted. The fact didn't seem to discourage the man. He issued an order. "Take this time to more securely pack your belongings in preparation for our trek to the mountain of God in Sinai. There we will offer a sacrifice of the best of our flocks and of our grain. On Sinai, you will meet the God of your fathers who has brought you out of Egypt."

There were grumbles but most of the men nodded at the wisdom of the advice. Everyone set about repacking. There was time to wade in the shallows along the shores and wash clothes coated with desert dust. The children thought it a great treat to be allowed to wade out and gather the supple reeds, which were swiftly woven into new baskets.

Caleb was the first to warn of the impending danger. It was midday when he ran into camp looking for Joshua and Moses. I knew his news even before Joshua started to his feet and ran to the rock outcropping south of camp. Moses also stood. He looked at the water, still lapping at the shore. The level had not gone down noticeably. Then he stared north. The well-patrolled highway lay along the coast. The soldiers from the Way of the Philistines could join any troops Pharaoh had approaching from the west.

Somehow, word of the approaching troops filtered through the camp. I heard cries of fear from the women. Children were hurriedly called back from the water to be held safe by frightened mothers.

"What leadership is this?" Not surprisingly, it was Simon who led the angry mob to confront my brother. "We are trapped! Pharaoh and his army can destroy us at will."

The assertion caused the women to cry out. I found myself walking toward them.

"Listen to me." Somehow my calm tone cut through the wails and sobs.

They stood bunched together but turned to stare at me when I scrambled into the front of a cart. Dozens of pairs of frightened and tearful eyes looked at me. Most of the women wore veils, a few left their hair uncovered and braided in the Egyptian style. They waited for me to speak. Behind me, I heard the men challenging Moses and Aaron. I saw Joshua climb down from his vantage point and walk toward my brothers. Then the words came to me even as I saw the dust cloud on the horizon.

"God will not forsake us." When I said the words, I realized I believed them. "The One God is not capricious and will not turn on us like the gods of Egypt."

"The Egyptian soldiers are coming." A sobbed statement from the middle of the crowd created a whirlpool of nods and whispers.

"What can God do against an army?" The question came from one of the women of Succoth. "I have seen the soldiers of Egypt. Their swords are sharp and their spears are long."

Her eyes glinted maliciously. I stared straight at the woman until she shuffled uncomfortably and lowered her eyes.

"Do not forget what God has done already. His arm is not shortened," was my reply.

"Our children will be safe. The One God of our fathers and mothers did not spare them when the Angel of Death visited the land to allow them to die by Pharaoh swords." I felt a prickling in my skin. Slowly I turned to face the menace approaching from the southwest. "Look and you will see the saving hand of our God."

I pointed to the massed troops of Egypt. The sun struck the spear points and reflected off the chariots and horse trappings. They had stopped a couple of miles away.

"Wait," I repeated when fearful sobs began. "You will see the hand of God."

Even as I spoke, the cloud of God descended between our camp and the armies of Pharaoh. Curses of surprise and even fear were heard from the soldiers beyond the towering pillar. A cheer erupted in our ranks. Then I heard Moses.

"We will go forward in the name of God."

I turned in time to see him stretch out the rod toward the water. A violent wind sprang up from the east. Anything not tightly bundled up began rolling across the ground or flying through the air. The power whipped my clothes around my legs and took away my breath. Mothers grabbed their children as they staggered in the gale. Still my brother faced the sea. Aaron stood on one side and Joshua on the other. I was not surprised to see Caleb standing next to his hero.

"Gather your things," I shouted to the women struggling in the wind. "We will be leaving this camp and crossing to freedom."

Stunned faces turned to me. Some women stared at the foaming water. Others looked to where the Egyptian hosts were hidden from sight by the towering cloud that blazed brighter than the sunlight. Even through the flying dust the light from the column could be seen. Beyond the pillar, darkness was falling as Ra sank toward the horizon. Impatiently, I tugged and pushed.

"If you don't hurry, you will have to leave your things behind."

Finally, my words penetrated the fear of a few women. They began gathering together their bundles. More followed. The men gaped stupidly at us until I placed myself in front of them.

"If you don't pack the tents," I pointed to the hides flapping wildly, "we will not have shelter on this journey."

Only then did a small group start to dismantle the canopies. By shoving, cajoling, and ordering, I got the dumbfounded people ready. They were still gathering up scattered items when a scream from a child alerted us to God's latest intervention.

"The water!"

We all looked to see that a path was opening in the water. Dry land was appearing amid the reeds. The last light from the setting sun topped the dripping reeds with gold.

Moses turned to address the crowd. The company stood silent and immobile with awe. His face was lit by the pillar's glow. Then he spoke. The deep tone resonated through the camp. My brother waved toward the now dry crossing.

"Come, we will leave Egypt. After this night, you will see Pharaoh no longer."

We all stood as though rooted in place. Caleb gave a cheer and ran into the path.

"Come on," he urged. "It's dry!"

The boy bent down and picked up a handful of sand. We watched it trickle from is fingers, not in muddy clumps but a stream of dry pebbles. I heard myself take a deep breath. It was like a signal. Everyone began to talk and move around. Joshua took charge.

"Herdsmen, take the flocks across, keeping to the north side of the path."

His order was obeyed somewhat hesitantly until the animals found the road. Then they contentedly trotted toward the far side.

"Finish loading the wagons."

The man's shout sent a crew to tying down the tents and equipment in the carts and hitching up the oxen.

"Come, my dear," Joshua gently urged a young mother toward the path. Caleb ran back to take the woman's hand.

"It's perfectly safe. You'll see!" The boy tugged her along.

Unafraid, the baby in her arms cooed and pointed to the sheep moving beside her. More travelers joined the procession. Fearful eyes looked at the water and the people began to rush through the path, dropping excess baggage along the road.

"Fire bearers, watch your buckets," Joshua cautioned as the bronze containers swung dangerously in the wind which still blew steadily.

Aaron took my hand and we marched down the road in the midst of the people. It was odd to see dry land where only minutes ago deep water stood. A few dead fish and sea creatures lay along the road along with abandoned belongings. To the north, the waves splashed and foamed against the wall of wind. A last glance westward reassured me that the cloud from God still kept the forces of Egypt at bay. Facing forward, I hurried through the passage. My action encouraged the waiting women. Children were grasped by the hand and families moved hesitantly toward the far shore. We tramped forward without getting our feet wet. I found myself turning back again and again to help some child who fell or to assist a friend with picking up a spilled bundle. A few at a time, members of each tribe gathered on the eastern side of the estuary. They called encouragement to those still standing fearfully uncertain on the west bank. Eventually the entire community was in the process of crossing or waiting for their friends to arrive.

Finally the wagons moved into the road, loaded with the tents, water, and other heavy items. The vehicles were only halfway across when the sentry on the east bank gave a cry and pointed behind us. Screams began when the people saw that God's pillar was disappearing from in front of the massed troops. The last of the flocks were urged toward shore with shepherd's crooks and shouts. Those of us still in the road began to run.

Moses stood calmly on a rock outcropping on the shore. He looked very far away. The rising sun was behind my brother. Thankfully, I scrambled up the last incline onto the verge. The ground looked the same but it was freedom.

"Is it better to die here rather than in Egypt?" Men from Succoth challenged the Prophet of God. "The soldiers will rush through the ford as easily as we did."

The men pointed to where the advancing soldiers marched toward the passage. Foot soldiers and chariots moved inexorably forward.

"Your God is weak!" Several groups surrounding Moses took up the shout.

Without responding or looking at the discontented crowd, my brother stared westward. The troops paused where the sandy shore turned to gravel washed by the sea. I saw the men pointing fearfully toward the roiling water on the north. Shouts and orders from the officers drifted across the distance. The last wagons and a few final sheep hurried to finish the crossing. A war cry focused all eyes on the chariot that led the way into the road. Emboldened by the example, the rest of the troops charged forward.

Women screamed and raced with their children away from the crossing. Grimly the men took up staves and hoes or axes to defend their families. Still Moses stood silent and unmoving.

"Has not *I AM*, the God of Abraham, Isaac, and Jacob, said you will see Egypt no longer?" The words were clear.

All eyes swiveled to the man. He stretched out the staff in his hand.

My brother's voice broke with emotion. "Behold, the Living God completes our redemption. "

In the sudden silence of no wind, all that could be heard were the chariot wheels, the shouts of the drivers and the thudding feet of approaching men and horses. Then there was a loud whoosh. It sounded as though a thousand water baskets were emptied at once. The sea returned. I had to turn away from the terrified thrashing of men and horses in the swirling maelstrom. The screamed pleas to the gods haunted my dreams for months. When the water stopped foaming and rested between the banks, a few floating shields and pieces of chariots were all that could be seen. Some of the horses managed to struggle out of the water dragging only reins. Chariots and charioteers, troops and horses had been pounded to pieces when the surf reclaimed the land. We watched a few soldiers crawl from the water to lie retching on the shore.

"You! Catch the horses," Joshua ordered a couple of the men standing openmouthed nearby.

Signaling to Aaron and Caleb, he moved to attend the Egyptians. Gently the trio brought the dazed and frightened men to a freshly kindled fire.

"The horse and rider God has thrown into the sea," Moses proclaimed the truth.

Before he could continue, I stepped forward. A song of praise to the One God poured from me. Soon other women joined me. The men began clapping in rhythm to our chanting. It was an event like I had never experienced. The ecstasy of the spirit of the Living God filled me as I danced and sang. It was a song of triumph and freedom. For that moment I forgot the dead of Egypt and could only rejoice in the power of the hand of *I AM*. After my song ended, my brother came to me and put his hand on my shoulder.

"Miriam, the Lord has spoken through you." Pride shone from his eyes. "Truly the nations will hear of the blessings that *I AM* has provided. All will know and fear the power of God for his chosen."

The day passed in celebration. The pillar of God rested outside the camp. Children laughed and played until called to bed by smiling mothers. The men gathered in small groups to joke and slap one another on the back.

I urged my brother to eat a piece of flat bread with nourishing goat cheese and bean curd on it. After he ate, the man slipped away to the tent Joshua and Caleb prepared. He spoke briefly to the young men before disappearing behind the flap. Joshua stood watch over the tent where my brother slept.

Caleb came to sit with me. "Moses says we will head into the wilderness tomorrow." He pointed south away from the sea. "We will head away from the trade route toward a mountain."

"It is where my brother met God," I explained. "He promised to bring the children of Israel there to worship."

My mind wandered over the many details of a long desert journey. The boy seemed to read my mind.

"It will be a long trip and there won't be much water." For the first time, I heard uncertainty in the young voice.

"Then we must tell all the women to be certain that they fill their water baskets." My practical suggestion had the desired effect.

The well-loved grin flashed in the moonlight. "That is what Joshua said."

With a laugh I squeezed the hand I held. "He told you to tell the women, didn't he?" The young man ducked his head and I laughed again. "We'll tell them together. Everyone will listen to a woman and a man together better than to one alone."

Proud to be called a man, Caleb stood up. Together we visited each campfire and gave the people Joshua's order. There was some grumbling about not following the trade route.

"God stands ready to lead us," I pointed out, indicating the glowing column south of the camp.

For a long time that night, I stood alone staring at the pillar and beyond to the dry route we would take into the unknown.

"God of my mother Jochebed," I whispered into the night, "she believed when there was no hope. Lead us, for you are the One who fulfills all that my mother expected."

There was no response except a brush of the sea breeze at my back. I shivered a little at the chill. My dreams of being the one to rescue my family floated briefly in my mind. It was my brother who God chose. For a moment I felt envy.

"Why can't I be part of the deliverance?" The words were barely whispered into night.

Perhaps it was only my imagination but the glowing cloud seemed to brighten and I felt warmth surround me. Tears rolled down my cheeks unheeded. Into my heart came a peace. I understood my part in the journey.

"Moses will need my support now more than ever. You healed my grief when I began to recite the stories of your mighty wonders, so must this people learn of all that God has done," I whispered through my tears.

I AM would not desert the people or my brother or me. God would be with us.

Chapter 18

It was not easy to lead the people. They longed for the remembered ease of Egypt. The complaints started almost immediately.

"There is no road here."

"It is hard walking in this sand."

"Where will we find water?"

"Moses is leading us into the desert to kill us."

"How can we be sure he knows the way?"

My brother never answered angrily. I saw his eyes grow more sorrowful each evening when greater numbers of the people assembled to complain.

Patiently he repeated, "We follow the leading of the One God. This is the safe route to the mountain where *I AM* will meet us. There you will see the radiance of the God of Abraham, Isaac, and Jacob."

In response to the inquiries about water, the man stated, "Those who filled their water jars carefully will have enough to reach the oasis."

The crowd was unsatisfied with the answer but Moses turned away to his tent with Aaron and Joshua. Caleb took the food I prepared to the men in their council. It took three long days to reach the promised water at a spring we called Marah.

"At last, here is water!" one woman told me. "We can refill our jars."

Several mothers sent their children to draw a fresh supply before we even set up camp.

Young Elim came running back. "It is bad." His contorted face told the story. "The water is bitter and undrinkable."

Then everyone circled Moses in a rage. Joshua stood to the right of my brother with Aaron on the left. They looked pitiful against the frenzy of the gathered people. The injustice of their complaints made me grit my teeth in anger.

"You have brought us out of Egypt to die of thirst in the wilderness!" Dathan shouted. "We would have been better to risk the Way of the Sea. It is faster to die by the sword than by thirst."

Murmurs and nods of agreement encouraged the angry man. He stepped forward to confront God's prophet. Moses did not shrink back from the wrath emanating from his challenger.

His silence brought Dathan's scornful words. "No answer, Deliverer? We were settled and comfortable in Egypt. There we had food and water in plenty."

I could contain myself no longer. "Have you so soon forgotten that with the food and water came whips and death?"

My passion was as great as the mob's. Even Dathan took a step away from me when I hissed my questions.

"Do you seek to return to the rule of Pharaoh who kills your children? Do you desire a land where our young women are raped and the finest young men die on the scaffoldings?" I paused for a panting breath.

"Miriam." Moses' gentle reprimand brought me up short.

All eyes turned to my brother. He led the way to the pool of water. I saw the man bow his head over the staff of God.

"Prayer isn't going to help." The taunt came from somewhere within the crowd.

A clump of mud struck my brother on the shoulder. I looked around seeking the perpetrator. No one looked me in the eye. Then I saw it.

"Caleb." I motioned to the lad. "Cut down this bush." My hand pointed to a small shrub. "Take it to Moses. He must throw it into the water. It will make the spring sweet."

The boy tilted his head to one side. Dark brows drew questioningly together over skeptical eyes. I nodded confidently. With a glance at his hero, still lost in prayer, Caleb shrugged and followed my instructions.

The company was a nest of murmurs and complaints. Small groups talked together with angry gestures. No one noticed Caleb approach Moses. From the angle of his head, I knew my brother doubted the solution. Finally, his eyes sought mine. I nodded and pointed to the water. Shrugging, the man took the bush from the boy. He walked toward the water. Conversation stopped when one by one people noticed the action. Almost casually, the plant was tossed into the spring.

"You may fill your water jars," Moses stated, facing the mass of frowning faces. "God has provided a way to turn this brackish water into drinkable, clean water. Behold the action of *Jehovah-roha*, the God who heals."

Still no one moved. My brother stepped toward the pool. Bending he picked up a gourd lying on the ground where some child had thrown it in disgust after tasting the water. Crouching, he scooped up a full cup of the liquid. The sigh when the man didn't gag or spit the water out told me that I was not the only one holding my breath.

Moses held out the gourd. "Is no one thirsty?" There was a smile on his face that I had not seen since we started the journey.

A baby cried. Men shuffled their feet but no one moved forward. At last, Helagar, grandmother of Simon, moved forward. She and her grandson were chief among the troublemakers in the camp.

"Give me a drink," the order was wheezed through toothless gums. I knew if she rejected the water, Moses would be doomed.

"Gladly, my mother." The smile grew as my brother held the gourd for the old woman to drink.

"It is sweet!"

The astonishment in her tone caused Moses to burst into laughter. I grinned when everyone began to crowd forward to taste the water. My brother sought me out where I stood listening to the exclamations of amazement and delight. Brown eyes were curious even though he smiled at me.

"Miriam." Linking his arm with mine, the man drew me away from the community. "How did you know about that bush? One minute you are a raging lioness ready to take on all my detractors. The next you provide the solution to the dilemma."

"I have learned things in my years as a healer." I smiled up at my brother. "Once a trader told me of a certain tree that makes salty water good and another that makes iron float."

An incredulous look crossed the man's face.

"I too thought they were tales for children and the gullible." My smile was rueful. "Today I saw that bush and knew it was the one he described."

"You didn't know it would work?" Aaron spoke up behind me.

"Why wouldn't it?" I defended myself. "God led me to it."

Moses pointed to the now cheerful travelers preparing their meals. "*I AM* has acted. Our sister was the instrument. Come my brother." He ushered the man toward the campfires now dotting the area. "We will eat and then rest. Tomorrow we will journey on toward the mountain of God."

I watched in wonder as his face took on a look of eager anticipation. Moses looked years younger whenever he spoke of meeting God. Almost jealously I wished that I could know such closeness with the Living One.

We spent several days at Elim. The twelve springs were only a day's journey from Marah. Repairs were made to wagon wheels. Flocks were rested and several lambs were born. Some women completed new baskets or made patches with the reeds gathered at the sea. A few set up looms and wove new blankets since the desert nights were cooler than we expected. The stars seemed closer than in Egypt, too.

One night I gathered the children to tell them the story of God's promise to Abraham that was shown in those stars. I sang it just as Jochebed had sung to me and to Aaron and even to Moses. Wide-eyed, the children hung on every syllable and stared up at the night sky.

> "You are a promise kept,
> Stars hung in the sky,
> God has not ever left
> For God cannot lie."

I finished the saga with the vow. Slowly the older girls gathered their siblings and friends. Still caught in the music they wandered off to waiting beds. Then I noticed that many of the adults had gathered to listen. Quietly, hand in hand, couples moved to the tents. Moses squatted near me.

"I remember that song," he said staring unseeing at the fire and into the distant past. "Our mother sang it."

"Yes." I touched the bearded cheek. "She taught you of Abraham and Isaac, and Jacob before you went to Pharaoh's house."

"Strange I forgot for so many years," the man pondered softly and sadly.

"The Living God made himself known to you in his time and in a special way. He himself prepared you for confronting the King of Egypt. *I AM* told you his name. Even our father Jacob did not receive that blessing at the Jabok." I pointed at the glowing pillar. "God is with us daily." Then I assured him, "You never really forgot our mother's song. It simply needed to be reawakened."

The man remained silent, lost in memories. I too thought of the long years and the lifetime I had lived. Tears of remembered grief clouded my eyes.

"It has been years since I have sung the story of the children of Israel. After Joel died, I was adrift myself," I admitted to the man who was my brother. "I lost myself, first in anger and grief. Then I immersed myself in healing the wounds of the people." A sigh rose at the memory. "There were so many lash cuts and broken bodies to tend as the treasure cities rose for the King. When you returned I had almost forgotten why I believed in the One God. Then I saw all God did …" My voice trailed off thinking of my jealousy against my brother, the chosen leader. Even if I had not joined in the complaints of my neighbors, my heart had cried out at the injustice of God's choice.

"Miriam?" The man spoke my name and roused me from the reverie.

"Tonight I understood." Tears rolled down my cheeks.

Moses brushed them away with his thumb.

"What did you understand, my sister?" Gently he asked.

"The saga of Abraham did not stop under Pharaoh's lash. God never abandoned his people. We will come save to the land promised to Abraham so long ago. The people must learn to know the God of our fathers. They need to hear the stories. It is how they will find faith and become a community." My voice rang with unexpected conviction.

Like a mural, I saw the story of God's deliverance and love stretching from the past into the future.

"The road will be long," I warned. "This journey will last until the ways of Egypt are left behind and forgotten. Only then can we claim our inheritance."

Moses took my hand. I was surprised when he pressed it to his heart. Looking up at the man, I saw him smile. He took my face between his hands and pressed a kiss to my brow.

"My sister, you have spoken aloud what God revealed in my heart. The Mighty One has opened your lips to speak in his name. You are the one who knows the story of God's works in Abraham, Isaac, and Jacob. You will encourage the people by reciting the deeds of *I AM*. Give glory to our God for he will accomplish all he has promised." My brother's words were an affirmation for me.

"Blessed are you, Lord of all," I exulted in response. "You keep your people secure in your hand. Praise to the Almighty One who triumphed over the gods of Egypt and will give victory over all gods. May your Name be forever adored!"

Sleep was far from me that night. Even after Moses sought his blankets, I sat by the embers. I knew that God would preserve the children of Israel and bring them to the Promised Land.

"Abraham received your promise, Living God, Isaac was saved by the ram in the bush and Jacob saw it in the ladder to heaven. Truly, you reveal your glory to this generation," I murmured in awe looking at the pillar just beyond the tents.

A serenity long forgotten surrounded and filled me. I felt as safe as when I lay in Jochebed's arms, before my brothers were born and Pharaoh became the scourge of the Hebrews. All the songs I lost for so many years now came flooding into my memory.

"Almighty God, you have given me back the song of your glory." With reverence, I committed myself to the call I felt in my heart. "Make me a faithful instrument to sing the saga. Speak through me so that the people will remember to trust your promises."

Morning light found me dozing by the embers of the fire. Caleb was surprised to find me there.

"Miriam, my mother, are you ill?" In his concern, he knelt beside me and touched me gently on the shoulder.

"No." My smile reassured the young man. "I was praying last night and fell asleep."

He looked a little surprised but asked no further questions. Together we walked to the oasis. I drew water to go with the morning meal of barley bread and goat cheese. Moses was deep in conversation with Aaron and barely nodded at me when he accepted a piece of bread spread with the cheese.

Chapter 19

Daylight brought resumption of travel. Packs were shouldered and wagons loaded. We set out toward Sinai. When the grain began to run low, the people began to complain.

"God will provide," I stated again and again when neighbors tried to engage me in censure of my brother. Sometimes it was hard not to agree. With an effort, I set aside my own jealousy to support the man chosen by God as Deliverer. After a while, I was no longer approached with complaints. A delegation came to Moses. Rude words were shouted.

"Where are we to find food for our families?"

"Where is the rich land you promised?"

"At least we had food in Egypt."

My brother appeared unaffected by the complaints.

Calmly he replied, "*I AM* will give you food."

When the man turned away there were a few grumbles of frustration. He climbed a nearby hill to pray.

"Let's wait and see what this God of his will do." I heard Korah tell the crowd.

It was much later when Moses returned to camp. His face had the glow I associated with my brother's relationship to God.

"Do not be afraid." The man stood before the community.

His words rang out over the bustle of animals, children, and chatter. Curious faces turned to look. Joshua and Aaron hurried to stand near the leader.

"God has heard your pleas for food." Moses stared directly at Korah. "You will have bread."

A buzz of interest rolled across the crowd as each person asked how this could be. Eyes again focused on my brother when he continued.

"In the morning you will find bread from heaven on the ground."

Gasps greeted this announcement. Women looked at each other with astonishment and hope.

"Gather only as much as you will need for one day." The warning was brief. "Do not save any for the future. Each day God will send the food you need."

"How do we know this will happen?" Dathan from Succoth stepped forward.

Moses sadly looked at his antagonist. Slowly he nodded his head.

"Tomorrow you will see and know that God cares for the children of Israel."

In a whirl of robes, he strode through the people to his tent. Caleb trotted behind followed by Aaron and Joshua. Their faces also were curious although they restrained their questions.

I gathered the women. "Have your baskets ready for the morning. We do not want to waste this gift from God."

Like the men, some doubted.

"What will this bread be like?"

"How can we be sure it is good for the children?"

"Why can't we store some for the next day?"

"How will we survive if the God of Moses forgets?"

The last question was the one I addressed. "Sisters, the Living God is not like the gods of Egypt. They are shadows manipulated by men. The God who leads us," I pointed to the pillar, "is the Living God, the same God who spoke to Abraham and gave Sarah a child in her old age."

"That was long ago. Such things do not happen now."

I heard the skeptical whispers and tried a different approach. "Can you forget your children?"

The answers were emphatic.

"Of course not!"

"How can you suggest such a thing?"

"Neither will the One God forget us." When there were still dubious faces and frowns, I explained," *I AM* will care for us as you mothers care for your children. The One who promised descendants to our ancestors will not abandon us." Looking around at the faces, some old and wrinkled, others smooth and young, I saw some nods of understanding. "God has preserved us in Egypt and through the sea," I pointed out. "There will be bread for as long as we need it." The assurance in my voice seemed to convince the women.

With the admonishment, "Go and prepare for the morning," I turned away to prepare my own baskets for the bread from heaven. Elisheva worked beside me.

"How can you be so sure?" the woman bent close to me to ask. "Just because Moses speaks, you believe."

Setting down the basket, I took her hand. No longer the soft child's hand that had held bandages on an Egyptian road so many years before, this hand was rough from the work of raising a family and washing and baking. The woman beside me was seeking to understand something beyond her comprehension.

"Elisheva, my sister" I began, "I believe Moses because he speaks for the Living God." The grimace on her lips told me that was not enough of an answer. "The True God of Abraham, Isaac, and Jacob is the One who leads us now. It is not Moses. My brother is only the messenger of God."

She shook her head. "It is not enough," the woman stated. "I do not understand how a murderer can be God's Deliverer."

"You have seen all the signs." I felt frustration at my friend's stubbornness. "Remember how the water turned to blood and insects came. You saw the darkness and the night of God's passing over the homes in Goshen. Can you forget the dividing of the sea?"

"Some of the women from Succoth have explained how these things happen. Even without Moses, there have been hordes of locusts. It was a wind that dried up the water and an eclipse darkened the sun."

I felt my jaw tighten against angry words. Instead I spoke gently, trying to patiently explain what I believed.

"My sister, wife of my brother, does not the God who created all things also control them? God uses the things of this world to work his wonders. *I AM* does not force our faith, it is something we learn in response to his care and love."

Still the woman shook her head. Her lips trembled. I thought she was going to march away. Instead, she faced me. Suddenly the real reason for Elisheva's discontent tumbled out.

"All the God of Abraham, Isaac, and Jacob has done is steal my husband. Namanah says that Aaron doesn't love me any more. Since Moses arrived, he doesn't even come to me. Why couldn't God have chosen someone else?"

The question was wailed as the sobs began. With tears in my eyes, I drew my sister-in-law into my arms. Rocking the woman as though she was again a little girl, we wept together. Months of loneliness and rage flooded from my friend as I held her. There was no answer I could give.

"All I know," my response was tender, "is that the God of our fathers brings good out of what may seem bad. If it had not been for Moses' intervention, I would never have had the joy of Joel's love." The memory of the long ago morning made her nod hesitantly against my shoulder. "Moses fled into the desert and there learned from God that he must return to lead the children of Israel from bondage. Aaron was called to be his brother's aide."

"It isn't fair," Elisheva muttered rebelliously.

"This time of separation will bring greater joy in the end," I assured the woman in my arms.

I felt the shaking of her head against my breasts. "How?"

"I do not know how," the admission was humble. "What I do know is that after darkness comes light and after sorrow, joy. I thought I would never smile again after Joel died." Even now I heard a catch in my voice at the memory. "Now God has given me peace in my heart and the will to sing of the mighty works of the Living One."

She had to be satisfied with that. I knew my sister-in-law considered the answer almost contemptible. Later, after the women were asleep, I sought out my brother. I stopped him as he walked toward Moses.

"Aaron." His frown might have deterred me but my tunic was still damp from his wife's tears. "My brother, you wrong Elisheva by ignoring her."

The statement made him scowl. "What do you mean?" It was almost a snarl.

"Your wife misses your company." My reply was a bald statement. "Other men in the community spend time with their wives and children."

"I am Moses' assistant." My brother's brows drew together in anger while his chin lifted in pride.

"God does not want you to abandon your family," I insisted. The tears in my voice almost choked me. "How can you turn your back on Elisheva and your sons?"

"Moses needs…" the man started to protest.

I cut him off abruptly with a raised hand. "Our brother's wife left him so he could carry out God's will." Frustration at the blind obstinacy of both men made my words harsh. "Do you want to lose your children and wife, also?"

Abashed by my rage, Aaron took a step back. I caught his sleeve.

"She still loves you." A gentler tone was in my voice as I pleaded for my friend's happiness. "Do not let that die."

The man was torn. I saw him look toward the tent where the leaders met each night then toward the smaller structure that housed his wife and sons.

"My brother." We both jumped in surprise when Moses stepped out of the shadows. "I have heard what Miriam has said. She is right. Go to your wife. I wrong you and all my faithful counselors by keeping you from your families."

When Aaron still hesitated, the younger man gave him a gentle shove. I saw my brother take a deep breath and start across the camp. His footsteps grew more rapid as he approached his wife. Elisheva saw her husband approaching. My brother held out his arms and the woman threw herself into them. Tears filled my eyes and I turned away. Moses was looking down at me.

"My sister, I forgot that others in this company have wives and children." His confession came with a sigh. "Zipporah left and took a part of my heart with her. Selfishly I have tried to fill that hole with meetings to discuss our travel and other concerns."

"You will see her again when we come to the mountain of God," I insisted.

His hands balled into fists at his sides. He shook his head and sighed, "Will she have me? My quest for God and his call to me caused me to neglect the woman I truly love. I may have lost her love."

I took one of the clenched fists in my hands. "Zipporah loves you. She left so you would be free to obey the Living God."

"I pray you are right." For a moment my brother looked forlorn in the light from the moon and glowing pillar.

I sent up a brief prayer myself that my sister-in-law would welcome her husband back. To divert him, I asked, "What will the bread from God be like?"

A small smile tugged the corner of the Deliverer's mouth.

"I don't know any more than you, Miriam. We will have to wait until the morning." Then he surprised me with a quick hug. "My sister, God has again spoken truth through you. I will go and tell my friends to go to their families."

I watched my brother stride across the camp. A brief discussion ensued before the men scattered to their wives. A wave of loneliness washed over me. For the first time in many months, I missed Joel terribly. Entering my tent, I spent most of the night sorting and folding bandages and herbs even though they really didn't need the attention. My skills as healer were used for blisters from walking in sand instead of whip cuts. More often I tended sunburn or an animal bite rather than broken bones. Eventually I dozed but only fitfully. I didn't want to miss the bread from heaven, but it came while I was asleep.

I rose as the sun was just barely lighting the eastern sky. Curiously, I peered from the tent. The ground was covered by what looked like hail. Tentatively I reached out and picked up a handful. It was not cold and didn't melt. Selecting one of the round, white objects I tasted it. The sweetness surprised me.

"Sister, is it good?" The smile in Moses' voice told me he was teasing.

I stood up and offered him a bite. He smiled and held out his own handful. Then I laughed.

"God is bountiful!" I exclaimed spinning around to see the entire camp covered with the food. My sorrow was gone with this morning miracle. "Wake up!" I called out to the still sleeping camp.

"See what the Living God has provided! Give praise to the God of Abraham, Isaac, and Jacob who supplies bread in the desert."

Drowsily men and women emerged from tents to stare in amazed silence at the substance on the ground.

"It is the bread from heaven," I assured everyone holding up my handful. "Taste and see, it is good."

Hesitantly a few women bent down and picked up some of the stuff.

"What is it?" Little Ruth, daughter of Malchi and Hanna, asked.

Moses chuckled. "*Manna* is what we will name this bread because we do not know what it is."

Then everyone was smiling and talking. Baskets appeared, to be filled for each family. We quickly learned why Moses ordered us to only gather one day's supply at a time. Those who thought to save themselves work by collecting extra found the stored manna consumed by worms on the second morning. Their screams of disgust and horror roused even the soundest sleepers. After that, we were all careful not to store any leftovers. Laggards learned that the bread dissolved in the morning sun. Late risers on the second and third day had to borrow from friends because the supply had disappeared.

In the weeks and months that followed, we learned many ways of preparing the manna. It was mixed in goat's milk. We ground it like flour and made bread. Manna was mixed with dried fruits and nuts to go on flatbread. It was almost a contest to see which woman could discover some new and exciting way of fixing the endless supply of manna.

We traveled onward into the unknown land of sand and cliffs. I continued to gather the families each evening to sing the songs of our ancestors. As I retold the stories of Abraham, Isaac, and Jacob, I felt God's presence near me. Caleb loved to sit close to me and hung on every syllable. He seemed to be trying to memorize the words himself.

"God is amazing," he told me often. I had to agree.

Chapter 20

We became seasoned nomads. The men were adept at erecting a tent city when we found good grazing. Efficient hands packed the equipment when we moved on. Whenever we stopped, Moses listened to complaints within the community. There were important issues. One man claimed another had stolen a gold goblet. Another insisted that his daughter had been lewdly accosted. Most were small problems, involving a missing blanket or a strayed sheep.

"You should let the tribal elders deal with such petty things," I suggested.

My brother shook his head; "I speak to the people for God. It is right that I hear all the disputes."

I had to grit my teeth against an angry reply. It was foolish for one man to take on all the responsibilities. Aaron would have been happy to help him and so would I.

When we heard word that the Amalekites were to the south we turned northeast at Dophkah. Travel became more difficult as we headed into the uplands toward the mountain of God. We followed rocky valleys and scrambled up and then down low hills covered with small trees. After a few days, we came to Rephidim. This was a well-known watering place, but when we reached it there was not a drop to be found. Immediately the familiar complaints started.

"Give us water."

"Did you bring us into the desert to kill us with thirst?"

"The children will perish."

"Living God," I prayed, "show my brother what to do. The people you have given him are angry."

Moses looked very tired as he stood before the crowd. He bowed his head over the staff. When the man looked up, he scowled at the crowd and strode toward a rocky outcropping. His face was flushed with rage and the hand that gripped the staff was white-knuckled.

"Behold, I will give you water." As he spoke, his staff struck the rock and water gushed out. "This place will be called *Massah* because you sought proof from the Lord." Moses' voice was filled with bitter rage. Slamming the staff into the ground so that more water burst out, he announced, "Behold *Meribah*, the water of contention."

A gasp of awe and joy greeted the bubbling up of water. When the leader turned and marched away leaving the flowing springs, everyone hastily gathered water jars and baskets to collect the precious liquid. I almost followed my brother but he stormed away from the camp past the herds and was lost to sight in the nearby hills.

Soon after we left the springs, we heard that the Amalekites were again threatening.

"We cannot continue to try to evade this enemy," Joshua spoke to Moses when scouts brought news of the approaching menace.

I continued to set out the platters of food and arrange the pillows. Deliberately I moved slowly to hear the news.

"They can move more swiftly than we can." Concern was in the young man's voice. "This location is defensible," the young aide continued. "We are on higher ground. The women and children can be sheltered in the caves."

The leader looked up for the first time. My brother frowned. "The people have no skill in fighting."

This obvious problem caused Joshua to grimace. Still he persisted. "If we continue on we will still have to fight the Amalekites and it will be on their terms. Let them come to us here where we have some advantage."

"Won't God protect us?" I could keep silent no longer.

Both of my brothers and Joshua stared at me. They had forgotten my presence in the tent. Moses tilted his head and cocked one eyebrow in my direction.

"Woman, you know nothing of such things," Aaron spoke roughly.

Joshua seized the idea. "Of course, your sister speaks the truth." The excitement in his voice reminded me of a child with a new toy. "God will fight with us!"

I never got a chance to explain what I really meant, because the young man rushed on eagerly. "Remember what your God did to the armies of Egypt. Why should we be afraid of a handful of desert warriors?"

"My brother," Aaron picked up the enthusiasm, "what Joshua says is true. You have often said that the God of Abraham, Isaac, and Jacob will not forsake us. God must fight for us."

Slowly the leader began to nod in agreement. "Truly we should not doubt that God will be with us."

I slipped from the tent when the men began to discuss strategy. Later all the tribal elders were called to a meeting at the fire in the center of the camp. Joshua explained the advantages to our position.

"God is with us," he proclaimed. "Therefore we cannot fail."

Morning light found the men arrayed along the battlefront. Joshua moved up and down the line of husbands and sons and fathers.

"We are fighting for our wives and children. When we defeat the Amalekites the way will be open to the mountain of God. Then we will proceed to the land promised to the descendants of Abraham, Isaac, and Jacob. Do not waste your strength in futile thrusts with the sword and random arrow shots. We will wait until the raiders are upon us and then strike."

A cheer greeted the words. It was accompanied by brave waving of the few swords and spears we possessed. Most of the men were armed with short daggers and slingshots. A few even carried hoes and mattocks as weapons.

"What will happen?" A frightened whisper from Elisheva caused me to turn my head.

Many of the women were grouped with me watching their men prepare for battle. Fear was etched on every face.

"Look, there is Moses."

I pointed to the nearby hilltop where Moses stood with Aaron and Hur, leader of the tribe of Judah. Hur was too old to bear a sword but he chose to support my brothers and stand with them rather than remain in camp with the other old men, invalids, and women.

"He will intercede with God for us," I spoke to the women with encouragement in my voice. "See, he holds the staff God gave him."

All eyes focused on the man. He stood tall in the morning light. The staff of God was in his hand. Even as I spoke, I heard a war cry from below us. We all rushed to peer down the mountain.

Half-naked warriors confronted the sons of Israel. I felt a shiver of fear looking at the armed and vicious looking men.

"Do the dogs and refuse of Egypt seek passage across Kadesh?" The challenge rang out from a broad-shouldered man on a horse.

No one responded. There was some nervous shifting in our ranks but the men remained in their lines.

"Come on then," the Amalekite leader laughed and gestured obscenely. "We will give you a welcome you won't soon forget."

Then Joshua spoke. "We come in the name of the Living God. Grant us passage to the mountain of God and beyond. Then your lives will be spared."

The derisive laughter from the ranks of Amalek angered me. I felt Elisheva slip her hand into mine. She was trembling. There was weeping behind me. I turned to comfort the women.

"It will be all right," I asserted looking at my brother on the hillside.

"Did you see them?" Hysteria edged the words.

"My Jacob will be slaughtered and then..." fresh sobbing broke out.

"Trust God," I commanded.

Below me I heard a war cry and then the clashing of metal against metal.

"Trust God?" someone repeated my words in a derisive tone. "While we watch our men die?"

"*I AM* will not abandon us to the hand of these warriors." My voice rang out authoritatively. Hopeful eyes turned to me.

"What can we do?" Elisheva asked tearfully. I knew she feared for her sons standing with the young warriors.

"We will pray," the answer came readily to my lips. "The God who promised descendants to Abraham and Sarah will defend the children of Israel against the Amalekites."

Glad to do something, the women gathered around.

"God of Abraham, Isaac, and Jacob," I began, "you have brought the chosen people from the Black Land to this desert. Your pillar of fire has led us. Manna has been our food. Defend us, we pray, Living God, let your glory and might overpower those who block our path to your holy mountain."

Soon other women joined my voice until we were all lifting up petitions to the One God. All day long we prayed for protection. I didn't look toward the battlefield. My eyes were fixed on Moses and beyond him the distant heights where the mountain of God was.

My brother did not waver. He stood tall on the heights. The staff of God was outstretched toward the fighting. When his arm drooped, Aaron and Hur held the arm steady. Late in the afternoon, a rock was brought for him to sit on. Still the rod never wavered. As the light faded, the sounds of battle died down. Cheers told me that the children of Israel had won a victory. Only then did I look down the mountain. Joyful women ran past me to greet husbands and fathers and sons. On the plain before the mountain, the Amalekite army lay slaughtered.

We were not without casualties, but they were surprisingly light. Still, I was kept busy with herbs and bandages throughout the night. In the morning, we buried our dead. The sobs of the women, now bereft of their men, were hard for my brother. He visited each one in turn to offer comfort and assistance. I heard the men bragging of their prowess.

"Moses has led us to a great triumph."

"Our skills destroyed the Amalekites."

"Who can stand before us?"

"It was God who won the victory," I reminded Caleb when he repeated the boast.

"Was God on the battlefield?" the boy asked with his brows raised in confusion at my sharp tone.

"How else would you have defeated warriors trained in the art of war?" When he still frowned, I added, "Slingshots and daggers have never before overthrown swords and spears." The young man considered for a long moment before slowly, and not too happily, nodding. I risked a quick hug, saying, "Truly all you men fought valiantly. The Living God brought success from your courage."

I was rewarded with a broad smile before he hurried off to fall in step with Joshua and Moses.

Chapter 21

After a few days of mourning our dead and allowing the injured to recover, camp was struck and we set out again. The mountainous terrain was hard to walk in, although the air was cooler now that we were higher. Our flocks found more plentiful grazing in the valleys. Moses led the people slowly southward.

I rejoiced one day to see Zipporah ride into our midst. An old man rode a second camel. My nephews shared a third beast. Gershom held his little brother securely.

"Father Jethro." Moses came forward with a *salaam* of welcome.

When the animals knelt, he helped first the old man then his wife from their saddles. He held Zipporah for a long moment until clamoring sons claimed his attention. He swung first Gershom and then Eleazar up in joyful greeting.

"My sons! You have grown tall! Let me look at you!" The father grinned joyfully as he tousled dark curls on one boy and smoothed down the straight black hair of the elder.

"Even in Midian, I have heard what the One God has done for the children of Israel. I have come to see for myself," Jethro commented when my brother turned from his family.

"You are welcome, sheik of Midian, father of my wife." Formally, Moses bowed again with his hand over his heart. Then the two men embraced. "Come, we will feast together. I will withhold nothing from you."

Graciously the man bowed his father-in-law into the nearby tent. I hurried to greet Zipporah.

"It is so good to see you." I hugged the woman. "Welcome, my sister, Moses has been missing his family. I've seen him watching the other fathers and sons. He will be content now that you are here."

"I have missed my husband." A sigh of longing reinforced her words. The dark eyes strayed to the closed tent where the men sat together. "It took much pleading to convince my father to travel here to meet you."

Linking my arm through hers, I led the woman to my tent. Together we prepared a meal. I was glad that Jethro met us at an oasis. We had more than manna to offer our guest. Roasted kid and doves, bread made from manna with cheese, a salad of herbs and greens gathered from around the water and honeyed dates made a passable meal, I decided while surveying the bounty. Zipporah and I took the trays to the men before sitting down to visit.

Gershom had already renewed friendships with the children he met in Goshen months earlier. Zipporah smiled to see them playing a game of toss with a hide ball.

"The boys have been lonely," she remarked. "After living with you it was hard to return to the desert. My father's camp has no other young children. My sisters have all gone to live with their husbands."

"I am glad you have come," I repeated placing my hand over hers.

"Father was concerned that Moses hadn't sent for me," the woman confessed with a sideways glance. "I think he didn't want to come, for fear ..." her voice trailed off.

I was glad to reassure the unspoken concern. "My brother has wanted you near, but the strain of being in charge of such a contentious group has left no time for his own desires." After a moment, I added, "It will be good for Moses to have you with him. He takes his duties almost too seriously."

Zipporah relaxed and smiled, "Then I am glad we came. It is not good for a man to bear such a burden alone."

It seemed that Jethro had the same thought. He advised Moses to divide the leadership among the elders of the tribes. Before we left the oasis, my brother called everyone together. He appointed lieutenants over each tribal unit.

"These men will judge minor concerns," he announced. "If something is too difficult, the problem can be brought to me. In this way you will all get justice more swiftly."

A cheer of approval greeted the arrangement. I was not surprised at how well the procedure worked. It was what I had suggested weeks earlier. My brother had more time for his family and the people seemed more content.

Daily we traveled south through the hills and valleys. I wondered if we would ever reach the mountain of God. At night the people gathered around the fires. I sang the songs I learned at my mother's knee. The promises of God to Abraham, Isaac, and Jacob came to life.

"Someday my children's children will sing the songs of Israel because you have taught them so well," Zipporah commented one morning as we walked together.

She carried her spinning whorl and spun yarn as we walked. It was a skill I had never been able to master. I learned to spin while sitting in a quiet room. The whorl insisted on dropping too far and dragging in the dirt or the yarn would tangle rather than fall smoothly as I walked. My sister-in-law had always spun while following the flocks. It was easy for her to form a smooth strand of yarn even as we walked up and down the hills.

"I hope they will remember all that God has done for this generation, too." With a sigh I glanced at the community around us. "They seem oblivious to the mighty acts of God even now."

"Write the story for them," suggested my sister-in-law.

I stared at the woman. "Wha … wha … what do you mean?"

Astonishment at her suggestion made me stammer. Deep inside I hid a dream that I could do just that, but I knew that I was just a woman and didn't dare suggest such a thing. To have Zipporah speak in such a matter of fact way took my breath away.

A smile was my answer. "You have the words and the skill."

Openmouthed, I could only stare at the woman from Midian.

"Remember, you told me that the princess gave you lessons when you visited the palace."

It was true, although even my parents never knew the extent of my training. For a moment, I almost felt the quill in my hand.

"I … no … that … no … how … no … who … no." My mind played with the idea even as I rejected it. Emphatically I shook my head.

Zipporah put her hand on my shoulder. "Sister of my husband, we will see what God has planned."

I felt a rush of excitement and longing when she spoke. There was no time for further conversation. Moses joined us. For a change, he was alone. My brother had news.

"Miriam, look, you can see the Mountain of God! In less than a week we will be at the base of Sinai." Moses pointed out the cloud-covered height not far away. In the evening light, the summit seemed to glow.

"You should tell the people," I urged, thinking that the news would improve the once again lagging morale.

Moses nodded. Joshua assembled the children of Israel in the evening. They stood in ranks behind their tribal leaders. Beside Moses stood Aaron, with Joshua on the left. Caleb joined me. His eager look was matched by my nephew's excitement. Gershom recognized that the mountain in the distance was our destination.

"God is indeed gracious. Has not the God of our fathers been with us on this pilgrimage?"

A cry of assent answered the Prophet's question.

"Now, my friends, we are nearing the very mountain of God. There we will offer sacrifices of thanks."

Another cheer made the man smile. Then he looked serious.

"Leave behind now any idols that you still cling to. We must approach the dwelling of the Living God with pure hearts and minds. Before the moon is full, we will encamp at the foot of Sinai."

The announcement set the camp buzzing with speculation.

"Do you think he knows of the teraphim in my pouch?"

"What right does Moses have to tell us to leave behind the gods that keep us safe?"

"He's just a man. How will he know whether we have abandoned the gods or not?"

"How can they still doubt?" Scowling at my neighbors, I spoke to Zipporah. "They are still depending on pieces of wood and stone. Night after night, I sing of the love of the One True God. Still they do not believe."

Rage and frustration poured out in a low complaint. I was embarrassed to hear myself. Tears sprang into my eyes at the childishness of my complaint.

"That is why they need to have them written." Persuasively my sister-in-law brought up the subject of our earlier conversation. "It is hard to give up the familiar until they are taught the greatness of the Living God. Each generation will need to be reminded of the works of *I AM*. Who will carry on the words when you are gone?"

"Surely the miracles and the manna and even the pillar of God's presence should be reminder enough that *I AM* is with us," I pondered half to myself.

"There are those who see the signs and believe," Zipporah assured me. "I have seen the faith, especially of the younger members of the community. Still," she gave a half smile, "a god that can be touched is easier to accept than an invisible one."

Slowly I nodded.

"Miriam, my sister, God speaks to those who are willing to listen. He gave you the song of the history for the children of Israel."

At her reminder, I smiled and took my friend's hand. "Yes, and renewed my belief in *I AM*. If God can reawaken my faith, nothing is impossible."

We talked of many things on the last day of our journey to Sinai. Zipporah pointed out familiar landmarks and told the story of meeting my brother at a well we passed.

"Amalekite herdsmen were trying to intimidate me and my sisters. A sheik, even a priest like my father, who has only daughters, is not considered strong. Jethro has seven daughters but no son. My first memory is of herding the sheep. As each of my sisters grew old enough, they joined me." She smiled proudly. "Our flocks grew. My father became wealthy from the wool and hides of our healthy animals." With a chuckle she added, "There was some jealousy from the neighboring tribes. It seemed inconceivable that girls could raise such a flock."

I agreed. "Men doubt that women can achieve great things. Even the King of Egypt didn't find it necessary to kill the girl children, only the male babies of Goshen. We bring life into the world, but that is our only use in a man's eyes."

With a toss of her head, the woman shook her head. "Yet we are stronger than men know." I saw a twinkle in the dark eyes. "What man could bear children?"

We laughed together. Then Zipporah continued her tale.

"We girls tried to stand our ground but the bandits and their herds were forceful and numerous. Suddenly a man stood up from that pile of rocks." She pointed at a tumbled cairn near the well that our own herdsmen were drawing water from. "None of us had ever seen him. When he spoke it was with authority."

Unconsciously we both looked at my brother. He stood talking to Aaron while animals and people milled around him. Love softened my companion's eyes for a moment.

"What did he say?" I asked curious to hear what happened. My sister-in-law gazed past the well, remembering events of decades earlier.

"He said, 'Whose well is this?'" The woman repeated the words in imitation of my brother's tone. "I was astonished that a man, obviously an Egyptian from his clothes and accent, would care about seven girls standing against the rough Amalekites. Still I answered, 'This is Jethro's well. He is priest of Midian and our father.' I was even more astonished by what happened next. The stranger ordered the shepherds to leave. I was afraid they would strike him down. It was one man against a dozen." The woman's smile broadened at the memory. She looked again at her husband, now talking to Caleb.

"Moses stood calm, even arrogant. Amalekite bravado melted before his stare and they slunk off grumbling."

"My brother was raised a prince," I commented, grinning at the picture in my mind. "No one had ever questioned one of his commands. It probably never crossed his mind that he wouldn't be obeyed."

"True," with a giggle the man's wife added, "sometimes he falls back into that habit. Humility has not come easily to my husband. It was months before he was comfortable with all the aspects of tending the sheep and living in a tent."

"It must have been hard," I mused. "Leaving my simple home in Goshen for this nomadic way of life was difficult. My brother was used to tiled halls, golden bowls, and servants to anticipate every need."

"I think the daily bathing and shaving was what he missed the most," Zipporah responded. "Let us draw water for our evening preparations."

Suiting action to words, we lifted water jars and carried them to the well. Other women joined in the talk with questions and comments. Together we began to prepare the evening meal. It was manna again. There had been complaints that we had no onions to flavor the bland diet. I occasionally wished for a change, until I remembered that the manna was food provided by God. It was a daily reminder of the loving care of the One whose name is *I AM*.

I reviewed my sister-in-law's words even as my hands worked to prepare the food. Never before had I considered how difficult the transition must have been for Moses. He was forced to leave the comforts of the Egyptian court for a shepherd's life. Perhaps it explained his patience with the incessant whining of the people. While I grew impatient and angry with my neighbors, my brother understood their feelings of confusion in this new life.

Zipporah and I resumed our conversation that evening.

"My father has returned year after year to this camp near Sinai." She pointed to the hill visible in the fading light. It looked very tall and rugged. "Even before Moses saw the burning bush and heard the voice of the Living God, the mountain was known to be holy."

In silence, I studied the barren heights above the bushes that dotted the lower areas. Could it be that God really did live there? I recalled the times I felt the peace and assurance that could only come from beyond me.

Turning to Zipporah I stated, "God does not *just* dwell on that mountain. *I AM* is life itself in all creation."

"True," my companion agreed, "but here is a place where God comes very near to man. You sing of Bethel where Jacob dreamed of his father's God. It is a holy place, too. There are many other such places."

"God has made his home with us on this journey," I whispered gesturing toward the glowing pillar.

"Yes," the breathed word was a prayer itself; "the children of Israel have been sanctified by God's presence. There has never been another such nation so chosen. The responsibility is great." After a moment of silence the woman added, "It took Moses a long time to realize that he was chosen, even blessed, by God."

"Tell me," I begged.

"My father made the Egyptian stranger welcome in his tents. He didn't tell us much about himself. I learned bits and pieces of the story as we tended the sheep together. When Moses asked my father for me as his bride, it was a sign to us all that he was letting go of the past. I rejoiced because the loneliness began to vanish from his eyes."

Zipporah paused to locate her husband in the midst of the camp. Gershom and Caleb were close behind. I smiled at the camaraderie the boys had developed.

"Still he was troubled by his memories of the man he killed. The beaten man he intervened to save and the rage directed at him from his own people haunted him. Moses believed himself to be a man without a country or kin."

My sister-in-law's eyes showed gentle compassion as she looked at the man who had been her husband for so many years. My own thoughts turned to bloodstained sand on a road by the Nile. Joel's unconscious body and Moses' intervention were forever etched in my soul.

"My poor brother. He never knew that in saving Joel, he gave me the joy of a husband."

A comforting hand rested on my arm. "It was a path he had to follow. Moses was drawn to find the Living One. The gods of Egypt he knew to be manipulated by the priests. The God of his fathers seemed deaf and unknown. 'Why does the God of Abraham, Isaac, and Jacob leave the children of Israel in bondage?' The question was asked of my father, of me, of the black night sky during long sleepless nights. Even though the man thought himself alone, God was with him."

"It seems that the further we think we are from God, the closer he is," I mused, thinking of my own desperate prayers and cries for explanation that were answered, it had seemed, by silence.

The woman nodded. "It was that way for Moses. There was no response from God. Our son was a great blessing to him. 'He is a sign that God is pleased with you,' I told my husband when Gershom was born." A smile softened my friend's face, "He said, 'It

is true, for I have been a visitor in this land. Now I have a home.'
For a while he was content and quit seeking answers. In teaching the
boy to tend the sheep, I thought he forgot about Egypt."

She sighed for the simple years before the Living God spoke to
my brother. I thought about the love I saw between Moses and both
his sons.

"He is a good father." The statement was answered by a
softening of Zipporah's eyes.

"Yes, then God appeared and it all changed." I could hear the
envy in her voice. "My husband became God's voice and hands. I
almost thought him mad until I saw the signs he did and the miracles
of God."

In silent understanding, I laid my hand over hers. Her next
words were hesitantly spoken. The confession came as a surprise.

"Even before he went up on the mountain, I tried to seduce
Moses away from his insane desire to confront God. Eleazar is the
result of that night. The baby was born just before we left for
Egypt. Moses said, 'God save me from the sword of Pharaoh' when
he named the boy. I was so angry that I barely spoke to the man for
a fortnight. I was still seething when we left my father's tents." She
seemed to be trying to decide whether or not to continue. "We made
camp one night." She paused again. The words were so soft I had
to lean toward my sister-in-law to hear. "Moses was attacked in the
night."

I heard my own gasp, "Who?"

"Maybe it was God. Perhaps bandits. I don't know. Moses was
ill from the beating. In terror I circumcised my son hoping to
propitiate God." Zipporah had tears streaming down her face. "I
was angry at my husband and his God ... and so afraid."

I imagined what it must have been like to be alone far from her
father's tents tending her badly beaten husband.

"Sister, you did what had to be done."

"I suppose so," she nodded, "but my spiteful words still trouble
me. 'You are a bridegroom of blood,' I told Moses. I circumcised
my son and blamed my husband for the baby's cries."

Gathering the sobbing woman into my arms, I rocked back and
forth until the weeping ceased. "You saved his life." My words of

comfort gradually penetrated the anguish. "Perhaps the deed was done in desperation, but God worked good through your action."

"I never thought of it that way." A ragged sigh issued from tremulous lips. "Miriam, how is it that you can see God in all things?"

"Do I?" The idea had never occurred to me.

"Anyway, Moses survived and you know the rest. Aaron met us at the edge of the desert and we came to Egypt."

"Now here we are at the holy mountain." I spoke with wonder for the setting sun seemed to set the summit ablaze.

All around I heard awed whispers. "Surely God is in this place."

"We will camp and worship here for many days," Moses announced.

The meal was prepared and fires dotted the site. The glowing pillar of cloud that had been our guide seemed to merge with the radiant swirling haze that rested on the mountain.

"Prepare an offering and sanctify yourselves. Wash your garments and do not go near a woman." Moses' order seemed harsh until he explained. "On the third day we will give thanks to *I AM* for bringing us here in safety. I will go up to meet God in the heights and learn God's will for us all."

Zipporah clung to her husband after the meal was consumed.

With a kiss, he set her aside. "My love, I must obey the decree I have set out. No man may go near his wife in this time."

Tears formed in my sister-in-law's eyes. She turned away with head bowed. Then the woman rounded on her husband. The whisper was desperate.

"What comfort will I have if you die on that mountain?"

"I will not die," Moses assured his wife with a gentle kiss on her forehead. "Go with Miriam."

I too feared for my brother. "Aaron," I spoke to my sibling, "How could a man do such a thing and live?"

The man shrugged and shook his head. "Moses is set on this course. Neither Joshua nor I could dissuade him."

"I will pray for him. We must all pray for him." The statement came from my heart. Aaron looked at me. There was a hint of respect in his eyes.

"Yes, my sister," he nodded, "we will all pray."

On the third morning, the community assembled. Moses prayed for the sanctification of the nation and then left the camp. Joshua and Aaron accompanied the man part way up Sinai. Then Moses continued to climb alone. Zipporah clung to my hand. Gershom stood beside her and Eleazar was held tightly in her arms. Caleb took his place beside me. Together we watched the figure grew smaller and smaller until he was lost in the roiling clouds spiraling around the heights.

Chapter 22

Aaron returned to the encampment. "Moses will come back with God's laws," he told the people. "We must go about our daily lives until he returns."

Joshua made a small camp for himself on the hillside. At night we saw the small fire he built. Each of us tried to pretend that life was normal but the constant clouds around the summit seemed to be lit, even during the day, with some kind of fire. I fell into the habit of saying a prayer each time I looked at the hillside. Nerves were stretched to the breaking point. Day followed day and became one week and then two. Inevitably rumors and murmurs started.

"Moses isn't coming back."

"He's gone away because he doesn't know where to go."

"There is no 'Promised' land."

"We will die in this desert."

"Maybe we should go back to Egypt."

"I am sick of the manna all the time."

"This God of Moses is a lie."

It was only a short step from doubting the God of Abraham, Isaac, and Jacob, to desiring the gods they all remembered. The ceremony sanctifying the people before my brother ascended the mountain was easily forgotten.

"The gods of the Nile have true power."

Somewhere within the crowd of discontented people the whisper started. Then each man and woman had something to add.

"I have seen the image of Ptah answer questions."

"Remember how Hari always brought the Inundation?"

"There is true power in the gods of Egypt."

A delegation came to Aaron after Moses was gone for an entire moon cycle. The full moon shone in the night sky. It glittered in the eyes of the leaders. The mob was dangerously determined.

"Up goldsmith," the voice of Dathan shouted. "This brother of yours, this Moses, has tricked us."

"No, my friends, Moses has gone to learn God's will for us," the man tried to placate the growing crowd.

"Then 'his God' has killed him." The claim was greeted with cries of agreement.

"He has not returned as he promised." Rage simmered in the snarled words and in the seething mass that continued to increase in size.

"He will be back," my brother pleaded, "give him time." A clod of dirt smashed at Aaron's feet. Still he tried to reason, "Perhaps the God of our fathers has much to tell us."

"You are old, so you believe such things as a god with no name who cannot be seen but who is everywhere." Dathan's mockery drew laughter. "We want a god we can recognize."

"Yes, give us a god!" The mob took up the cry.

Aaron raised his hands in horror and looked toward the fiery mountain. I knew he was hoping Moses would appear. All that could be seen were the ever-present clouds, lower on the mountain than usual. They almost merged with the small glimmer of Joshua's campfire.

"No, such an abomination will bring punishment." The sound of my voice surprised me.

Aaron looked around in astonishment although he agreed. "Miriam is right. The Living God does not need images. The One Lord who made all things cannot be reduced to a block of stone or wood."

"Old fool," Dathan moved closer, "do not pay heed to this woman." His sneer dismissed me as nothing. "We don't want an idol representing an invisible and very likely imaginary god. What we demand is an image of a god we can recognize." The community responded with shouts.

"Give us a god like those we knew in Egypt."

"My friends," Aaron's plea was lost in the growing uproar.

"Give us a golden calf. That will appease the god Apis. We can return to Egypt under his protection." Dathan stood face to face with my brother.

I stood forgotten just inside the tent. Zipporah grabbed my hand partly in fear and partly in support.

"Yes, a golden calf." The throng took up the cry.

Again, I could not keep silent. "Would you return to Egypt where you were beaten and killed? Have you so soon forgotten the graves …"?

"Woman, be silent," Dathan's hand met my cheek.

Korah shouted, "At least in Egypt there are graves. Bodies are not buried in the shallow sand to be eaten by jackals. How can the *ka* survive if the body is lost?"

Despite my stinging cheek and Zipporah restraining hand, I stepped forward past Aaron.

"The *ka* of Abraham, Isaac, and Jacob is not lost," I stated, anger overriding any fear I might have felt at confronting such furious faces. "They live among us." I raised my voice as hisses began. "Our fathers are alive when we remember the acts of the Living God in their lives. They are more with us than the Pharaohs, buried and forgotten except for writing on a scroll. How can you dare to affront the very One who rescued us from Egypt and provided food and …"

My speech was cut off when a well-aimed stone hit my mouth. The sharp edge left my lip bleeding. Zipporah dragged me into the tent. In grief, I tore my tunic and sprinkled dust on my head. As though in mourning, I unbraided my hair and pulled the gray and brown strands over my eyes. I would not let Elisheva clean the dirt and blood from my face. She knelt beside me sobbing when I pushed her hand away. Aaron continued to plead, but I heard the wavering in his voice as the demands grew louder.

"Very well!" At last, my brother conceded. "Bring me the gold and jewelry you brought from Egypt."

Dathan's triumphant laugh echoed in my soul like a knell.

"God of Abraham, Isaac, and Jacob, Living Lord, you who speak to Moses, have mercy on this stiff-necked people." I prayed, rocking back and forth on my knees. "They have forgotten your redemption so easily. They desire the slavery of Egypt over the freedom you offer. You are the One who keeps the promises you make, even to the third and fourth generation. Remember, I beseech you, the love you bear for the children of Israel."

Tears were streaming down my face. I covered my face in desolation and moaned in agony. I sensed my brother standing near me. He looked lost and years older than at the evening meal.

"They would have killed me ... us." He offered the excuse with his hands held out. The man reminded me of a child who knows he has done wrong but still hopes to be forgiven.

"It is not me, but God you need to appease if you continue on this path." My voice was stern with warning.

Still my brother tried to placate me, "By the time the gold is gathered and melted and an idol made, Moses will have returned."

"Aaron." I stood up and took the shaking hand. He seemed very old and frail in the filtered moonlight coming through the tent flap. "Your skill as a goldsmith is well known. It is a gift that should be used to glorify the True God, not make an image of a false god."

"You are just a woman. I don't know why I attempted to explain." Jerking his hand away, the man raged at me for speaking the truth. Frowning he stated, "This plan will give the people something to do while waiting for Moses. It makes perfect sense."

"Aaron bar Amram," through tears I spoke his name. "I cannot live in your tents while you turn your back on *I AM*."

My heart broke as I piled my kneading trough and spindle onto my blanket with the only other tunic I owned. Rapidly I wrapped my meager possessions into a neat bundle and walked from the tent. Tears poured down my face. Through the veil of my hair, I could see the men and women hurrying back and forth searching for their jewelry and other precious objects. I ignored the comments and questions as I walked away from the camp. Against a low hill part way to Sinai, I sat down.

"Living God, even though the people turn from you, do not remove your favor from them," I interceded in despair.

There was great commotion in the camp all night and throughout the day. My friends and neighbors were sorting through their possessions to bring out all the gold objects taken from the Egyptians.

"God of Abraham, Isaac, and Jacob, you rescued this nation from bondage, do not hold this defection against them. You passed over the homes of those who believed your promise. Help them remember that salvation."

I rocked back and forth in my misery. The setting sun brought Caleb with Zipporah, Gershom, and Eleazar. The young men erected a small tent.

"We will keep watch with you," my sister-in-law said offering me a cup of water.

The liquid felt good pouring down my parched throat. I was glad for the company and grateful for the hide covering when the night grew cold. Caleb and Gershom took turns keeping watch by the fire.

A week passed. From our vantage point, we could see the smoke from the raging fire needed to melt the gold. The sounds of hammering and shouted orders floated on the desert breezes to our ears. I could only imagine how miserable it would be to be near the blaze. The summer sun beat down each day. Even higher up and near the mountain, we felt the heat. Daily my eyes searched every rock for signs that Moses was returning. Zipporah often stood beside me. I felt her fear when no figure appeared from the heights.

"God will not fail Moses," I assured the woman. "He will be back soon."

"What if the Living One punishes my husband for that?" Agonized eyes glanced at the activity below us.

Her words voiced my secret fear but I insisted, "The One God is just and will not punish my brother for something done by others." She seemed comforted.

One afternoon Gershom informed us, "They have finished the golden calf. The festival will begin tomorrow. Dathan has assured everyone that even if it isn't yet the new moon that Apis will honor their prayers."

Neither Zipporah nor I questioned how the boy got the information. Both boys slipped in and out of the camp at will. They brought us food and news. We could see the idol set on a pile of rocks that formed a rough altar. The creature was nothing like the smooth and shining gods in the temples along the Nile. Women

were busy arranging garlands around the feet and horns. The smell
of baking drifted to our nostrils.

"The god will eat well," Caleb mentioned ironically.

"Lord God, don't you see what your people are doing?" I
turned away to face Sinai. The lowering cloud cover seemed
menacing in the midday heat. "Send Moses before they bring your
curse on themselves." My plea came from a full heart.

The sound of tambourines, pipes, and laughter awakened us in
the predawn. From our hillside, we could see the crowd circling
around the golden shape. The rising sun reflected the brilliance onto
the excited faces.

"Ra! Great is Ra! Praise to Apis." The shouts came clearly to
where I stood beside Zipporah.

Eleazar clung to his mother. Caleb and Gershom placed
themselves slightly in front of us. When I saw Caleb's hand on his
dagger I understood that they meant to protect us if necessary. My
heart swelled with pride.

There was no threat from the camp. A lone figure began to
walk toward us. It was Aaron. His steps dragged and the gray head
was bowed. The man was almost to us when he stopped. I turned
to see what my brother was staring at with such fear. Moses was
pacing rapidly toward us. Joshua strode beside him, sword at the
ready.

"What is the sound of debauchery in the camp?"

Brother faced brother. Aaron's eyes dropped and he fell on his
face.

"You delayed to return ... the people were restless ... the gold
... fire ... a calf ... emerged ..." the words became more incoherent
as he tried to explain.

The Prophet stared at the man groveling at his feet. There was
such sadness in the tone that I found tears in my eyes when he
spoke.

"My brother, the people have sinned."

With one hand Moses drew his brother up. Aaron would have
prostrated himself again but Moses held his arm.

"Forgive me." Wretchedness was evident in his attitude and
plea. "I have failed."

"God has given us his own laws." Moses held up the two stone tablets he carried.

With a gasp, Aaron fell to his knees and covered his face. I stared with awe at the slabs of rock inscribed with odd letters. They were not written in Egyptian or the Canaanite alphabet I learned in the palace.

"What is this writing?" I breathed the question.

"The Law of God in the hand of God," was the reply.

I dared to reach out one finger to touch the edge of one of the rough tablets. Moses turned to look at the singing and dancing now raging throughout the camp in the valley.

"The people would not even wait. They have turned from the Living One." There was such despair in my brother's voice that I moved forward to comfort the man. He did not look at me. "Now they will feel the wrath of the God they scorn!"

Rapidly the sorrow turned to rage. He stormed toward the encampment, the brown robe flapping behind and dust puffing from beneath his rapidly moving feet. Moses' voice carried over the music and laughter.

"Behold the law of God!"

A few people at the edge of camp turned. When they saw the man, fear began to eddy inward through the crowd. In a very short time, everyone was staring at the man of God in his wrath. My brother held the tablets over his head as he strode through the path formed in the crowd.

"By this Law you are judged and found wanting." He stopped beside the altar and brought the stones down on the idol, smashing into the golden calf. The figure teetered and then toppled to break into rubble. The tablets split and fell from the Deliverer's hands.

"The Living God will crush you in just this way. Then will you know and believe that *I AM is* GOD!"

A cry of horror rose from many throats when they saw the destruction of their idol.

"Aaron." At his name my brother tottered forward to cringe before the leader. "Your hands formed this abomination. Your hands will destroy it."

"Yes." Total submission could be heard in that one word.

"Grind the gold so fine that the people may drink and be tested by the Lord. Those who will not drink will die." Still the righteous indignation burned hot. The man looked around at the now silent assemblage. "Who will stand for God?"

A few men, mostly cousins from the clan of Levi, stepped toward Moses. A rustle of apprehension started at the center of the crowd and moved outward when the men strapped on their swords and took their stand beside Joshua.

"By this willingness you consecrate yourselves to God," Moses stated. "Because you are not afraid to strike down those who sin, it will be counted to you as holiness."

I barely recognized my brother in his rage. For the second time in my life, I saw in him wrath unmitigated by any pity. Enraged royalty glared at the congregation and they fell back before the condemnation. Even I was afraid to approach my brother. For an eternity he studied each person through eyes that were mere slits. Some fell to the ground sobbing in fear. Others tried to stare down the man only to lower their glance. Many of the women wept openly and clutched their children. A few whispered pleas for mercy were heard. Mostly the community remained silent in fear-filled awe.

Gradually his fury was replaced by grief. Shoulders moved in a great sigh. He turned away and began to walk back toward Sinai.

"As for me," the deep tone was tired and no longer filled with wrath, "I will intercede with God so that you are not all blotted out for your lack of faith." The man seemed to have picked up a heavy burden. He stumbled like a blind man. I saw him stoop down to grasp a fist full of dust and pour it over his head. In the stunned silence, we all heard the ripping of his robe and the grief-stricken cry.

"Lord God, do not blot our your people. Let me take their sin and die in their place. God of Abraham, Isaac, and Jacob have mercy. Let your wrath fall on me alone." Still stumbling, my brother moved toward the mountain. The clouds on the summit seemed ominously black and heavy.

Elisheva broke the silence with a wail. "We will all die!"

A hubbub broke out.

"Our god is destroyed. We have no gods to protect us."

"There is nothing left to make another idol."

"We are lost."

"The God of Moses will strike us down."

Surprisingly, it was Aaron who stood up and silenced the crowd. He climbed onto the pile of stones and dirt left from the altar for the calf. Nothing remained of the golden figure except a pile of golden flecks. The man had been crushing the idol even as the people argued.

"We must all drink the gold dust from this abomination." In his statement my brother included himself in the corporate guilt. "The Living God will purge us all."

Something in the solemn tone silenced all opposition. Caleb brought forward a large jar of water. I watched as the gold dust was poured from the platter in Aaron's hand into the water.

"I will be the first." Suiting action to words, the man dipped a small gourd into the water and poured the liquid down his throat.

Then I took the gourd and drank also. Caleb, Joshua, and Zipporah followed. The contingent from the tribe of Levi stepped forward next to drink of the gold-flecked water. Slowly and fearfully, the remainder of the people came forward. Each accepted the dipper from Aaron's hand. Some stared into the vessel before sipping the liquid. Others gulped their portion without looking.

Those who tried to avoid drinking faced a sword and met a swift end. Far from the joyful crowd of the early morning, it was a subdued group that began to dig graves for their slaughtered friends. Even the sky seemed darker as the afternoon drew on although the only clouds in sight hovered steadily on Sinai.

The cramping pains started as the sun set. The gold laden water caused some in camp to moan and curl into helpless huddles of agony. My soothing herbs seemed to have no effect. Aaron was one of the first stricken. He refused my offer of help.

"No, Miriam, I must bear this purging. Surely it is fit punishment for forming the calf. I allowed myself to be persuaded to deny the Living God."

Only a few died from the gold sickness, but Zipporah and I were kept busy tending the ill. Nearly everyone had recovered by the time Moses returned from the mountain.

Caleb whispered the news to me as I wrung out yet another pile of blankets soiled by the affliction. I left the washing and followed the boy. We skirted the camp and met my brother near where my tent was still pitched. There had not been time to bring it into camp. Winds over the past weeks had left the posts tilted. The hides were torn and flapping. It was not the devastation of my small campsite that made me stop in shock.

"Moses?"

The tentative whisper barely made a sound. The man's face was transformed. I had seen the glow of God's peace on his countenance before when my brother spoke of encountering *I AM* at the bush. This was a more awe-inspiring change. His skin seemed to radiate light.

"Moses?" Again I spoke, slightly louder.

Cautiously I approached and reached out a finger to touch my brother. He seemed closer to being an angel than a man.

"Miriam, my sister, it is me." The voice was the same. "God has returned favor to his people. The Living God has restored his laws to us."

Only then did I notice that the man held two newly inscribed stones in his arms. "Come, I must tell the people the commandments of the One God. *I AM* does not forsake his own, nor forget the promises to Abraham, Isaac, and Jacob."

Chapter 23

Moses never referred to the golden calf again. It was as if the incident never happened. Side by side, we walked the short distance to the tents of the tribes of Israel. I stood beside my brother when he stopped at Aaron's tent. Zipporah hurried to her husband. They were only allowed a brief embrace. News rapidly spread throughout the encampment that the Prophet had returned.

It was the radiance of the man's face that drew the community to the Deliverer. Soon everyone was gathered around. He held out his hand to draw Aaron to his side. In that hand clasp my brothers were reconciled. I sighed; relieved that Aaron's fears of being rebuffed were unfounded. Joshua joined the team of leaders followed closely by Caleb. Zipporah and I stood in the background with my nephews beside us.

"Hear the Word of God." The command penetrated to the furthest tents.

Moses stood in the center of the camp. He held up the slabs of stone.

"These are the Laws of our God. There is only One God who made the heavens and earth and everything that is part of creation. The God of Abraham, Isaac, and Jacob spoke to our fathers and chose the children of Israel to be bearers of the truth. *I AM* is Loving-Kindness from generation to generation. Remember the promises and see how they are fulfilled at this time. The Living God has led you from Egypt and will bring you to the land promised long ago to Abraham."

The man paused in his recital to look around. The entire congregation hung on every word.

"All that is asked of you is to remain a steadfast community and trust in *I AM*, holy is his Name."

The sigh of relief made me smile a little. My brother looked at the sea of faces. Some showed confusion. There were a few nods of agreement. One or two looked disturbed. Moses continued to speak. One by one, he read the commandments to the gathering.

"*I AM* is the One God who brought you out of bondage in Egypt. You shall worship no other gods. There are no other gods."

I expected an argument from Dathan or one of the other rebels but they remained silent.

"You must not make any image of anything in creation." Sternly the words were spoken. "Everything was created by *I AM*. Do not worship illusions but Truth." The man looked around at the listeners. No one moved. "The Name of our God is holy. Do not swear or curse by the name of God or invoke the Name of the Holy One to harm another. Surely the Lord will find guilty any who misuse his Name."

Without moving his head, my brother gave the impression of seeing each person.

"Remember the Sabbath day," my brother continued more gently. "Six days you must work but the seventh day is for God. In six days creation was completed and then the Lord God rested. So has *I AM* hallowed the seventh day as a day to rest and pray to God."

I saw nods of agreement and smiles at the thought of a day of rest. Moses glanced at me before he continued with the fifth law.

"Honor your father and mother." I saw the man smile. "Then your days will be prosperous in the land the Lord gives us." The next few commandments needed no explanation. One by one, Moses stated the ordinances. "You shall not kill. You shall not commit adultery. You shall not steal. You shall not lie about your neighbor or yourself. You shall not covet anything that belongs to your neighbor, whether it is wife or servant or beast."

When the man stopped speaking, there was no sound. Not even a child or animal stirred. In the distance, the clouds on Sinai rumbled with thunder.

"What *I AM* has commanded, we will do," I felt compelled to speak into the silence.

Aaron looked at me with irritation. Moses laid a hand on his arm to forestall any anger. My words were repeated tentatively at first and then enthusiastically.

"What *I AM* has commanded, we will do." Over and over the chant rang out. Looking at the community gathered in the valley, I hoped that faith was in the response.

My brother turned with his two lieutenants to enter the tent. I breathed a prayer.

"God of my brother, look with compassion on your hesitant people. Help them learn to follow your commandments. Give to Moses and Aaron and Joshua the wisdom necessary to encourage this stiff-necked congregation."

We had a festive meal as the sun set. Zipporah rejoiced that Moses had returned safely. I too was glad. As we ate, I stared at the man who was my brother and yet still a stranger. The radiance was gone from his face. He looked like any contented husband in the camp, with his wife on one side and Eleazar cuddled close on the other. As he talked, Moses absently tousled the boy's hair. Gershom hung back, slightly in awe of his father. The man finally noticed his oldest son standing near the tent entrance. He stood up and walked to the young man. My nephew grinned at something his father said. Together they returned to finish the meal.

Caleb's eyes never left Moses. He hung on every word. I wanted to ask what it was like on Sinai with God but my brother didn't seem to want to speak of that.

"We will remain here by the mountain of God while a Tabernacle is built," we were told. "The people need a tangible reminder of the presence of the Living God. *I AM* has placed the design in my heart." The man gazed past us seeing his vision. "There will be no image of God."

"God dwells among his people," I whispered, and saw Moses smile at my words.

I treasured his nodded affirmation.

"True, but the people need something to remind them of that presence."

In the morning, a council of the tribal leaders assembled. This included the elders of each tribe as well as the men appointed as judges. Aaron and his sons were present. Caleb stood proudly beside Joshua like an honor guard behind my brother.

I made sure my tasks kept me close to the men. Moving my loom close to the side of the tent was the work of a moment. My shuttle lay idle rather than moving across the blanket. In my mind I saw the design my brother described. Eventually my hands fell into my lap as I imagined the beauty of the gilded box. It would be carried on poles. At night, an enclosure made of curtains would surround the Ark. Altars and fire pots of gold and bronze would be within the sanctuary.

"Gather those skilled in woodwork to construct the ark," Moses decreed. "Anyone skilled in the casting of gold and beating of bronze must work on the accoutrements of the holy place. Those who know how to work with fine jewels shall collect donations from the people and make the priest's breastplate and decorations for the curtains. Shepherds must find the purest of their flocks to present before the Lord." Moses was not done. "No one will be left out of the construction. Women skilled in fine weaving will make the curtains and hangings. Those who can sew will make garments for the priests. Even children can card the wool needed."

My heart sang, delighted at the chance to make something to honor the One God. From a distance, I heard the men moving away to explain the plan to the people. Lost in thought, I didn't hear Moses until he spoke.

"My sister, are you pleased?" The teasing note in his voice told me that he knew I had been eavesdropping.

"You have included each person in this plan." The admiration in my voice was sincere.

"God is for all people." The man squatted at my side. "Perhaps as they work on this shrine the people will find God and not doubt."

"It is hard to leave behind the old ways," I reminded my brother looking up at him.

"The God of Abraham, Isaac, and Jacob has done so much for us" With a sigh Moses shook his head. "And still they waver."

"It takes a long time to trust in a Loving God who cares for the people." I laid my hand on the man's arm. "Zipporah has told me of your struggle with the Living God."

"True." A small smile creased the face. "I have fought against God longer than I have followed him."

"Not so, my brother." Taking the bearded face between my hands I looked into the man's eyes. "God has loved you and been with you all through your life." When he looked unsure, I stated, "Even when you challenged God, *I AM* has been with you. The God of our fathers will not desert us now even though the people falter and fear."

"Miriam." In his turn, my brother took my face between his hands. He looked deep into my eyes. "Where do you find such faith? You gave up your life to care for Amram and Jochebed. You watched Joel die under Egyptian rock and worked daily with the wounds of slavery. My sister, from your heart, you bring forth such comfort and faith that I am humbled."

He pressed a kiss to my forehead. I felt tears filling my eyes.

"From God comes the healing," was the only response I could make to the unexpected affirmation.

Each day the sound of sawing and hammering filled the camp. Smoke from the fires used to melt the gold and brass drifted from nearby hills when the wind shifted. It was choking and smelled awful. I preferred the smell of the freshly cut trees that were dragged to the work site. In an amazingly short time, the round trunks were split and split again into lumber. Then the sanding and planing began.

I worked on the looms with the other women. We smoothed lamb's fat into our hands to make them soft enough to work on the delicate cloth. It was soothing to have the finely spun thread to weave rather than the coarser wool I usually used. We talked together while the cloth grew on the looms. Sometimes we discussed children and husbands. Often I was asked to sing.

"Tell us again of our father Abraham."

"Let us hear of Joseph the governor."

So, the days passed happily and productively. Caleb kept me informed of progress in all areas.

"The brazen bowls have been made," he told me only a few days after work started. "You should have seen the men pounding the sheets of brass into the right shape. Now the polishing will begin." The young man's enthusiasm was contagious and I smiled when he added, "The wood has been cut to length for the ark. Tomorrow they will start smoothing it and notching the pieces to fit together."

A couple of days later I heard Moses talking again to the elders. The men gathered every evening to discuss progress on the work.

"Will you be the priest in charge of the holy place and the worship?" Horem raised the question one night.

I paused in my task of folding away the clean garments. All the women had spent the day washing out clothing and drying it in the sun. The stream that flowed from Sinai had more water than usual thanks to a recent downpour and we took advantage of the freshet to clean the dusty robes and tunics. Barely breathing, I listened for Moses' reply.

My brother didn't even pause to think. He must have been expecting the question. "Aaron and his sons have been chosen as priests and guardians of the presence of the Living God among the children of Israel. The tribe of Levi is set aside for service of the sanctuary. They will not receive an allotment of land in Canaan. Each of the other tribes will provide for the priests from their bounty."

There was a murmur of approval from the elders. My heart leapt at the honor given to my brother, even as I felt a twinge of jealousy.

"I, too, have kept the faith," I whispered into the darkness of the tent. The dancing shadows on the hide wall moved as the elders went to their beds. "I sent Aaron to meet Moses. I didn't make the golden calf either." A tear of self-pity slid down my cheek. Like a petulant child I stamped my foot and muttered, "It is not fair."

The hand on my shoulder made me start and I felt my face flush in the dark. It was Aaron.

"Miriam," for once he did not sound angry with me. "It is true that you have been more faithful than I ever have."

"No, Aaron, I'm sorry." I turned toward my brother wishing I could take back my petty words.

Moses stood beside him and I was glad for the night, which hid my reddening face. Embarrassment at being caught acting like a child kept me silent.

"My sister," the Prophet spoke. "To you has been given the greater responsibility. Miriam, God has a different task for you."

I tilted my head and stared at the man in confusion. White teeth glinted when he grinned at my look. My fingers were grasped between the strong hands that had born the staff of Prince, killed a man, tended sheep, and carried the staff of God. The fire's glow lit our faces through the open tent flap.

"Miriam," serious now, my brother continued, "to you is given the task of keeping the story of this people. You alone remember the songs of our history. It must be written down so that no one will be able to forget." I found my head shaking in denial even as I wondered if I could remember how to form the letters. The lessons in Pharaoh's palace seemed long ago.

"Yes, my sister," Moses spoke to my doubt, "you have the skill. What you learned in Egypt is to be used for God's glory." Soberly the man folded my hands together between his. "This is what *I AM* wants from you. Each day you sing the songs to the women. The people are encouraged by the stories of God's love for his people. It needs to be written so that all generations will remember our history."

I felt unsuited for the job placed in my hands. A quick kiss on the forehead and the man strode into the night followed by Aaron.

"I believe the Living God calls us to do things we feel incapable of," my brother, chosen by God as priest, paused, "but then we are given the strength to accomplish whatever it is."

I hoped he was right. In the darkness, all I remembered were my years of rage and doubt.

Chapter 24

When I was alone, I pondered the command. In the hide tent at the foot of the mountain of God, I held my hands out in front of me. Then, with the end of my finger I began to form the letters in the sandy floor. The memory of each letter came back to me and I smiled. Begun on a whim, almost as a game, the Princess had instructed her own scribe to teach me. Who could have dreamed that lessons learned in Pharaoh's palace would be used to write the story of the captive people. Still I doubted myself. I once thought I would be the one to rescue my family, but I was wrong. Perhaps this was an illusion, too.

Early the next morning, I found Moses. I was surprised he was alone.

"My brother, why have you given me the job of writing the story of the children of Israel?"

The man rested his hands on my shoulders. Steadily we looked into each other's eyes. I don't know what he saw in mine. The Deliverer appeared older now. I had not noticed the many lines surrounding my brother's eyes. His eyebrows were gray and so was much of his hair and beard. The fire in his eyes, though, was that of a young man. Deep in them I saw a peace, even in the midst of the bustle and complaining and demands, which could only come from God.

"Miriam, my sister, I have known that *I AM* would seek you out for a special purpose. You, like me, have come through the fires of doubt into a place of abiding faith."

It was not an answer to my question

"You gave me an impossible job," I reproached my brother. "Why?"

196

"I will send you the papyrus, quills, and ink you need for the writing," I was told before Moses was called away.

My heart desperately needed assurance from my brother. I needed to know why he chose me. Caleb brought me a pile of papyrus scrolls and a supply of quills and ink.

"Moses said you would need these."

The young man's curiosity and amazement made me feel even more unsure. Unable to form a reply I simply nodded. After I was alone, I fell on my knees.

"God of Abraham, Isaac, and Jacob, this is an assignment far beyond my abilities. My brother has set me to writing the history of the children of Israel. Is it just a diversion so I won't complain?" Another doubt grabbed my throat. "Perhaps he wants me to fail. I cannot do this!"

Tears flowed down my cheeks and I felt a lump of resentment building. The longer I thought about Moses' request, the more I became sure that he meant for me to fail in the impossibility of the task.

Still, I was drawn to the blank scrolls. Hesitantly at first, I began to practice the letters learned so long ago in the tiled and golden halls of the Egyptian palace. Memories of the princess and of my parents came to me. One day I wrote down the song of creation. I could almost hear Jochebed singing the words as the quill moved across the papyrus.

The cadence of the refrain, 'God said, it is good,' rang in my ears and almost seemed approval of the work before me.

Caleb's arrival with the daily report of progress caused me to roll the scroll up rapidly so he wouldn't see my work. Later, in the moonlight, I unrolled the papyrus and touched the lettering. My mother's words lay before me on the page. I marveled at them. For the first time I wondered if I might actually be able to accomplish what Moses asked, but my doubts remained.

Every afternoon I unrolled one of the papyrus sheets. I tried to start the story of Noah, a man called to build a boat in the desert. The account I wrote seemed lifeless. The words had no significance. Finally, I laid the quill aside. The responsibility of writing the story of God and his people would have to wait.

"No sense ruining the scroll," I told myself. "There are important things to do. The women need my help with the weaving."

It was not true. The curtains and the sacred garments were complete. The altars and basins were finished. Men worked on the poles and final gilding of the tabernacle itself. The cherubim on the cover of the ark were amazing. Their golden wings stretched out across the lid. I wondered where Moses had conceived of such creatures.

"They are not idols," the man assured me when I questioned him. "Cherubim are guardians of the sacred things. They are not the Holy One."

"Won't the people be confused?" I asked.

Irritably he brushed me aside. "Woman, you know nothing of such things. Have you been face to face with God?"

For a moment he looked every inch the prince he once was. I stepped back in outrage and opened my mouth to respond. Then I paused. My brother was furious because I voiced his secret fear.

"Moses." Although my tone was conciliatory, he strode past me.

Sadly, I looked after him. Zipporah greeted me with a warm embrace later in the day.

"My sister, I have been neglecting you lately." I apologized.

"Tell me what task does my husband have you doing that keeps you so busy?" Her smiling question brought back all my doubts and suspicions.

"It is …" I shook my head and frowned. I was appalled by the bitterness in my tone when I answered. "My brother felt I was interfering more than a woman should, so he set me to writing the story of this people."

"It is what you should do, just as I told you before we arrived here!" Zipporah was delighted. "Don't you remember? I said you needed to write down all the songs before they are forgotten."

"Yes." I remembered with a half smile. "And you told Moses that I knew how to write." Still, I sighed. "I cannot seem to get past the fear."

My confession surprised the woman.

"Fear?" Her brows drew together in confusion. "What are you afraid of?"

It sounded foolish when I replied in a whisper. I felt a tear slide down my cheek. "How can I dare to write down the story of this people and of God? What if I get something wrong? Everyone will laugh at me."

Zipporah did not laugh. She drew me into her arms again and held me as I sobbed.

"Have no fear," she crooned. "If this is what God calls you to do, you cannot fail."

Over and over, she repeated the words until I stopped sobbing. I had never believed that this responsibility might really be from God. Since the beginning, I thought Moses himself wanted me to write the stories. Drawing back slightly, I stared at my sister-in-law.

"I never thought of it that way. Do you really think that this is what God wants me to do?"

"Did I not say so before we reached Sinai?" The woman tilted her head to the side like a sparrow and smiled at me.

We talked of other things, but I pondered her words. Later in my tent, I unrolled the one scroll I had completed. Slowly I reread the story of Creation and the Garden of Eden. Jochebed's words came back to me, 'The Living God has been acting since the beginning of time. Even now in this slavery, God is active.'

"Yes, Mother," I breathed into the night. "God has indeed acted. We must not forget."

In that moment I dedicated myself to doing what Moses, and perhaps *I AM*, had ordered. Now that I was ready to begin, I was unable to settle to work because the final preparations for the dedication of the tabernacle and people were in motion. Moses himself oversaw the last details. However, he refused to be considered as one of the priests.

"I am only God's messenger," he insisted when the elders tried to convince him to accept the mantle of priest. "Aaron and his sons have been set aside for this duty."

The day finally came when the work was done. Each man sanctified himself. The women baked and prepared mountains of food for offerings and for feasting.

Bright sun greeted us on the morning of the dedication. To the awe and amazement of everyone in the camp, the fiery cloud seemed to rise from atop the mountain to settle on the Ark and Tent of Meeting. I felt a thrill and my heart beat faster at the sight. Caleb stood beside me with Zipporah and Moses' sons. No one spoke. To one side a group of sheep and goats was penned. These were the sacrificial animals.

Moses stood near the entrance of the Sanctuary. With a flourish he lit the fire in a huge bronze basin standing at the entrance. He nodded to Aaron. My brother slowly walked forward. He wore only a plain linen loincloth. Nadab, Abihu, Eleazar, and Ithamar followed their father. They lay on the hard ground in front of the Deliverer.

"The God of our fathers has chosen you," Moses proclaimed to the men. "You will keep the holy things and you will bless the children of Israel."

The man turned and dropped some sweet smelling incense onto the coals of the brazier. Smoke billowed up, swirling over the men and floating upward to merge with the cloud hovering over the sanctuary. The Prophet took Aaron's hand and drew him to his feet. Brother faced brother.

"This is what **I AM** has commanded for your consecration and ordination," the Messenger of God spoke clearly.

Lifting a bowl of water from the table Moses washed his brother and his nephews. They stood dripping in the early morning light while the man dressed each of the priests in a clean tunic. The cloud of God seemed to reach out and enfold the men. The priestly garments were brought forward. Each man was dressed in a robe of finest cloth. Around the hem were bells and pomegranate decorations. The women had done their work well. I smiled for my friends. Moses was speaking.

"My brothers, you have been set apart by God from your kinsmen and neighbors to minister before the Lord. Each of these garments is a sign of your consecration to the True God, the God of Abraham, Isaac, and Jacob. Wear them when you serve before the Lord, so that the offerings of the children of Israel may be acceptable."

Each man bowed low. The last item was a turban for each man's head. Five priests stood proudly before the congregation. A cheer erupted from thousands of throats. When the acclamation subsided, Moses raised aloft a golden signet. The medallion was placed in the turban of Aaron, newly consecrated High Priest. I knew that on it was the name of *I AM*.

I remembered the first time I heard my brother say the name of God. It seemed a lifetime before in a different world. Did that woman still exist? The journey had changed me, I decided. I was no longer jealous of Moses' designation as Prophet and Deliverer. It was enough to see the Living God fulfilling the promise made long ago to Abraham, Isaac, and Jacob.

"Wear this always when you enter the holy place. By it you will find favor for the people for any guilt they unknowingly have committed in their offerings." The Prophet's words interrupted my thoughts. "Aaron bar Amram, you will carry all the tribes when you enter into the sanctuary,"

I gasped to see the jeweled breastplate that Moses held up and lifted over his brother's head. The names of the twelve tribes were engraved on the stones, one on each of the precious gems. The onyx stones set in gold that rested, one on each shoulder, also bore the names of the tribes.

"Aaron, priest of the One Living God whose name is *I AM that I AM*, you are charged with judgment of the children of Israel. When you go before the Holy One, you will wear the breastplate with the names of each of the tribes. In that way each man will be represented before God."

Aaron bowed low. I held my breath until he straightened. The exaltation on his face brought tears to my eyes. The priest faced the gathered congregation. A cheer rose. Moses stepped in front of his brother. In his hand he held Urim and Thummim, the stones of prophecy.

"My brother." The man's voice was choked with emotion. "In these stones, you bear not only judgment but the destiny of your brethren."

Only after he placed the objects into their position on the breastplate did he allow himself to embrace his brother. Then the Deliverer ushered the new priests forward to enter the courtyard of the holy place. The cloud lifted slightly when the curtains were drawn aside. We could see the altars and candlesticks. Faintly behind the further curtains, the outline of the ark with the cherubim on the mercy seat was seen. A sigh of reverent awe rose from the community.

Aaron and his sons stepped forward and took up their positions at the altar. Nadab blew the ram's horn. A bull was brought forward for the sin offering of the priests. Oil and grain and bread were offered along with the animals. When the ram of ordination was killed, Moses dipped his finger into the blood.

"May you hear the word of God," he intoned touching Aaron's right ear with the blood. "Keep your hands holy to the service of the Lord. Walk always in the way of *I AM*." Blood was placed on the right thumb and foot. The ritual was repeated for each of my nephews. "You are anointed for the service of the God of Abraham, Isaac, and Jacob," Moses spoke to his brother. "For seven days you and your sons will remain here at the entrance of the Tent of Meeting. Your food will be the meat and bread dedicated to the Lord."

"What God has commanded, we will do." The men's response brought tears to my eyes.

For a week, while the rest of the camp went about the daily routine, Aaron and his sons remained in prayer just inside the Tent of Meeting. Then Moses called together all the people again. Aaron offered a goat for the sin of the people followed by a ram and an ox for a peace offering. Side by side, my brothers stood before the tabernacle to bless the people.

"The fire of God!" A cry rose from many throats.

Something like a tongue of flame shot from the cloud hovering over the Ark. The offering on the altar was consumed entirely. As one, we all fell to our faces.

"You are set apart for *I AM*," Moses warned his brother and nephews. "Do not be drunk when you enter the sanctuary. You will teach the children of Israel the ways of the Lord. The Ark itself will be carried only on the shoulders of the priests."

Moses instructed the leaders of each tribe to prepare their offerings of dedication to the Lord. Standing before the congregation, my brother looked around at the sea of faces.

"Sanctify yourselves." The words were stern. "You have been chosen by *I AM* for the honor of bringing the offering of dedication before the Lord. One day is set apart for each tribe. On that day, the clan will assemble and the sheik will bring forward the offerings so each tribe will be consecrated to God."

"In the morning, you must bring your offering," Moses told Nahshom of the tribe of Judah. "The others will follow in order."

The man pressed his hand to his heart while bowing in homage.

For twelve days this continued. Each man brought a huge silver plate and a gigantic basin with oil and flour as well as a golden dish full of incense. Animals for the burnt offerings and sin offerings were herded forward. The smell of burning flesh and incense hung over the camp day in and day out. The dedication of the nation was finally over. Life returned to a routine.

Aaron and his sons learned the rituals they were expected to perform. Many intricate laws were expounded about cleanliness and purity. I was amazed at the number of them. Moses spent part of each day writing down the principles to govern our lives.

Daily we expected Moses to announce that we would move on. Instead, we remained camped by the mountain of God through the dry winter months. Occasionally snow dusted the ground and covered the heights of the nearby hills, including Sinai. The darkest night of the year came and went. As the weather began to warm, Moses strode out into the fields to walk among the ewes and check the multitude of new lambs.

New babies were born to many of the young couples. Each firstborn son was dedicated to *I AM* by circumcision. It seemed to reinforce my unspoken belief that the laws were more important than the history of the people.

"This covenant was given to our father Abraham," Moses reminded the congregation. "It is also a reminder that by the death of the firstborn of Egypt, God redeemed forever all the sons of Abraham."

"That is the way to God," I told myself. "If we follow the rules as Moses has set them out, *I AM* will be with us."

I often looked at the scrolls in the basket in my tent. Despite Zipporah's encouragement, I couldn't settle to the task of writing the saga. Each day I came up with a new excuse.

"After the blanket is complete, then I'll start."

"I am needed to assist with Debora's birthing."

"Tomorrow, if the weather if clear, I will begin."

Zipporah shook her head at each pretext. "Miriam, you cannot evade God forever," she warned. "You have been chosen to do this thing."

"The Laws Moses is writing are more important than the saga of the past," at last I blurted out my real reason.

"Who is to say which task is greater, slaughtering animals for sacrifices or keeping the memories of the people so they don't forget their heritage."

"I will do it. The time just isn't right." My obstinate declaration brought a smile to my friend's lips.

Chapter 25

One day Moses called all the camp together. "This is the first month of our second year of freedom," the Messenger of God announced.

I was amazed to realize that a full year had passed. Egypt seemed so far away. We no longer even looked like the same ragged group of refugees that stumbled and limped from Goshen to Succoth and then to the Great Sea. We had become skilled nomads. Memory of the victory over the Amalekites gave us new confidence. The Ark of God in our midst was a constant reminder of the care and presence of *I AM* with us.

"God has commanded us to keep the Passover as an everlasting memorial to the actions of the Living One in bringing us to freedom. Prepare yourselves. On the fourteenth day at sunset, the Passover will begin."

It was as a community that we prepared for that first Passover as a free people. Everyone wanted to be part of the celebration. Even those who found themselves ritually unclean petitioned Moses to allow them to participate. The answer from the Man of God pleased everyone.

"Even if you are found to be unclean because of touching a corpse or if you are traveling, you may still keep the Passover of the Lord," Moses announced to the entire camp. "Visitors or strangers in our midst may also eat the Passover if they keep it as a holy feast."

I wondered if the caravan from Cush that was camped with us influenced my brother's decree.

Zipporah was troubled by their presence. "How can Moses include foreigners? The One God has set apart the children of Israel. Now my husband includes outsiders in the holy celebration.

Look at him." Angry eyes followed the progress of man and girl around camp.

I felt sorry for my sister-in-law. The young daughter of the trader hung on every word my brother said. Her adoring eyes followed him everywhere. The man was not immune to her dark charms. He preened at her questions and devotion. Moses was obviously explaining the reason for the elaborate Sanctuary with its curtains and altars. The young woman did not appear bored even when the explanation stretched on and on.

"The man is a fool," Zipporah hissed. "What makes him think that child wants anything except the prestige of associating with the Prophet of God?"

Turning on her heel, the woman stormed into her tent. I heard weeping and hesitated at the entrance.

"Leave me alone," the sobbing voice sent me away.

The seven days of sanctification began with Moses' proclamation, "This is a time for men to purify themselves from women."

During the week, Aaron led the men in prayers of thanksgiving reminding the people of their freedom from slavery. Many sacrifices were prepared. All the women kept busy baking and chopping for the festival. Zipporah kept to her tent and ignored the presence of Petrama among us. Finally, the day arrived. The sound of the ram's horn trumpet summoned everyone to the Tent of Meeting as the sun was setting.

Caleb stood beside me. His eyes were wide as he watched the ceremony. "Why is this night different from all other nights?" Barely, the whispered question reached my ears.

I remembered that he had not participated in the first Passover.

"On this night God smote the sons of Egypt and passed over the firstborn of Israel." It was all I had time to say.

"On this anniversary let us remember the mighty acts of ***I AM that I AM***," Moses recited. "The God of Abraham, Isaac, and Jacob visited us in Egypt. By a mighty hand and outstretched arm we are a free people."

"This is a perpetual feast of remembrance," Aaron responded formally.

"AMEN," the community cheered with one voice.

"Tonight we eat the roasted lamb and unleavened bread in memory of the saving act of our God," Aaron explained in dismissal.

When the ceremony was over, each family dispersed to its tent for their meal. Zipporah and her sons waited for Moses. The man signaled to Petrama and her father to accompany him. My sister-in-law lifted her chin proudly and turned away to walk beside me. My own heart broke for the pain I knew she hid. Caleb walked beside me to the tent where Elisheva waited proudly for her husband and sons to complete their duties.

"It is good." She smiled, indicating my brother walking toward her. "See how content Aaron is to serve God?"

Absently, I returned her smile as I watched both brothers walk toward us. As usual, the young Cushite girl pressed close to the Deliverer.

"Welcome to this humble tent, my friend." Moses ushered the trader through the opening with a salaam.

All the men settled onto cushions around the rug. Petrama smiled adoringly at Moses and tried to be the one to take the jar of wine. I frowned at her presumption and handed the jar to my sister-in-law. No one else noticed when Zipporah slipped away after pouring the wine. Silently, Elisheva and I brought out the lamb with herbs and unleavened bread. As at every meal, each man reached into the central platter to select what he wanted. For the trader, my brothers recounted the events in Egypt that lead to our freedom. Caleb hung on every word.

When I sought Zipporah out later, she refused to be comforted. "My husband is blind. That girl feeds his ego. He no longer cares for me though I have borne him sons." The words were cold and bitter. "It would have been better for me to have never returned to the man." Angry eyes looked into mine. "God stole part of my husband. Now this dark-skinned foreigner has taken the rest."

"The caravan will move on soon," I counseled. "Wait. When we move on toward Canaan, Moses will remember you and his sons."

Although she shook her head, my friend agreed to stay with me. A few days later, we set out from the mountain of God. Our route lay to the north and east.

"We have eaten the Passover in the very presence of God," I told Zipporah. "We are now a consecrated people."

"Yes." The abstracted answer made me look at the woman.

She was watching her husband. He was not alone at the front of our snaking line of travel. Aaron led the way. My nephews carried the Ark. The wagons with the curtains, altars, and other equipment followed surrounded by the sons of Ithamar as guards. Then came Moses. He walked several cubits behind the wagon to stay out of the dust. Petrama accompanied him, rather than his usual lieutenants, Joshua and Caleb. Her hand rested on his arm and she was listening raptly to his words.

"Oh!" I gasped in a mixture of sorrow and outrage.

There was nothing I could say. We walked in silence all day. Inwardly I seethed. How dare Moses act so carelessly? This was not the way to lead the people of God. That night I tried to find a chance to speak to the man alone. He was busy receiving a report from Joshua of the day's travel. I was distracted by Caleb's arrival. He told me that Hannah, wife of Beliah, was in labor.

"The midwives bid you hurry." Anxiety was in the voice. "They sent me to find you."

The young woman was a tiny, slender child, almost too young to be having a baby. I had been concerned about her throughout the pregnancy. With my herbs I hurried to attend the woman. Dawn broke when the infant was delivered. Hannah lifted her head weakly to look at the tiny girl before turning her face away.

"A girl." The statement was more of a moan than words. "Beliah will hate me now." Tears slid down the white cheeks.

"The child is healthy and strong." The bracing words of encouragement from Marah, one of the midwives, didn't bring comfort.

"It does not matter." The voice was weary.

Quickly I mixed a potion of soothing herbs and wine. "Drink this."

The girl was too weak to resist my command. When she slept, I took the newborn from Marah. Rocking the baby in my arms, I looked at the other women. We knew that Hannah spoke the truth. Beliah was a rough man, boasting about the camp that he would have a fine son. He picked his bride carefully, as much because she had ten brothers as for her sweetness and beauty. 'From such a family, of course I will have many sons,' he boasted many times. The blow to his pride would be great. I feared he would take it out on his wife.

Now it was time to confront the man. Squaring my shoulders, I stepped from the tent. Beliah was not alone. I glimpsed Caleb in the group of waiting men.

"My son, give me my son." Stepping forward the big man held out his hands.

Still cuddling the small bundle, I replied, "Your child is a lovely girl."

"That cannot be." So incredulous was the tone that I nearly laughed.

A few of the men weren't so polite. Chuckles were heard. Enraged the man glared at his friends before towering over me.

"How dare you lie to me?" The snarl was ugly.

Bravely, I stood my ground. I was taller than the baby's father by a full head was. Even his menacing fists did not frighten me. Only after his hands unclenched did I unwrap the child to show to her father.

"God has given you a beautiful daughter." Tenderly I rocked the baby.

Each time I held a newborn, I was awed just as when I held my brother after his birth. I smiled down at the infant and received a gurgle in response. The tiny child did not soften her father's heart.

"Take her away and drown her." As though disgusted, the man turned his back on us both. "Sons are needed to settle the Promised Land, not girls."

When I did not move Beliah turned toward me with one hand half raised to strike. I did not flinch even when the man threatened me.

"Go! Do you not hear what I say, woman?"

Caleb intervened, stepping in front of the irate husband. Bristling, he spoke in defense of the baby.

"This child is a blessing from *I AM*. You have no right to order her death." I was proud of the young man and amazed when he continued. "If you deny your daughter, I will be her protector."

"Bah, take her then." With a sneer the man looked at his friends, silent now at the drama being acted out. "What do you know of taking care of a baby? You are nothing but a stripling, an errand boy for Joshua."

I saw the muscle in Caleb's cheek twitch as he gritted teeth against an angry response.

All he said was, "Miriam will teach me what is needed." Looking around at the assembled men, he stated, "You have all heard this man give up his daughter to me."

"We have heard."

By the affirmation, the orphan boy became guardian for the rejected girl child. Arm in arm we walked away from Beliah and his friends. I realized that the young boy was now a man whose head reached my shoulder. Marah and the other midwives stared openmouthed before hurrying to spread the news throughout the camp. My day was spent with Caleb and the infant. We named her Sarai.

"It means princess," I told the young man, "like Abraham's wife. May the Living God bless this child with the joy of husband and children."

Zipporah and Elisheva hurried to my tent when they heard Marah's announcement. In helping care for the baby, my sister-in-law forgot her distress. There was an almost contented smile on her lips as she rocked the dozing baby. I had no time to talk to Moses, although he came to see the new addition.

"Caleb, you have taken on a great responsibility." The pride in my brother's voice made the young man blush. With a glance at Sarai, now held by Elisheva, he teased. "I am sure you will have plenty of help. Every girl in the camp will want to play nursemaid to your child."

Morning came and I expected us to strike camp and finally set out toward Canaan. Instead, Moses had an announcement. The entire company gathered at his order. I was surprised to see my brother in festive garments.

"He looks like a groom," I whispered to Elisheva.

"Shanal, the Cushite, and I have agreed," proudly the man spoke. "Petrama, daughter of Shanal, will become my bride."

I felt almost physically ill and immediately reached for Zipporah's hand. She gripped my wrist as if it was a lifeline.

Proudly she stared forward refusing to let anyone see her devastation. Her husband spoke.

"Gifts have been exchanged. Look here is the bride."

Pointing toward the nearby tent, he indicated the girl. All eyes turned to watch. Shanal led Petrama decked in veils and dowry chains, out of tent. The rich display irritated me.

"Who is she trying to impress?" I muttered under my breath.

The trader led his daughter forward and placed her hand into Moses'. With a low salaam he bowed backward.

"May the God who you follow give you many sons." I heard the words through a mist of rage.

Zipporah tightened her grip on me and I heard shallow angry breaths coming from her parted lips.

"My father," the Deliverer bowed in response, "I will honor your daughter with my life."

Aaron hurried forward. "God has made man and woman for each other. From the beginning this has been true. May the blessing of the God of Abraham, Isaac, and Jacob be with you both."

When the cheers and applause started, I led my sister-in-law away. A glance back showed me that Moses was kissing his bride. We did not travel for seven days. The time was given over to celebration. The Deliverer and his bride occupied the festive tent in the center of camp. Zipporah closed herself away behind her veils and would not speak. My heart ached for her sorrow. Angrily, I began to complain to anyone who would listen. Everyone in the camp commented on the leader's actions. Small groups clustered together to talk about his marriage. Day after day, I fed the discontent with self-righteous looks and remarks.

"Just because he was a prince, he thinks he can marry whomever he wants."

"The woman isn't even a daughter of Abraham."

"Poor Zipporah …"

"Someone should tell our grand leader what we think of this marriage."

Even Aaron was heard to comment, "Surely God does not want us to marry anyone outside the tribes of Israel."

My campaign brought Zipporah many expressions of sympathy. Now that I no longer held myself aloof from the whispers, everyone came to me with their complaints about my brother.

The camp became a seething hive of rumors and gossip. My anger at the man's actions blinded me to the destruction of the community. With satisfaction, I watched the discontent grow but Moses seemed oblivious to the undercurrents. He didn't even notice my cool demeanor toward Petrama when we moved camp toward the northeast.

From criticism about my brother's marriage, it was only a short step to agreeing with the protests against the endless diet of manna. It was the question of food that always caused the most frustration for my brother. The whining started again as summer ended and the nights became shorter and cooler. It was Dathan.

"I wish I had some meat."

After a few days of ever-increasing grumbling, Moses lost his temper. We had paused to water the flocks at a well when Dathan took up the refrain.

"Give us meat, Prophet of God," he challenged.

Several nearby men took up the demand. Moses stared at his adversary for a long moment. His eyes narrowed dangerously.

"You will have meat," he finally snarled. "There will be so much meat it will make you sick!"

The complainers stepped back from the rare display of rage.

With that threat the Prophet stormed from the camp. Joshua and Aaron stood stunned and immobile. Caleb stared after his hero with wide, aghast eyes. After a few minutes, I followed the man. I found him flattened on the ground beseeching forgiveness from God.

"Living Lord, I am not worthy to lead your people. I do not have the patience to bear their complaints and whining." The deep voice broke with emotion. "God, it is too great a burden. How can I provide for this people meat for their cravings?"

Kneeling beside the prostrate form of the servant of God I laid one hand on his shoulder in support. Beneath my touch, I felt the sobs of remorse.

"Send peace to this man," I pleaded, tears sliding down my own cheeks.

For a moment I forgot my own exasperation with my brother. Gradually the emotion ebbed. Moses stopped weeping. Still he lay face down waiting for some sign from his God.

"My brother." Gently I stroked the man's hair as though he was a troubled child. "God has heard the protests and desires of the people. Just as we have manna to eat, *I AM* will provide meat as you have said."

After a heavy sigh, Moses sat up to look at me. His eyes were weary and full of despair. "Miriam, my sister, I spoke in anger and frustration not in faith. My words were not prompted by God." His head lowered in shame. "I wanted to harm those who incessantly complain."

"Moses, you are the chosen of God, but you are only a man," sternly I reminded my brother. "You have borne the criticism of the nation for all this time. The One who called you to this task is still with you."

Moses took my hands and held them between his big palms.

"My sister, you bring consolation again. You are right to remind me that *I AM* will never leave me or this people."

The desolation in the brown eyes eased. He stood up and drew me to my feet. Guilt smote my heart when I remembered my own voice grumbling about his actions.

"We must prepare to move on. God will act when the time is right."

No one dared question the decision to move, even though the day was well advanced. As we made camp the following afternoon, a cloud appeared from the east.

"Is it going to rain?" Aaron asked. Joshua shook his head, squinting at the approaching storm.

"That doesn't look like a storm cloud."

"It is a huge flock of birds." Caleb's young eyes picked out the flying forms.

He had barely shouted the news when quail began to fall from the sky. They appeared stunned and were easy for the children to capture. Everyone was kept busy slaughtering and cooking the bounty. Still the birds rained on us. I was sick of the sight and smell of quail before the onslaught ended. The entire camp reeked of cooking birds mixed with the smell of the offal and plucked feathers.

I couldn't stomach the taste of the birds. After a tiny nibble, I picked up a piece of bread and wandered away from the feast. Living birds staggered around under my feet pecking up scraps of bread and even meat. Eventually, they recovered and flew off toward the south.

Moses stood in front of his tent.

"*I AM* has provided meat," I commented, coming to stand beside my brother.

A half smile creased the man's face. "And in such a way."

"Perhaps there will be less murmuring, now." My suggestion was made without much hope.

"Miriam, this is a petulant people." He shook his head not in frustration but with a loving look. "They remember too well the ease of Egypt."

"Ease?" My question was sharp. "Slavery to Pharaoh was not easy."

"We quickly forget the bad and remember only the good." A gentle hand rested on my shoulder. "The people have forgotten the whips and scaffoldings. They prefer to think about the security of homes and plentiful food."

I gave a rueful nod. There seemed nothing more to say. We stood together in companionable silence, watching the people gorge themselves. I spent the night ministering to those who became ill from the surfeit of meat.

Even with my herbs and the help of those women who weren't ill, many of the community died there. We named the place *Kibbroth-hattavah* for the graves we left behind.

Chapter 26

When we finally set out, it took two days of travel to arrive at Hazeroth. I seethed impotently about my brother's preoccupation with the Cushite girl and grumbled to anyone who would listen.

Moses was never away from his new bride. Zipporah mourned in silence. She had not spoken since my brother made his announcement. Even her care of Sarai was mechanical. I saw her bury her face in the baby's blankets more than once when she thought she was alone.

Everyone was glad to reach the oasis. Tired, dusty feet soaked in the water. The days of sickness had left many in the company weak. Muscles ached from tramping through the sand and climbing over rocks. Even the animals seemed glad to stop. The herds drank happily and the oxen lay in the shade chewing their cud. Children ran giggling and wet through the camp.

Only Zipporah remained silent and withdrawn. I missed her bright comments and laughter. My brother had no right to make her suffer so. That my brother dared to insult one that I loved was more than I could bear. He must be brought to understand his error. It made no difference that the man spoke God's Law to the people. There was a greater law of honor that he betrayed.

"I will speak to Moses." The announcement did not draw any response from my sister-in-law.

She bent over Sarai and shut out the world. I hugged her firmly. Her lack of animation fueled my rancor. Standing just outside the tent, my eyes scanned the area for the man. At last I saw him, near the Tent of Meeting, talking to Aaron. Quickly the camp was crossed.

"Moses bar Amram." My angry hiss made both men look at me. "You have sinned."

His surprised and confused response only made me angrier.

"Miriam, what is my sin?"

"You have cast aside Zipporah to marry that child!" Sympathy for my friend made my voice harsh. "She is faithful and believed in you even before you had any faith or knew anything about God or heard *I AM* say 'Let my people go'. It was Zipporah who taught you of God." I was panting with emotion but plunged on. Toe to toe with the man I snarled, "She has walked beside you in danger and borne you two sons. What right have you to reject her for a foreigner?"

Breathless and almost crying from rage, I spat one final accusation. "You prate of the Law of God while betraying God. Doesn't God talk through me and even by Aaron? You said *I AM* wants me to tell the stories because I retain the memory of the acts of the Living One in loving relationship with his people." My voice rasped with rage. "Now you yourself discard the love of the woman who has given up her life to follow you. You wed another wife and leave Zipporah alone. Will you so easily reject God too?"

Moses hung his head. I wished he would respond. Aaron stared at me, although I had seen his slight nod as I spoke. The silence stretched out. Then the man of God looked toward the nearby Tent of Meeting that surrounded the Ark. Slowly I turned to face the curtained Sanctuary. The cloud of God's presence glowed. Moses moved toward the holy place. Aaron followed. Slowly, ever so slowly, I inched my way after the men as though drawn by a cord.

I knew that in my denunciation I had gone too far. Moses would never reject God, but my voice would not speak the words to ask forgiveness. Inexorably, I was pulled forward until I stood at the entry to the Sanctuary. I cringed from the fiery cloud even as I raised my chin in defiance.

"Moses is wrong," I told myself. "It is right that he be reprimanded. Zipporah should not be made to suffer because my brother considers himself above his own laws."

Afterward, I was never sure if I heard the words in my ears or just in my mind. That it was God I had no doubt.

"With prophets I make myself known in visions and dreams. Moses is my servant. He is steward over my house. I speak to him face to face and he has seen me." There was a moment of awful silence. *"Why weren't you afraid to speak against Moses, my chosen messenger?"*

Then the cloud dissipated to return to the Ark where it remained. Aaron stared at me in horror and threw himself at Moses' feet.

"My Lord, Great One," he begged, reverting to the princely titles of Egypt, "have mercy! Do not punish us for our foolishness. Heal my sister. Do not let her be an abomination and an outcast. She will be as one dead."

Unsure of why my brother groveled in the dirt, I reached out to touch him. My scream of horror when I saw my hand must have reached the farthest edge of the oasis. White, blistered pustules covered my skin. In a panic, I pulled up my sleeve. My arm too was leprous. Crying in terror, I ripped open the neck of my tunic. Every inch of my body was covered with the evidence of the dread disease. Tears fell on my hands but I couldn't feel them. I felt my breath coming in gasps. Dimly I heard Moses praying.

"O God, have mercy, heal my sister."

Again, in my mind or ears came the answer.

"Put her outside the camp for seven days. It will be as though her father spat in her face to curse her. She will bear the shame for seven days."

I heard hysterical sobs and realized they were coming from my lips as I collapsed onto the ground in front of my brother.

"Miriam, I am sorry." The pity in the man's voice only made me weep harder.

His feet moved away. I heard him order a tent erected for me. Moses himself returned to take me to my exile. Head bowed and entirely covered by my veil, I followed my brother past, it seemed, hundreds of pairs of bare and sandal-clad feet.

"Look away, she is cursed by God."

"A woman, daring to speak against Moses."

"Who does she think she is?"

"Serves her right."

The whispers made me want to lash out in fury. Countless times the same voices murmured against Moses themselves. I had plenty of time in the next week to rage against God.

"It is not fair," I challenged in my seclusion. "Others in the camp complain about Moses. Yet it is me you single out for punishment! I might as well be dead with this affliction! My brother rejects his wife and I am the one disciplined!"

Alone, very alone, I wept and cursed. In frustration I pounded my hands against the dirt floor until they bled. Each morning Moses came with food and water. Every evening he took it away uneaten.

"Do you delight in testing me? I have kept silence all this time. Now when I speak in defense of my friend, I am punished. Yet Moses is safe from your judgment."

Once started, I couldn't seem to stop ranting at the Living One. I almost wished to be struck dead.

"Why is Moses your chosen servant?" I heard the bitterness in my voice. "What about me? Does it matter that I am a woman? Didn't I cry out to you in grief even before Moses was born? Is it wrong to seek good for those I love? My own mother had her son restored to her because I spoke up at the palace. I endured the shame of Egyptian rape and my own grief when the Deliverer did not come. I had to nurse my beloved husband back to life and then you allowed him to be crushed under the stone." Memory of the dark days after Joel died flooded over me and I wept anew.

"Yet you chose my brother, the murderer. You set him even over Aaron, elder son of Amram bar Levi." I almost screamed at the unfairness of the choice. "Moses could not even speak for you. He needed his brother to speak to Pharaoh. How dare one man get all the credit?"

Anguish burst from my lips in a wrathful torrent. "God, you left your people in bondage for four hundred years. Now we are homeless wanderers. Are we any closer to your Promised Land than a year ago?"

All the frustration of years of silence boiled out. Eventually, exhausted from days of raving, I fell into a restless sleep. I saw again the ceaseless lines of my neighbors trudging ever forward under the weight of mud and straw and brick. Again and again the lash brought the bright red blood down backs and legs. In my dream, I held my parents as they died. Joel's lifeless body lay in my arms. My hands moved to cleanse the bodies for burial. Even as I wept in my sleep, the scene changed. I was not alone. Another hand washed the bodies with me. A pair of hands worked with me to cleanse the whip cuts. The strong hands lifted the stone off Joel's lifeless body and gathered us both into a comforting embrace.

Then I saw the graves we just left at Kibbroth-hattavah. Only one pair of hands dug the graves. They were not mine. I reached out to help with the work. My fingers encountered the rough hide of the tent. It woke me up.

I held up my clenched fists, white with the awful disease. Understanding flooded through me. A moan of grief poured forth from my soul. Anguished tears began to fall.

"You struck me with leprosy so that I might see the blight on the congregation that my jealous fury brought about. The wounds caused by my unreasoning rage are just like the sores that cover my skin. Like an infection, my virulence spread throughout the congregation. By speaking against Moses, I injured the Children of Israel. My sin is great for I brought division within the community. Forgive me, I did not care that my words would harm." Silence and the wind outside the tent were the only reply.

"God of Abraham, Isaac, and Jacob," I sobbed in remorse. "My repining brought your punishment on the people. They died from the surfeit of quail that I encouraged them to desire. I did not understand ..." For a long time I wept for my offense against my brother and the congregation. Eventually I curled into a dejected ball, whimpering softly. "Let me die for my part in sundering the community," I offered. "Living God, your punishment is just."

Miserable and repentant I waited for death. Instead, I felt peace envelope me as it had in my dream. It was like being enfolded in my mother's arms long ago when I feared Pharaoh's swordsmen. Overwhelmed, I knew I was loved and that God had forgiven me. Seamlessly I slid into a doze. When I awoke, I was not surprised to see the leprosy gone from my hands and body.

"Living and True God, forgive me. My pride has led me to doubt your power and forget your loving care. I am nothing without you, Almighty One. It was not my tears or Moses' words that freed the children of Israel from Pharaoh. Only you, *I AM that I AM* from before time, could have brought us from bondage and led us to your holy mountain."

"*You have not been abandoned.*"   Clearly, I heard the gentle assurance in my heart.

For a long time, I lay on my pallet of blankets. The peace lingered with me. I knew now that God had been with me even when I doubted and turned from him. In my darkest moments, it was the hand of the Living One that comforted me.

In the quiet of the ending night, God gave me a great gift. I saw the action of *I AM* from the beginning of time. The *Ruach* that breathed life into all creation, the *EL* who spoke to Abraham and wrestled with Jacob was the same *I AM* that now led the chosen people with the cloud of glory. My fingers itched to write the words. No longer did I doubt that the stories of the Living God would convert the people. Only by hearing of the actions of the God of Abraham, Isaac, and Jacob could the congregation find unity and identity.

"I will write the words you give me." And, in that declaration, I fully consecrated myself to God's task.

I reached out and picked up the flat bread and cheese my brother had brought. Now I was hungry. I didn't know how long I had lain in the tent. The crunch of feet on gravel led me to peer out. Moses saw my face. His grim expression broke into a joyful grin. Hurrying forward, he knelt beside me. Taking my hands, he caressed the smooth, unmarked skin.

"You are well, Miriam!" the man exclaimed.

His joy and relief made me sob in remorse. I could not look at my brother.

"Forgive me for bringing division to the camp and causing the deaths of so many at Kibbroth-hattavah. I was jealous because I thought I did not matter." From the corner of my eyes, I glanced at the brother I had wronged. "You spoke to Pharaoh and led the people from bondage. In my resentful malice, I caused division within the congregation. The Living One has been with me and shown me my transgression. My actions were as much a disease within the community as the leprosy was an illness in my body. Can you forgive me?"

I held my breath and did not dare look at the man. The Prophet drew me close. Weeping, I clung to my brother. Finally, he gently tilted my head up to look at him.

"My sister, you are more important than you know." The tears in the man's eyes surprised me. "Time after time you remind me of the path God set before me. I have needed your counsel. The people, too, depend on your wisdom. Each of us has our part to play in the saga of the God of Abraham, Isaac, and Jacob. Only as the congregation hears and learns of the One God will the nation be ready to forget the gods of Egypt. My sister, your stories of God and his people will encourage generations."

I shook my head. "I will only seek to teach that God is faithful, so they may enter the Promised Land and find peace."

"You must also write of this journey," the man told me, "so that others may hear of all that *I AM* continues to do for those who follow him."

I could not speak. Gazing past the Prophet I saw the glowing cloud resting on the Tabernacle. Moses turned to stare at the visible symbol of the Living God in our presence. His hand rested on my shoulder.

"Miriam, you are chosen by God for this task."

"Now I am ready to do it," I replied. "My heart was not in the work before."

I was rewarded by a grin of understanding. "I know what it is like to resist what God wants you to do."

He briefly held me against his shoulder. "It is fitting that you be brought back into the community with a festival," Moses told me.

"No." Fearfully I drew back.

The thought of facing many curious faces terrified me.

"I will send Zipporah to you with fresh clothes." My brother ignored my dismay. "We will celebrate your return to the congregation."

Although the question hung on my lips, I didn't ask him if he was reunited with his wife. Zipporah's relaxed smile told me that they were.

"My sister," we spoke together and gripped hands before embracing.

"I have missed you," my sister-in-law exclaimed stepping back to look at me. "Moses said you were healed. It is more than that. You are confident and have the same look that my husband has. You have been with God!"

"I … God … I … dreamed and God showed me that he has never forsaken the children of Israel or me." Haltingly I affirmed her observation. "I will write the mighty works of the God of all creation."

"I am glad for you," there was no jealousy in her tone. Unselfconsciously, the woman hugged me again. She picked up the small bundle dropped in her haste. "Here are fresh clothes."

"All is well?" Finally, I voiced the question as I washed myself and dressed in the clean garments.

My sister-in-law responded, "Yes. Truly, my sister, we are content."

"I am glad," was my only comment. The subject was closed.

Zipporah gently combed my hair, tangled from the days of struggle with God. At last I was ready to return to the main camp. Suddenly I felt very hesitant.

"I … I … cannot …" Grabbing Zipporah's hand, I held her back. "I cannot bear the stares and whispers."

"You will not be alone." The woman tried to console me. "Here come Moses and Aaron."

Ashamed of my fearful tears, I drew my veil over my face and turned away.

"Miriam," Moses spoke kindly, "it is time to rejoin the people. They are eager to welcome you back."

Still I hung onto Zipporah's hand.

Aaron spoke up, "Everyone knows that God has healed you. They are celebrating."

It was true; there was music and laughter from the camp. Gently my sister-in-law drew back the veil.

"Let all see that your are no longer a leprous outcast."

Moses nodded his approval. I walked between my brothers with Zipporah following close behind. Our arrival at the Tent of Meeting was the signal for musicians to begin. A cheer of welcome surrounded me.

Aaron stepped forward to announce, "Miriam, child of Amram and Jochebed of the tribe of Levi, is cleansed of the disease that *I AM* laid on her." He took my hand and pulled me forward. "Rejoice for this daughter of Abraham is alive again."

Another cheer rose and I felt my cheeks flush at the sound. We feasted long into the night. Although the main course was manna, there were also greens from the oasis and even meat. It felt wonderful to be part of the family again. Caleb hugged me with joy and I happily cuddled Sarai. She seemed to have grown a span in the time I was exiled.

Chapter 27

In the morning, we set out again. Ever to the north and east, the ark and cloud of God led us. We moved much more slowly than on the way to Sinai. For whole months we camped when we found good grazing.

Petrama had her own tent apart from Zipporah and her sons. Moses seemed to spend more time with my friend than before he married the Cushite girl. He included his sons when he strode through the camp. Eleazar learned to herd sheep beside his brother. I rejoiced at the happiness my brother found.

Caleb and Joshua became close friends. I was glad to see the young man learning from the man who kept order in the march and in camp. It barely seemed two years since the boy joined us at Succoth. Now a broad-shouldered man stood before me. He was unaware of his good looks. I was not surprised that his appearance made the girls giggle with excitement. As Moses predicted the young women used Sarai as an excuse for being near when he played with the baby.

Sarai grew strong. I knew her mother watched her from a distance and wished I dared allow her to play with the baby. Beliah would have beaten her for such an action. Already she was pregnant with another child. I prayed it would be a son.

Zipporah, Elisheva, and I enjoyed the baby who too soon began to toddle around after us. Her little hands were always reaching for the dough or the needle. Time slipped by as we moved slowly toward the Promised Land.

When we paused, I worked on the scrolls. I was happy to draw the letters that formed the words of the story of the chosen people of God. In the long summer evenings, I told the saga to the people.

"God has always been with us, hasn't he?" Caleb asked the question one afternoon when we stopped early.

All around us tents were being pitched and preparations for the night begun.

I nodded, "It is true, my son."

The endearment slipped out naturally. A warm smile told me the young man heard it.

"My mother," he responded, taking my hand. "You have taught me so much."

With a quick hug, he was gone. The glimmer of tears in his eyes explained his haste. My heart was full. Not only had God restored me to the community, but I had a family, too. Sarai and Caleb were the children I never bore.

"*I AM*, you are the One who restores all things." I began the prayer in a whisper. "Glory to you, God Almighty, you give us bread for our sustenance. Praise to you, Mighty One, you provide us with water. Honor to you, the only True and Living God, for you cause all of life to be. Everything flows from you. You keep your promises to those who love you for a thousand generations. God, you have been with us always. Because you love us, you will never forsake us. Help us to be faithful to you and remember your abiding love."

The paean of praise rang from my heart. Standing outside my tent, I lifted arms in praise. Peace and joy filled me as I stood there.

"My sister," Moses startled me, "truly *I AM* is faithful." We stood together in silent communion for several minutes before he spoke again. "The people are still rebellious." The man's sigh was deep. "They do not understand all that God has done. You tell the stories and the young people hear and understand. The generation that remembers Egypt cannot let go of those memories."

"They will not enter the Promised Land," I stated sadly.

"I know." It was an admission filled with grief.

I could find no words of comfort. My brother moved away to Zipporah's tent.

Moses was right about the continuing resistance from some of the people. I found it difficult to resist the attempts to draw me into the various protests, but I remembered the chastisement of the

Living One. The community would not be divided by my criticism again.

"God will continue to supply everything we need. Moses is his chosen Prophet," I repeated with deep conviction until the people quit expecting me to join in their complaining.

We traveled north along the shore of the sea. At Jotbathah, we turned west into the Wilderness of Paran.

The autumn began when we reached Kadesh Barnea. This low-lying oasis was near the head of the Brook of Egypt, which divided Egyptian possession from the tribes in Canaan. We were also not far from the trade route called the Way to Shur. Instead of running close to the Great Sea, this route clung to the foothills of the high desert. Caravans traveled into Canaan through Beersheba and north to Hebron. Some even went as far as Damascus and Haran. I felt a thrill at being within a day's travel of the route our father Jacob used for the journey to Egypt four hundred years earlier. It was obvious that Moses planned a long sojourn at this oasis. The tent stakes were driven deeply into the sandy soil.

"Caleb." As usual, the young man was pitching my tent. "What is the plan? Will we follow the trade route to Canaan? How soon will we leave?"

My eager questions tumbled over one another. I knew that all around the camp the same queries were being whispered.

"Scouts will be sent into the land," the handsome young man responded. With a proud lift of his head, he announced, "Joshua chose me to go with the group. I am the youngest of the men entering the land. There is to be a representative from each tribe. We will bring back a report. Moses has given us strict instructions to look and act like traders."

I wanted to warn my beloved foster son to be careful and swallowed the lump of loneliness already building in my throat.

However, I held my tongue except to inquire. "When do you leave?"

"As soon as Moses gives the word." The young man was almost prancing with impatience.

Less than a week later, my brothers stood together in front of the Tent of Meeting.

"The Promised Land lies before us," Aaron announced.

He wore the sacred garments of the high priest. My nephews stood to one side as assistants.

"Scouts will be sent into Canaan to see where we may enter."

Moses began a role call of the men chosen to represent each tribe. Each man stepped out of the assembled ranks when he heard his name. At one name, my brother couldn't repress a smile.

"From the tribe of Judah, Caleb son of Jephunneh."

I grinned too as the young man stepped forward. He looked so capable with the leather belt around his waist that held a dagger. On his head was the new turban, my present to him. In imitation of his hero, a beard sprouted on his chin. I heard more than one sigh from the young women nearby.

"Joshua, son of Nun will lead the men and represent the tribe of Ephraim."

All around were nods of agreement. Who else but Joshua would lead the scouts?

My brother paused to look around at the strong, dedicated faces standing to one side. They were an impressive group. Broad-shouldered and strong from desert travel, the men were not all young but each was well respected. I believed they would bring back an honest report. When the twelve men were arrayed, Aaron stepped forward to bless the chosen ones. He addressed the men.

"God has set you apart for this task. You will enter the land promised to Abraham, Isaac, and Jacob and bring back a report of the richness and the defenses of the inhabitants."

Ithamar held out the censer. Aaron took it from his son. When he moved toward the group of chosen men, they fell to the ground in homage to God. With great ceremony, the priest moved among the prostrate forms. The scent of the rich incense floated from the brazen cup over the entire crowd. Eleazar and Ithamar now cast more of the incense into the coals. The brazier in front of the Tent of Meeting flared up. A great pillar of smoke billowed upward and merged with the still-present cloud of God that daily hung over the Ark. A gasp of awe came from hundreds of throats.

"Sanctify yourselves," my brother told the men. "Bring a young goat or a lamb for the sin offering. You must be holy to enter the land."

The priests kept busy accepting and slaughtering the sacrificial beasts all afternoon. The fire on the altar within the curtains burned brightly. Night was upon us when the ceremony was concluded.

"Keep yourself from women," warned Aaron to the men now standing before the altar. "In the morning you may go forth in the name of *I AM* to determine what sort of land this is that we will dwell in."

The normal babble of the camp was subdued that night. Everyone was thinking about the mission of the twelve men camped together near the Tent of Meeting. The stars seemed closer than usual and reminded me of the covenant made with Abraham.

I prayed in the stillness of the night. "God of Abraham, Isaac, and Jacob, remember your servants. Give them safe passage into the land you swore to give to our father Abraham. We are as plentiful as the sands of the sea or the stars in your heaven. Let the chosen men bring a good report of the land of Canaan."

The entire camp roused at dawn to the sound of the ram's horn. Walking beside donkeys laden with supplies, the twelve men set out. My eyes sought Caleb. He strode in the midst of the scouts with pride.

"He will return," I told Sarai who wiggled in my arms, more to console me than the baby.

When I put her down, she toddled after a dog wandering through the camp.

It was hard to wait for the scouts to return. Each day I saw Moses staring to the northeast. Finally, I could stand the tension no longer. A week had passed and I was impatient for word. I found my brother alone one afternoon.

"When do you think they will return?"

"I do not expect them back before a full moon cycle," the man told me. When I opened my mouth to protest he added, "They need to travel throughout the land. Joshua will lead them as far as the Jabok if he can. All the land that our fathers lived in shall be ours." The statement was emphasized by a firm nod of my brother's head.

It was over a moon cycle before the men returned. They brought huge clusters of grapes and reports of a rich land. Caleb came to me with an excited report. He picked up Sarai. She squealed when he whirled her around.

"Those who believe will enter the land," he told the little girl. "We will have a good home there. The fields are rich and the flocks are strong and healthy. We can prosper in this land. The other men will give a fearful account. They insist that the towns are too well defended for us to overthrow. Even though they saw the same rich grazing and vineyards, they have focused on the strength of the walls."

Stormy eyes glanced back at his companions, now answering questions from the excited crowd. I could hear the negative reports.

"The people live in cities."

"We cannot hope to defeat them."

"The land is too well fortified."

"What good is a rich land with walled cities and armed men that we cannot get past?"

Caleb scowled as his companions. "My comrades have forgotten what God did in Egypt and how we have prospered on the journey."

"Then you must remind them," I urged.

Fear increased throughout the camp as the scouts continued to recount what they saw. Moses was confronted by an angry mob.

"You brought us out of Egypt to kill us."

"The promises are empty!"

"There is no land for us!"

"We are doomed. "

"You, Moses, bear the stain of our children's blood."

"Let us return to Egypt."

Surprisingly, it was Caleb who stepped forward to speak. No longer was this the ragged boy from Succoth who begged to accompany the exiles. In his place stood a determined man. I was filled with pride for this, the son I didn't bear.

"Where is your faith?" he shouted. The deep strong voice overrode the clamor. "How can you doubt the Living God? Have you already forgotten what *I AM* did against the power of Egypt? Have we gone hungry or thirsty in the desert? Do you not listen when Miriam recites the deeds of the Holy One since the beginning? Why do you think God's hand would be shortened now?"

Some of the tension left Moses' face as he listened to Caleb's defense. Joshua too stepped forward to plead. "Listen, my friends, this is a rich land! It is the land promised to Abraham, Isaac, and Jacob. God will surely lead us and defeat those who stand against us."

The man's eyes roamed over the crowd. They rested on the other ten men. A couple of the scouts lowered their eyes and shuffled their feet. Others shouted back at the leader.

"The towns have stone walls. They are thick with battlements on the tops. You said yourself that we could not scale them."

"God will fight for us," Caleb insisted.

"You are only a boy. What do you know of warfare?" mocked Palti.

The response was instantaneous. "I remember how God defeated the Amalekites while you hid in the cave."

Drawing back, the accuser looked around to see if anyone heard his secret. Curious eyes were staring at him.

"What does the boy know?" he repeated before somewhat shamefacedly shuffling to the back of the crowd.

Before anyone could say any more, Marah gave a strangled cry and pointed toward the Tent of Meeting. Even before I turned, I felt the presence of God. The cloud had begun to glow as though with fire. There was crackling in the air. Involuntarily I took a step backward and dropped to my knees. Moses fell to the ground.

"Lord God, do not ..." His plea was anguished.

"How long will I endure this people?"

I heard the question and briefly wondered if everyone heard it. That my brother did, I knew. He cowered away from the pulsating pillar.

"They refuse to listen. Even now they doubt." The voice of God came again.

The community began to fall to their knees with cries of fear as the column towered higher and higher. I was reminded of the fiery shaft that held Pharaoh at bay at the sea. Now mothers grabbed children and began to flee to their tents. Husbands and wives clung to each other in terror.

"My God, have mercy." Moses was on his face before the Lord.

I froze in awe at the display of the glory of the Lord.

"I will destroy this obstinate people and make of you *a great nation!"*

Hearing the voice of God made my heart pound. My breath came in short gasps. Joshua, Caleb, and Aaron joined Moses on the ground in supplication.

"No, Great and Mighty Lord God." My brother dared to raise his head to argue with *I AM*. "All nations have heard of your mighty acts. If you destroy this people, it will be said that you were unable to bring the children of Israel into the Promised Land." The man knelt facing the blazing presence. "Please," he pleaded almost desperately, "do not kill this people."

All around me there were screams of fear and moans of despair. No one could doubt what God's plan was from hearing the Deliverer's intercession. I couldn't take my eyes off the cloud. There was no smoke, only flaming light brighter than you see when the sun sets behind clouds on the horizon. The light pulsated as my brother continued to beg for the same men and women who so regularly turned against him.

"Remember how you said, 'God is slow to anger, and abounding in steadfast love, forgiving iniquity and transgression, but by no means clearing the guilty'?" Softly Moses spoke.

I held my breath while the man prayed.

"Forgive your chosen people according to your steadfast love. You have pardoned this people since we before we left Egypt." When he finished speaking, the servant of the Lord flattened himself to the ground.

I too lay face down unable to bear the sight of the fire of God that raced up and down the pillar.

In my heart I added, "Spare these foolish and misguided ones. They are like children." The voice seemed to speak to me as well as to Moses.

"*I will forgive as you ask. However, this generation shall not enter the land promised to Abraham, Isaac, and Jacob. They have rebelled and tested me ten times. Therefore, none who saw Egypt will enter the land. Caleb, son of Jephunneh is faithful. He has not lost his belief. He will enter the land and possess it.*"

"Lord God, you are gracious and merciful." My brother bowed to the ground again and again.

I watched in awe as the cloud moved to cover the Ark and Tent of Meeting. Moses called the congregation together. Hesitantly they gathered again. Mothers held tight to their children and husbands.

"*I AM* will not strike you down for your lack of faith." The man spoke gently to the frightened multitude. "As punishment we will not be allowed enter and occupy the land at this time."

A great mourning sob greeted the announcement even as Aaron pronounced, "The Lord is merciful. Blessed be the name of the Lord."

My youngest brother was not done. Moses looked compassionately around at the mournful faces. "Thus says the Lord, 'Your children, who you said would die, will inherit the land.' We will be shepherds until the last of this generation is gone."

I heard sorrow in the man's voice. At the end of this speech, the servant of God turned and walked away from the camp.

Chapter 28

It was a subdued community that turned back from the northward journey. Our route now led us back into the Wilderness of Shur where we could find winter grazing. Word of bands of Amalekite and Canaanite raiders made us hurry along.

Elisheva sought me out. "Miriam, what will happen to us? God has deserted us."

Her words gave voice to the unspoken undercurrent of fear pervading the camp.

"No, my sister." I took her hand. "God has not abandoned us. He is preparing the children of Israel. Until we truly trust in *I AM* we are not ready to enter the land of our fathers."

"I do not understand," the woman stated with a shake of her head. "Why must we all be punished for the doubts of a few?" She looked past me to where the Ark led the way up a stony outcropping. Her next words were angry. "Your God demands that I have no fear when all around is danger. The God of Abraham, Isaac, and Jacob steals my peace of mind and my family. Yet I am expected to be happy about it."

The challenge caught me by surprise. For a few minutes we walked in silence.

"Living God," a prayer went up from my heart, "give me the words to soothe this woman."

No answer came. Instead, I drew my friend down on a rock beside me. Scalding tears soaked my robe and tunic.

"God has given you a place of honor in the community." Finally I began to speak as the sobbing eased. "Your husband and sons are honored above their kin by being priests before the Most High."

"But I want Aaron beside me." The weeping began again. "I dreamed that when we settled in Canaan that he would return to me and we would grow old together."

"Ah, my sister." I understood her grief.

Now that we turned away from the Promised Land, she lost hope and in her despair turned against God.

"Talk to Aaron," I counseled. "You can comfort one another. He too is saddened about not entering Canaan."

I never knew if she spoke to my brother. One day, not long after, I met him coming from the Tabernacle. The priest looked old and tired. New lines etched his face and more gray showed in the hair I saw beneath the turban. He walked slowly to his wife's tent.

"God grant them peace in each others arms," I prayed.

Moses too was grieved by the events. One evening, a week after leaving Kadesh Barnea, I stood in my tent door looking at the busy encampment. We had climbed up the lower reaches of Mount Hor to this place. Caleb brought me the leather trunk that held my scrolls. The young man only brought the writing tools when we were going to be in camp for several days. Looking around, I agreed that this was a comfortable location. Water trickled down the hillside in a small but sturdy brook. There was grass not only beside the water but also in the scattered nearby valleys. Our camp occupied a flat rise that gave us full view of any approaching travelers or bandits.

"Miriam," my brother came to stand beside me. He surveyed the arrangements.

"This is a good place," I mentioned, wondering why the man sought me out.

He nodded before looking at me. "My sister, I have failed God."

The statement amazed me. I gestured toward the bustling camp filled with the children of Israel.

"How can you say so? Look at the people. They have learned to live off the land and are no longer dependent on the bazaars of the occasional town for supplies. The young men are being trained in the ways of war and a new generation has already started to grow."

I pointed to where Sarai played with a couple of other children just younger than her.

Briefly, the Prophet smiled. Then he turned serious. "I allowed the people to doubt and rebel. Instead of strengthening their faith, I let my own frustration keep me silent. Caleb and Joshua have been more outspoken in reminding us of the mighty works of God. Even you, my sister," his smile was loving, "tell the stories of our fathers to encourage the congregation. Everyone is instructed in the ways of the Living God."

For a long time, he stared down the pass in the direction we came. Beyond our view was Canaan.

When he finally spoke, it was very low. "I will not enter Canaan. My slowness of tongue in reprimanding the children of Israel has led to this exile. Rather than patience, I raged with impatience against them, especially at the waters of Meribah."

"Dear brother." I wished I could comfort the man.

"Even now, the men who insisted on forcing their way into Canaan without the presence of God are fleeing in defeat. I should have stopped them."

Sad eyes looked at me and then back down the road. The man bowed his head low in agony. I laid a hand on his shoulder. There were no words of comfort. My brother was right. I had known that retreat was inevitable even when the troop set out valiant and full of courage. My thoughts roamed back to the scene at Kadesh Barnea.

"The Ark of God remains with the camp." Moses stood firm against the pleas of Palti. "Until the Lord gives the word, we remain outside the Promised Land."

The men set out to the cheers of the community. Moses went into his tent and lowered the flap. The next day we moved into the heights. The return of the warriors was ignominious. A few at a time, they stumbled into the encampment over the next several days. They told of cities that could not be taken because of their stone ramparts.

"We will need stronger weapons and more soldiers to attack this land," each man insisted. "The people are giants."

This statement was an exaggeration, I was sure.

Moses called the community together. "Why do you all look so downcast?" the man chided. "The Lord will go before you into the Promised Land. God will give you the fortified cities for your own."

"When?" The eager question came from many throats.

"In the time *I AM* has determined." The Prophet didn't flinch from the angry growl at his reply. "All of us must learn obedience to the will of the Mighty One who made the heavens and the earth. In the spring, we will move from here to find grazing for our flocks and herds. Our children will learn the ways of our fathers. We will be shepherds and nomads like Abraham, Isaac, and Jacob. They depended on God. The Living Lord did not fail them. The Almighty One, that he called *EL*, made a covenant with Abraham. That vow will be fulfilled in the lives of our children and grandchildren. Jacob went into Egypt with seventy men. He believed his God would bring the children of Israel out of the Black Land."

Moses paused to let his gaze roam over the multitude of men, women, and children gathered before him. With a sweep of his hand, he indicated them all.

"Behold, *I AM* brought us out of bondage to Pharaoh, thousands in number. The despised Hebiru have become a mighty and free nation."

No one dared question the leader further. He spoke with authority. The glory of God flared behind him as it covered the Ark and Tent of Meeting. I heard some comments of agreement.

"It is true, we are a great people now."

"I remember how scorned we were in Egypt."

"Moses reminds us that God has not failed us yet."

"Better to live as nomads than die in battle."

"We are free men now and do no man's bidding."

Ultimately, most of the people decided that it was better to wait for God. Some families slipped away each night for a few moon turnings.

"They cannot bear the thought of waiting for God," I told Caleb when he came to me with news that Beliah and two others had left in the early dawn hours. "God seeks to make a great nation of us. Some think they can force the hand of the One Lord." With a shake of my head I added, "It is better to wait for God's timing."

"Now Sarai will never know her father." The young man glanced sadly at the three-year old happily stirring the pot nearby.

I let her help me with the daily preparation of the manna. The morning light still brought the small white bits of bread from heaven. There were so many ways to prepare the stuff now that we hardly remembered that it was manna. We were able to augment the diet with herbs gathered nearby and small animals trapped by the children. Occasionally, an animal from the herd would be slaughtered and then we all feasted joyously.

"Sarai has the love of many. She will not miss the father she never knew." I soothed Caleb's fears. The next moment I laughed because the child brought a treat to my visitor.

"Ca-eb," she lisped, "'ith for you to eat."

The expression as the young man swallowed the raw dough was comical and again I chuckled when the girl looked affronted by his effort.

"Let us pour the mixture into the bowl," I suggested. "Then we will bake it near the fire. Caleb will like it better then."

After setting the cake to bake, I gave the little girl her spindle and suggested she practice spinning. With a look of intense concentration, the child set to work.

"She is growing quickly," Caleb grinned at his charge. "Sarai will enter the land of Canaan and find a home there."

"You and Joshua will lead the people into the land promised to Abraham, Isaac, and Jacob," I reminded the bold young man.

"My mother." The title of love and respect brought tears to my eyes. "When will that be?"

"I do not know." With a look toward the Tent of Meeting, I shrugged. "This generation must all die and their children learn to trust the True God before it can happen. The congregation will be united in their faith in *I AM*. You will see the fulfillment of the promise," I repeated taking the strong, tanned hand in my wrinkled one.

Before he left me, the young man dropped a tender kiss on my forehead. "I will remember your words," he promised.

I turned away to my tasks, knowing that he spoke the truth. The hand of God was on Caleb bar Zephunneh. He would do great things.

Epilogue

"That was nearly forty years ago." The old woman lay back on the pillows looking at her companions. "You know how we have wandered as nomads through the desert all these years. Aaron died while we camped at Mount Hor. Zipporah, too, is buried in these hills as is the Cushite girl, Petrama, and Elisheva."

A shade of sorrow crossed her face. Miriam looked first at the young man and then the young woman. Her eyes softened and she smiled.

"I have seen the two I cherish most in the world find love in each other's arms."

Sarai rested her head against her husband's strong chest. Adoring eyes looked up at the bearded figure beside her.

"It is true," she admitted. "There is only one man that I could ever love."

"I have seen your children born," continued the aged voice. "A whole new generation has come to know the ways of the God of Israel."

"We will never forget," insisted Sarai.

Caleb added, "You have taught us the stories of the One God. They are written and safely placed in their case."

The young woman stroked the fingers that labored long over the scrolls now safely wrapped in oiled leather. With the law that Moses had compiled, all the writings were placed inside the sacred Ark.

"Yes, I have completed the work God gave me to do." A contented smile lingered on the wrinkled face. With a slight shake of her head, she added, "Once I fought against the Living God and tried to rescue my family and the nation by myself. God's way is better."

"Without you we would have lost hope long ago." The strong man heard his voice catch with emotion as he spoke. "Again and again you remind us all of the love of *I AM*. The words you have sung are inspiration to all the children of Israel."

"My son, you are first of them all. You are the child I thought I would never have."

A loving smile softened the deep lines on the old face. The man buried his face in the blankets for a moment, overcome by emotion. Sarai pressed close to offer comfort.

"Then God gave me a daughter also." Miriam looked fondly at the girl kneeling beside Caleb. "Surely I am most blessed of women. Only Moses and I are left of the generation that lived in Egypt," she mused softly.

Looking past her companions, the woman let her gaze wander over the encampment. Men who were little more than toddlers so many years ago now tended their own flocks. Women who never saw the pyramids of the Black Land held children and grandchildren in their arms. The families in the encampment had never known the strange gods of the Nile. They worshiped the God of Abraham, Isaac, and Jacob. Aaron's family did not falter in its priestly duties. More and more, Moses allowed Joshua to make decisions.

"Now is the time." The statement was firm and she raised herself slightly to look eastward. "We have become truly a community with one belief. The people understand that the love of the One True God has been with us always. *I AM* will bring the congregation into the Promised Land."

"Yes, my mother, we will soon go forward," Caleb agreed.

The old woman pondered. "The people have fought against Edom and many other enemies. By the hand of God, you have prevailed."

"Once again we are on the edge of the Promised Land again, my mother," eagerly the scout reminded the women.

"It is time," she repeated with a nod. "You and Joshua will go ahead of the people. Moses and I will not cross over the Jordan. *I AM* will lead you. It is enough that I hear you, Caleb, tell me of the bounty and taste the grapes you have brought back."

She selected another small cluster of the succulent fruit to savor.

Sarai spoke up, "Mother, do not speak so. You will live to see the vineyards for yourself."

"My daughter, I am an old woman," was the response. "I have seen many things. God has shown me wonders in my lifetime. Since I had the leprosy at Hazeroth, I have known that my eyes will not see the Promised Land. It is enough that I have seen your joy and your children have played on my lap."

The young woman opened her mouth to argue. A shake of the white head stopped her. A wave of the wrinkled hand encompassed the camp.

"These families are the fulfillment of the word of God to Abraham, Isaac, and Jacob."

With a sob, the young woman buried her face in Miriam's lap. Stroking the brown hair, the woman looked at the man she considered her son.

"Caleb," she cautioned, "it will not be easy to march into the land and conquer the inhabitants. Only by the hand of *I AM* will you be able to succeed. Never forget that."

Nodding in agreement, the broad-shouldered man stated, "It is true, the cities are well fortified. Our spies have been to Jericho. The walls are wide with houses built into them."

"Yet, there is a way." Miriam smiled when the man paused.

"Nothing is hidden from you, here in your tent, is it?" he asked with a grin.

"Salmon has made a conquest already, I believe," the woman teased.

A nod affirmed her unspoken question. "Yes, my mother, the woman Rahab helped our spies. I believe she will spread word throughout the city of our astonishing prowess." Chuckling, and shaking his head, Caleb continued, "If they only knew how limited our fighting resources are."

"Never consider your armies insufficient," Miriam scolded quickly. "You march in the power of the Living God."

Sheepishly, the warrior ducked his head. "Yes, my mother."

"The God of Abraham, Isaac, and Jacob is the one who throughout our bondage and our wanderings has been the true deliverer. Even though I hoped to liberate my family, *I AM* used a shepherd's staff in the hands of my brother to redeem all the children of Israel. God always has a greater plan than we can see."

"My sister, your words are true," the voice of Moses, Deliverer of Israel, was heard.

He joined the group beside his sister.

"It is the Lord who will bring the victory. The people are ready to enter the Promised Land," Miriam stated with conviction.

"Yes, they have learned the ways of the God of Abraham, Isaac, and Jacob as they listen to your words." A smile of affirmation was for the Prophet's sister. "By the recitation of the manifold acts of the Living God, the people have been healed of their doubt. They are now a faithful nation ready and able to follow the laws set out by *I AM*. With your help, my sister, the Word of God has been given to these chosen ones."

"The story will give generations to come the faith to obey the Law of God you have written. In relationship with the Living One, the people will continue to find the faith and healing they will need." The old woman spoke confidently. Loving eyes surveyed the encampment.

Sarai and Caleb left the siblings together. Hand in hand, the young couple moved away to their own tent. The man held arms wide for his children. Happily, they raced to greet their father. The Deliverer settled beside his sister. Together they watched the community prepare for the night. They did not need words. In each heart held a prayer of thanksgiving to the One God.

Blasts from the ram's horn called the congregation together in the morning light. Moses stood in front of the Tent of Meeting. Joshua stood on his right and Caleb on his left. He raised the staff of God and the whispers in the crowd ceased.

All eyes focused on the old man when he intoned, "Hear, O Israel, *I AM that I AM* is the only God. Love the Lord your God with your heart and your soul and your mind that you may be blessed in the land you go in to possess."

"Amen, so be it!" came the shout from the assemblage.

"Remember the stories of *I AM* through all ages and the Law that is in your midst." He gestured toward the Ark that housed the scrolls bearing the law and the deeds of God. "Read them daily and bind them on your foreheads and on the doors of your homes. When you come into the rich land, do not forget *I AM* who brought you out of bondage."

Again the roar swelled, "Amen, so be it!"

The old woman sat in her tent. She could see Sarai with the children. Their eager faces were full of hope. Joshua and Caleb stood ready to lead the people into the Promised Land.

"The children of Israel are ready," as a prayer the old woman's lips moved. "Praise to you, God of Abraham, Isaac, and Jacob. You will bring them into the land promised to their fathers. My brother and I have accomplished the tasks you set before us." A contented smile crossed her lips. "It is good." Unconsciously Miriam spoke the refrain from the very first scroll she had written.

With a nod, she let the tent flap fall into place. Again she heard the community proclaim, "Amen, so be it!"

Faith born from the experience of *I AM* and on learning the acts of the God of Abraham, Isaac, and Jacob resounded. Another smile rested on the wrinkled face as she lay back on the blankets.

"It is good," she repeated.